DREAMS OF SAND

a novel by

ANNALISE BERNADETTE

Printed in the United States of America
First Print June 2013
ISBN: 978-0-9895415-0-3

Cover artwork by Joan Peters

Author photographs by Mirlie S. Green

ACKNOWLEDGEMENTS

Thank you to my beta readers, Kevin Turner, Melinda Bradford, Carolyn Ryan, and Janice Davis. Thank you to my friend and wonderful artist Joan Peters, who was able to quickly render the vision I had for the cover. Thank you to those writer friends, particularly Women Writing in Asheville, who provided encouragement and inspiration to me during this perplexing activity of trying to put a story onto a page. Thank you to my family and friends and all those persons who have supported me during this journey. If you have heard me talk about this project, then you know you are one of those to whom I am most grateful. Thank you for lending me your ear and your friendship as I struggled to write this story, my first, whose birth has been coming for a long time. I couldn't have done it without you.

In loving memory of Hubert, Gudrun, and Kurt.

In honor of Ryan and all those who have cared for me over the years.

Annalise

PREFACE

While this story is set in the time of the war known as Desert Storm, there are likely missed details about the experience and the conflict. It is the author's hope that this lack of detail or fact does not offend anyone or hinder the reader's appreciation of the narrative. This story is written with heartfelt respect and gratitude to all who served and continue to serve in times of world conflict. It is also written with respect and gratitude to all of the families and friends left behind to carry on with the daily responsibilities of life and sometimes child-rearing while they wait with uncertainty for the return of their loved ones.

The town of Sand Beach is fictional and represents a kind of place that is becoming increasingly rare - the small town where everyone knows each other, where residents have a face and a name - the pharmacist, the bartender, the officer. The story of Sand Beach reminds us that we are all connected. That one person's grief is everyone's grief and all it takes is one hero to inspire us. In a world of villains, mass murder, and man's inhumanity to man, we all need a hero and we each carry with us a responsibility and an opportunity to be a hero to someone else.

Annalise

ONE

Grace Moore tucked her hair under her black velvet riding cap as she contemplated the situation she now faced. That morning she'd returned to her bathroom six separate times to make certain, absolutely certain, that the test strip she had urinated on had in fact turned blue. She had kept this discovery to herself all day, cherishing it and protecting it from the reactions of others that might include comments about her life never being the same again.

She knew that her life was never going to be the same. She felt it. She felt the miracle inside her that was ever so small. On this day, she realized that life could change in a heartbeat. Had she known what was to follow in the subsequent days, months, and years, she would have gotten down on her knees and counted her blessings. She would have kept a journal and detailed each day, each conversation. And on this particular day, she would have memorized and documented in that journal each moment that had led to and followed her discovery in the hours just before coming to the barn on this bright October afternoon.

Her secret safe so far, she leaned forward atop Silver Glo and inhaled the crisp autumn air, thinking about where she would head to now that she had just completed the final ride of the day. Slowing

— *1* —

Glo to a walk, she approached the eight tired, sweaty horses that were still saddled and roped and waiting to be fed by her assistant, Sally, who was busy filling their buckets with grain. Following their meal, they'd be loosed into the pasture, a reward after hours of carrying inexperienced riders through the fields and down the well-worn riding trail in the Michigan woods.

Grace smiled at the familiar equine behavior, the whinny for food, the hanging head, the obedience and impatience, a hoof stomp, a tail swish or a quick snapping bite to ward off an occasional insect. Grace had been a trail-ride leader at Sand Beach Stables for as long as she could remember and never failed to appreciate the way horses behaved.

Grace leapt off the mare, removed the bridle, and replaced it with a halter. Then she fastened Glo's lead to the tie rail.

"Hey, Sally, I thought it was a pretty good day. You?"

"I think it was an excellent day! No falls, no injuries. Decent tips. Good weather. Couldn't ask for more! Too bad we have only two Saturdays left till we shut down for the winter."

"Winter, brr, snow and more snow. I am not looking forward to that."

"We got twenty dollars apiece."

"Thanks!" Grace meant it. Money was good. *Especially* now. Grace pulled off her riding hat and ran her fingers through sweaty cords of blond hair.

Working together, Grace and Sally unsaddled the tired steeds and finished filling their grain buckets as the noisy feeding commenced.

"Sally, you can go. Enjoy the day. I can finish up here. I think these guys are well under control."

"You sure you don't want help with the grooming? I didn't get to it this morning."

"No problem." Grace answered. "The routine will do me good."

"Thanks, Grace. Now I can get a shower, do my nails, and get ready for tonight." Sally pushed her hands deep into her jean pockets and looked down at her mud-caked boots.

"Ryan again?"

Sally blushed. "Yes."

"Better watch it, you two will become an item," Grace said with a grin.

After she watched Sally drive down the gravel road in her old Malibu, Grace pulled out the dusty bucket filled with grooming supplies and started brushing Glo. She removed the dirt from the horse's sweaty coat, combed her mane and picked her hooves. Then she repeated the ritual with each horse, moving quickly and steadily down the line. When the task was completed, she breathed a sigh of satisfaction.

"All right, guys, thanks for the hard work!" She smacked each horse on the rear and called out each one's name as she set them loose in the hundred-acre pasture.

Grace yawned and stretched, pulled her sweatshirt down over her faded jeans, and bent down to touch her toes. She found a spot along the fence and rested her chin on her folded arms. She looked over the rolling green pasture with the deep blue sky rising above it accented by cotton clouds. Like the seasons, she felt herself changing and knew that after today, her life was going to be very different.

She glanced at her watch. Walt would be home soon. And she needed to be there when he arrived.

TWO

Grace arrived at the duplex which was half of an older home located on a quiet, tree-lined street. She removed her damp, mud-caked English riding boots and put them in the foyer. Tossing her jacket and hat on the rack in the hall, she headed straight for the bathroom and showered. Even when she scrubbed from head to toe, she found that the smell of horses tended to linger under her fingernails, in her hair, and inside her nostrils. The familiar smell centered her, brought her peace, a sense of belonging. She wondered how long she would be able to ride while pregnant.

She exited the shower and dried, powdered her body, and wrapped her white fuzzy robe around her. Her heart fluttered as she lifted the test-strip off the tissue on the back of the commode. There was no doubt. The blue strip didn't lie.

She didn't have a baby inside her yet. No, at this tender stage, this life was a blastocyst, a fancy word she had learned in high school biology. But it was still the beginning of a family. She had never been able to understand how anyone who had seen those pictures or pondered the miracle of a new life could choose abortion. This was a human being. This was a miracle.

She was pretty sure Walt would be happy, but she worried that he'd be overly concerned with the financial aspect of having a baby. At times he seemed worried about money, especially when he paid the bills. He was a scrimper, a saver, always planning for a financially secure future.

After thawing Walt's favorite chili, Grace sat down with a cup of tea and began to leaf through her high school yearbook, which she sometimes did when she wanted to remind herself of where she had been and how far she had come. Her high school days hadn't been particularly happy. She hadn't been one of the popular girls, hanging out with a boyfriend and making out in the hall. She hadn't been a cheerleader with a short skirt and a slim figure who bared reddened skin on cold football nights. She hadn't been an honors student or a basketball player. But neither had she been a druggie or a drinker or one of those that skipped school and saw the principal's office more often than an open textbook. No, Grace had been anonymous. She had been pudgy and pimply and awkward most days.

The one thing that had made her feel happy was volunteering at the animal shelter on the weekends and working with the horses at the barn. And the one person who had held her together had been her best friend, Fran. Without the barn, the animals, and Fran, she likely would have suffered from loneliness and despair.

As she sipped the last of her hot tea, she closed the yearbook. Enough of looking through a book of memories of a time that was not so great. Those days were over, thank God!

She glanced up at the clock. She didn't like it when Walt had to work a Saturday, but he always said, "A little extra in the bank never hurts."

Grace changed into her blue jeans and t-shirt, pulled on a parka and stepped out onto the front porch. Restless and exhausted, she settled into the plastic chair and waited. The night was chilly and, as the darkness surrounded her, she realized that the only beings in the world who knew about the life growing inside her were God and the baby. Neither her mother nor her sister Beck were around to hear the news. Her connections to them were gone. Fran had called the barn earlier to see what Grace and Walt were doing next Saturday and had invited them to join her and Michael for a short trip to Morristown, a half-hour drive from Sand Beach. Grace had had to bite her tongue so as not tell Fran everything. And she had kept the news from Sally. And Dad. She hadn't even whispered the news to the horses, with whom she often chatted as she brushed their tails.

Although she had picked up the barn phone twice to dial Walt at work, she had quickly stopped, not knowing the exact words to use. She didn't want to blurt out her news on the phone. And she couldn't very easily interrupt his Saturday at the *Sand Beach Times* by barging into the office and making such an announcement in front of all the busy journalists. Walt was a man with a lot of deadlines.

This time Grace's ability to hold off, to be disciplined, was going to pay off. She wanted Walt to be the first person to know of his new title: *Daddy*. The man she loved, the father of this miracle, would be the first to know. And *Daddy* would hear the news in person. Every time, Grace thought about the word *Daddy*, she quivered.

She awoke with a start thirty minutes later to a stiff neck and the sound of a car door slamming. Her disorientation gave way to excitement.

"Walter!" She jumped up from the hard porch chair. "Hey... you!"

"Hey, you, yourself." Walt grinned that handsome, sexy grin. "Waiting out here on this porch in this cold? Let's go in and warm you up," he said, pulling her behind him.

Grace couldn't make small talk. Once inside, she went straight to the bathroom, her stomach fluttering. She took a deep breath and grabbed the test strip. Giddy, she went into the living room where Walt sat on the edge of the sofa, his jacket still on. She held up the little piece of paper.

"Walt, we are going to have a baby."

"Are you sure?" Walt asked.

"Yep," she said, waving the blue strip in front of his eyes. "Ninety-nine percent accurate."

She searched his expression for some clue of what he might be thinking. For what seemed like forever, he was quiet. The question about whether they would ever have children was answered.

"Wow," he said, seeming distant. "Wow." His eyes became wet. "I must be dreaming. You're kidding," he repeated.

Overwhelming joy washed over her. "No, *Daddy*, I'm not."

THREE

Monday morning came quickly, and Walt decided to make the one-mile trek to the newspaper. He pulled on his overcoat, grabbed his briefcase, and kissed Grace goodbye. He stepped onto the sidewalk, sucked in the earthy air, and started quietly singing "Silly Love Songs" by Paul McCartney. His step quickened as he made his way down Oak Street. As the sun made its slow, steady appearance and began shimmering through the leaves on the tree-lined sidewalk, he noticed all the porches adorned with carved pumpkins and pots of yellow and orange mums. His pace quickened and he got a little louder as he hummed the refrain.

"Hello, Walter."

Startled, he looked up to see Mrs. Givens dressed in slippers and an old flowered house coat. She beamed at him as she stepped into her driveway to retrieve the newspaper, followed by her overweight dachshund.

"Hi, Mrs. Givens." Embarrassed, he stopped humming and nodded, greeting his gray-haired neighbor.

"A nice warm day for once."

"Yeah, hard to believe it's almost Halloween."

Gathering his composure, he continued a few blocks down the road to Gloria's Cafe. He pulled a Detroit newspaper from the orange metal stand out front and stepped inside to take his usual spot by the window.

"Hi, Walt." Linda, his favorite waitress, smiled as she approached the table with coffeepot in hand.

"Black, please, Linda," he responded absent-mindedly as she poured his coffee.

"Since when does Walter Moore drink his coffee black?" she asked.

"Since I've been trying to quit drinking coffee altogether. I figure the worse it tastes, the easier it will be to give it up."

"Interesting theory, Walt."

Linda left him to serve other customers. He munched on his toast and studied the paper. The Gulf situation was heating up. Crime rate in Detroit steadily rising. Ford Plant Hires New Workers. He read Beetle Bailey and laughed out loud.

Linda served the others and came to sit with Walt. "What's up, Walt? You're not eating much." Linda noticed everything. "Nothing but toast and coffee?"

Walt looked up from his paper and nodded. "Hard to eat much when I've just had a very exciting development in my life." He paused to consider whether to blurt the news.

"I'm going to be a dad," he announced, avoiding eye contact. This was no time to give up coffee. He nervously ripped open a sugar packet and pulled the tab off the plastic creamer and mulled for a moment, stirring and stalling as the black coffee turned sweet and creamy.

Linda looked right into Walt's eyes, seemingly processing what she'd just heard. "A dad, really!" Her brow raised as her expression changed. "No kidding? Grace!" She averted her gaze as she processed this new information. "Wow, I'll have to call her!"

"You know, Walt, that your life will never be the same."

Walt realized that if anyone would know how children change your life, Linda would. She had four children under the age of ten. She and her husband, Bob, always managed to adjust their schedules so that one of them was at home when the other was at work.

"You will never look at motorcycles or vacations in quite the same way." She winked at him.

He looked at her quizzically. What did that mean? That he wouldn't have time? Money? That he couldn't take risks? His blood pressure rose as he considered her comments. All that work. All that responsibility. He filed away her remarks in his mind for future consideration and thanked her as he handed her three crisp singles plus a two-dollar tip. The restaurant door clanged as he rushed out into the clear blue day heading for his office.

When Walt arrived at work, Stu was waiting by the front door running his fingers through his thick black hair.

"How's that story coming?" Walt's boss was always on his case.

"Which one?" Walt fumbled to remember.

"The one about the dentist. The one you told me you would have ready by two o'clock today. You do remember, don't you?"

Walt hesitated. "I think I have the proof done," he said, hoping that this was the case.

Walt made it his personal policy to be a day early on all deadlines. He hurried to his corner office and pushed aside papers to find the article just where he had left it on Saturday—in the organizer. It was a four-column feature article about a local dentist who had spent his summers with his wife traveling all over the world on mission trips to tend to the dental needs of those less fortunate. It was slotted for the front page.

He breathed a sigh of relief. He wasn't losing his mind.

"Here you go, Stu." Walt handed his editor the piece for approval.

Back at his office, he picked up the phone and dialed the number of a local farmer who was always available for a good crop update.

"Mr. Marsh? This is Walter Moore from the *Sand Beach Times*. It's time to do our annual story on this year's crops. Can I stop by around one o'clock to interview you?"

After he hung up, Walt sat back and glanced up at the wall in front of him, letting his gaze linger on the framed copy of the first article he had written for the paper before moving to another frame that held the first printed copy of the *Sand Beach Times*. Next to that was his diploma from the University of Michigan with a Bachelor of Fine Arts in Journalism. Walt had been a shoe-in as a staff writer when he and Grace first moved to Sand Beach to be near Grace's father, who was newly retired after spending thirty years as the *Times*'s editor-in-chief. During high school, Grace had been a part-time weekend employee, collating the papers as they came off the press and proofing articles for punctuation. With his background and new father-in-law, Walt had no trouble landing a job at the paper. There weren't many residents in Sand Beach who were qualified or interested in a job at *the Times*. The biggest employer in town was the tire factory.

Walt had not planned to live in a small town, but Grace had been raised here and wanted to be near her father. He had envisioned a life in the big city as a big-time journalist, covering big-city politics. But when he met Grace, he knew they were going to be together and he would have to consider her needs as well. After he and Grace decided to marry, they had considered living in Detroit or Cleveland, where Walt's parents lived. But neither place appealed to her.

On one occasion, Walt went to Detroit for a major interview at the *Detroit News*. Not long after arriving, he promptly became the victim of a pickpocket as he stood out in front of his hotel waiting for a taxi. After the interview, he decided that even if he was offered the job he would not take it, even though it would have paid substantially more than he would get in a small town. He thought maybe Grace was right, when she told him they needed to live in her home town. A small town, though not full of opportunity, would provide them with a quiet existence. And that was how they had landed in Sand Beach.

The phone interrupted his daydreaming.

It was Grace. "Walt, do you know where my watch might be?"

"Hey, it's you!" He smiled, happy to hear her voice. "Why don't you look in the bathroom? I bet you've checked that blue stick a thousand times today."

"How did you know I still have the blue stick? Wait a sec, I'll go look."

Within a few moments she was back. "How do you always know everything?"

Walt took pride in having guessed right. "Bye sweetie," he said, smiling at her forgetfulness.

FOUR

Grace was scrubbing the toilet when the phone rang.

When she picked it up, she heard Fran's voice say. "Grace, I need to talk. You busy?"

"I'm busy cleaning toilets!" Grace laughed. "What's up, Fran?"

"I've got to talk, and I have got to get out of here. Can we meet at the swing set at Sand Beach Park in about half an hour?" Fran sounded upset.

As soon as she hung up, Grace hopped into the Jeep and drove off, wondering what was so urgent. When she arrived at the park, Fran was already there with her son.

"Pauly, you wanna swing?" Fran asked her son.

Paul jumped up onto the adult swing. Fran plopped down next to him and squeezed her plump rear onto the narrow rubber seat.

Grace noticed there were dark circles around Fran's eyes, and her mascara had run down her pretty face. Her expression was one of despair.

"Paul sure is growing up," Grace said.

The five-year old worked his small legs on the swing, pushing upward.

"Mommy, push me!" Paul said. Fran ignored him. Grace stood up and gave the boy a push.

"So, you okay?" she said to Fran.

Fran started crying, and Grace waited for her to gain her composure.

"I think Michael is cheating on me," Fran finally blurted out.

"Shh, Fran, you might want to keep this news from Paul." Grace gasped. Just listen, Grace thought, don't judge, and don't give advice. She continued to push Paul higher and higher on the swing.

"He didn't get home til two in the morning, and he smelled like another woman."

She went on to describe how distant he'd been over the past months, spending very little time with her. And there had been a few times she had stopped by his office and he hadn't been there when he said he was. And he rarely, if ever, wanted to have sex with her anymore.

Grace glanced at Paul, wondering if it was okay to say *sex* in front of a five-year-old.

"Daddy came home late, Mommy," Paul commented as he winced and sailed high upon the swing.

"And last night, everything I've been worrying about seemed to come true."

"Well, did he admit it?"

"No. He just said he'd been shooting pool at Sammy's and lost track of time. But if he'd been shooting pool, he would have smelled like smoke and not perfume."

Grace pondered this new information. "I don't know what to tell you, Fran."

"What would you do?"

Walt coming home late smelling of perfume, was one problem Grace had never had.

"I don't know, Fran," she said. "I'm probably not the best one to give advice. But I know it would hurt, bad. I *always* thought you guys were made for each other."

Fran started wailing, taking over swing-pushing duty from Grace. She pushed Paul so high, Grace was afraid he would sail over the top of the swing.

"And you know, Grace," she said through her sobs, "we finally finished the floors and all the renovations."

Grace and Walt had helped Fran and Michael Baker move into their first home five years earlier on a hot July day. At that time, the house was generic and unloved, with white walls and broken tiles in the bathroom and shaggy trees in the yard. It hadn't been christened by its new owners with smells of frying hamburgers, sounds of conversation, a crying infant or steam escaping from the clothes dryer scenting the outdoors. Or decorated with blue-and-white wicker furnishings and refinished hardwood floors. Or tainted by infidelity.

Grace had seen the results of Fran's hard work. Inspired by pictures in *Ladies' Home Journal,* Fran had carefully planned and executed a complete makeover of the house, painting everything in shades of blue and white to resemble a beach cottage. She had collected wicker furniture from yard sales. Paul's room was the only exception to the décor, with wallpaper decorated with red fire engines to match his red fire-engine-shaped bed.

"I thought we had finally settled into a good family life. The bills are paid, the house is fixed up, and Paul will be starting school next fall. Now what am I gonna do?" Fran looked miserable.

"One day at a time," Grace said, thinking of all the work that she and Walt needed to do on the duplex before the baby arrived.

"How's work?" Grace asked referring to Fran's new job over at Glamour Clips. Grace figured it would be best to change the subject.

"I love it, Grace. It's been a lifesaver, and I'm real glad to have it right *now*. I take Paul over to my mom's while I work." Fran's mother was a retired hairdresser who lived in an old clapboard house on the edge of town. Her dad had left the family when Fran was small. Grace had never seen him.

"Why don't you come over this weekend, Grace, you and Walt? Maybe the four of us can make fajitas. Maybe that's what Michael and I need. To have some friends over. I'll make daiquiris."

Grace considered the offer. "Sorry, Fran. Walt is at training all weekend, and I've got work at the barn. My doctor prefers I don't ride anything more than a slow trot, but I can still clean stalls and feed and groom. I can't lose my income right now."

"Well, at least come see me at Glamour Clips," Fran said, handing Grace a freshly printed pink business card.

Fran, now calmer, hugged her. Then she reached down to hold Paul's hand as they exited the park.

Fran had never looked so forlorn. Grace felt sick to her stomach. She wished she had stayed home to clean the bathroom. She felt guilty that Walt was slaving away at the *Times,* probably typing frantically to meet a deadline. She would make it up to him by cleaning the house and baking his favorite fried chicken with French rolls, salad, and homemade chocolate chip cookies.

And she would try to file away the dilemma of her best and most treasured friend.

FIVE

"Yum," Walt said as he grabbed a chocolate chip cookie.

The smell of fried chicken filled the duplex. In the corner of the tiny kitchen, the small round table was set with red taper candles and the Oneida dinnerware they had gotten as a wedding present from Walt's brother, Pete.

Walt washed his hands and then sat down at the kitchen table across from Grace. "You sure spoil me." He grinned. "How did you know I needed a good home-cooked meal?"

"Vell," she said, trying to imitate a German accent. "I just know I luff you and you are verth it." Grace glowed. She poured the ranch dressing on her salad and passed it to Walt.

"You are so silly," Walt said, taking a sip of Chardonnay.

"Don't worry, sweetie," Grace replied. "I save my accents for you only."

"Thank goodness! Can you imagine if everyone in town thought my wife had a rare malady that caused her to go into convulsions with multiple accents?" Walt responded, referring to Grace's occasional habit of tainting her speech with foreign accents. "To be honest, love, it kind of scares me. I had a friend in school who did a ma-

— 19 —

jor paper on Foreign Accent Syndrome."

"Actually, I felt guilty that you worked all day." Grace spread a thick layer of butter on her roll. "Fran called and wanted me to meet her at the park. So I spent a few hours there with her and Paul. She wants us to come have dinner with them this weekend. But I told her you would be gone."

Grace thought about being alone while Walt put in his weekend with the National Guard. She missed him already.

"Yeah," Walt affirmed. "Wish I didn't have to but got to. Maybe we can join Fran and Michael the week following," he added. "Haven't seen Mike in a while. Last time I saw him, he looked like he'd lost a few pounds. Wonder if he's been on a diet."

A diet all right, thought Grace. "Yeah, he does look like he's been dieting," she said. "Maybe we can get a rain check. I'll ask Fran." Grace smiled as she cleared the table.

"Whatsa matter, sweetie?" Walt breathed into the back of Grace's slender neck.

"Oh, nothing, Walt."

He gently brushed his lips against her ear.

"Yeah, right, I've lived with you eight years and suddenly you get quiet right in the middle of dinner. Are you mad that I'm leaving for the weekend? Is it something about the baby?"

"No, it's not about us. Or the baby." Grace knew that the worry was not about the two of them. "It was just something Fran told me today, and I'm worried about her. But I promised not to tell anyone." She looked up at Walt and met his gaze. "Even you, love."

She stood on tiptoe to grab a kiss. He bent his six-foot frame to make it easier for her to reach his lips.

They rolled up their sleeves to begin their after-dinner routine.

Walt filled the sink with hot suds while Grace put away leftovers and cleared the table.

"I've got to work now, Grace. I have a story that needs to be on Stu's desk in the morning."

"No problem," Grace said, though she had hoped they could go for a walk or watch a movie.

Walt found his way to the corner of the living room that he called his home office.

"Watcha workin' on Wal?"

He picked up the pile on the corner of the desk. The top page detailed the events leading up to the disappearance of a woman outside of Sand Beach.

"Oh," he said. "It's that story about Melissa Perkins. They never found the body." He rubbed his head, massaging his temples as though he was attempting to keep another migraine at bay. He gave Grace the rundown as he patiently described the details of the article. Then he gathered his notes into a pile and looked at Grace.

"Sorry, honey, I gotta be alone now. You know. Cross my t's and dot my i's."

Just then, the phone rang and Grace ran to get it.

"Grace!" It was Fran again. "I am going crazy! Michael came home and had dinner with me, but when I tried to talk about last night, he stormed out. He said I was a 'crazy broad.'" She sounded as upset as she had that morning. "Please come out for a ride with me."

"Walt?" Grace stuck her head into the living room after she hung up the phone. "Fran needs me again. I'll be gone for a while. Okay with you?"

"Sure." Walt nodded, engrossed in his work.

When she heard the sound of the car horn, Grace grabbed her purse and rushed out.

"Sorry about the mess," Fran said as Grace eased herself into the front seat of the Buick Skylark and tried to find a place for her feet amidst Twinkie wrappers and a juice box. "I know I shouldn't be doing this, but I can't help it." She spoke fast, out of breath. "He left so angry and I just can't sit at home alone with Paul waiting to see what's next."

Fran wasn't kidding. She was now on a mission. She looked worse than she had that morning and seemed much more upset.

Grace twisted her neck to look at Paul, who was secured in his booster seat, wedged beside magazines and stuffed animals. He looked small, pale and pouty.

"Hi, Paul. I like your Power Rangers." Grace held the action figure in front of Paul, hoping this would be enough to distract him from the chaos his Mom was going through.

"I *love* Power Rangers." Paul held up two action figures and began mimicking their fighting sounds.

"Pow!" The muscled blue ranger attacked the ranger in black.

"Zam," the other one replied as Paul maneuvered them in battle.

Grace tried to listen to Fran and entertain Paul at the same time, all the while wishing she were sitting by Walt's side as he wrote his articles rather than driving around with a distraught friend and a five-year-old.

"I just gotta know! I don't believe him. How could he lie to me? He doesn't love me! He's gonna leave me! What's the matter with me?" The drama of the moment and of the last twenty-four hours played itself out in the large Buick trailing up and down the side streets of Sand Beach in search of Michael's white Chevy truck.

Fran suddenly slammed on the brakes, and Grace felt herself fly forward. Thank goodness she had her seat belt on. Fran pointed to a white truck in a driveway visible from the corner.

"Maybe that's him."

Fran turned left onto the street. The truck was parked in the driveway of a bungalow whose yard was littered with children's toys. Both Fran and Grace knew who lived there.

"QRS 920. That's his truck!" Fran cried out. "Oh my god! Mavis? That slut!" Grace winced upon hearing a word she despised. "She has four kids all by different guys. What in the world would my husband want with her?"

"Fran, I know you're upset," Grace said in practically a whisper. "But do you think Paul should hear such language?"

"Paul, oh Paul, I'm sorry. I'm sorry, Paul." She went on repeating this apology to her son.

"And I'm sorry too, Grace. What can Michael possibly see in her?"

Fran was getting a little calmer, not much, but a little.

Truth is always a good thing, Grace thought as she tried to comprehend along with Fran the meaning of it all. Truth is sane. Real. Undeniable. Without valid facts, the imagination can weave tall tales. And tall tales can lead to trouble.

"Mavis Brown," Fran said. "What does he see in her? He must have done some work on that old shack of hers. I bet she seduced him while all them half-naked kids were running around the place. It won't last," Fran continued. "It can't! What does she have that I don't? She doesn't have a kid with Michael at least." She paused as if she wasn't sure. "I *hope* she doesn't have a kid with Michael. Oh, crap, Grace!"

"Well, whatever happens now, at least I know the truth. I'm not gonna say another thing to Michael. He'll have to tell me himself." Fran seemed calmer and stronger now.

Grace glanced at her watch. "Fran, I'd love to be able to stay with you," she said. "But I better get home to Walt. He's probably worried by now. It's been two hours. And your boy looks tired. Aren't you Paul?"

Grace looked back at the pale blond boy who had by this time dropped the Power Rangers onto the floor. He stared at her blankly and yawned.

"But call me if you need to, okay? If things get *really* crazy." She made sure to emphasize *really* so that if anything happened that wasn't *really* crazy, she wouldn't have to go out on another run like this one.

"Okay, Grace." Fran started driving back toward Grace's street. "I do feel better, though I'm not sure I'll live through this. I'm sorry. I don't want you in trouble with Walt. But I really appreciate you being my friend. What would I do without a good friend?"

Back home at last, Grace waved goodbye to Fran and shut the door quietly behind her. She sighed deeply and tried to clear her mind.

"Walt, I'm home." She suddenly felt a need to curl up at Walt's feet in the living room. She went over to his chair.

He looked up at her. "Hi, Gracie. Home so soon?" He apparently hadn't been watching the clock like Grace had been.

"Yep," she purred as she kissed the top of Walt's dark hair. "Mind if I sit with you while you write?"

She tossed a pillow on the floor along with a throw from the couch and curled up at Walt's feet.

"Of course not," he said. "You won't go to sleep on me will you?" He smiled.

"Nope." She yawned. "Just here to keep you company." She enjoyed the familiar hum of the typewriter as its keys tapped the page.

By midnight, Walt was finished with his work. He roused Grace and pulled her to her feet. Groggy, she stumbled beside him.

"I just dreamt that I was driving to California, and our wonderful baby was in the back seat and you were with me and we were oh so happy. And the sun was shining and the sky was so blue with puffy clouds. And I think the baby was a girl!"

"And I bet she was just as pretty as her momma." He led her to the bedroom, removed her shoes and tucked her up under the covers. She was too tired to undress and wash her face. This was a night where each of them plopped onto their own side of the bed.

"Night, hon."

Walt patted Gracie's behind. She turned away from him and within moments fell into a deep and dream-filled sleep.

SIX

Grace was determined to clean everything. She donned a mask and used vinegar and baking soda, as she had read that inhaling the fumes from commercial cleaners could hurt the baby. She cleaned the entire fridge inside and out, vacuumed under the beds, and eventually worked her way through the entire duplex. Each time she thought she was finished, she would start all over again. She did this between waves of nausea.

Each morning she would look at the calendar and note how many days remained until the baby would come into the world. In the third month, she started pulling out the tape measure and measured her girth every other day to see how much her belly was growing. Other than the time she spent listening to Fran rant about Mavis and to Walt reading aloud his news articles and the few days a week she still tended to the horses, her life was all about the baby.

One day, she discovered blood in her panties and immediately called Fran.

"Fran, is it normal to spot?" Grace clutched her well-worn copy of *What to Expect When You're Expecting*, the section on spotting now bookmarked.

"Spot, you mean bleed? I think I spotted some when I was pregnant with Paul. You might want to rest."

"Fran, I don't need to rest. I have too much to do. If I rested all the time, how would I get anything done around here?" She paused. "What about you, Fran, you okay?"

"Yeah, I guess I'm okay. Michael came home last night. And he didn't get on the phone and he never left, not even to go to the corner store. Maybe he's tired of Mavis. Maybe we can work this thing out."

"I hope so. You're way better than Mavis, and maybe Michael just has to come to that conclusion himself."

"Yeah, I thought of that too," Fran replied. "But really, this whole thing is just way too much for me. I keep thinking I'm gonna wake up and it will all be a bad dream. And Grace?" Fran added before she hung up. "You might want to check with the doctor about the spotting."

"Yes, Mom." Grace hung up the phone, sat down and propped her legs up on the chair.

Grace knew it was going to be approximately 198 days until their first child's birthday. She looked forward to a time when she no longer reeled from the smell of steak and hot coffee, two things she had once loved. She was sick of analyzing every little bodily function, wondering if it was normal or the sign of something serious. She looked forward to no longer opening up her book at every hint of a symptom, no longer worrying about taking a Tylenol or having a glass of wine with dinner. She looked forward to the day when she could once again gallop freely through the fields and lead trail rides.

Pregnancy had caused Grace to worry about things that could happen to her now that she had another life to be responsible for, another life that could not exist without her own. She thumbed through her address book to the *H*'s for Dr. Hays. Ten minutes later she had her answer. Dr. Hays told her that she didn't need to be concerned, that spotting was common in early pregnancy, but if she had other symptoms like pain or cramping, she should call again.

The spotting passed within days and Grace was able to leave that worry behind.

SEVEN

Grace shivered in the cold January air and even the bright sun didn't warm her as she and Walt walked toward the barn. She lived for these Saturdays when she had Walt to herself. She wore thermal underwear, a sweatshirt, two pairs of wool socks, boots, winter coat, a scarf, a hand warmer, and mittens.

"I do believe you're wearing every piece of clothing you own," Walt said with a teasing smile.

"It's times like this that Florida seems very appealing," Grace said as she shivered.

After leading Glo from her stall, she took out the bucket of grooming tools and worked her coat til it shone like silk. Then she placed a bridle on her.

"What are you doing that for?" Walt asked. "I thought Dr. Hays told you not to ride anymore."

"He said that he thought it would be a 'good idea' to stop riding, but he also said I should do whatever I feel comfortable doing. Surely, at three months it's not going to hurt me. Besides you're riding with me!"

"I am?" Walt looked hesitant. "Hey, you know how I feel about

— 31 —

trusting my life to a huge four-legged mindless bundle of nerves!"

"We'll be fine," Grace said. "There's way too much snow piled up to go very far or very fast. This may be my last chance to ride for a *long* time."

Walt hoisted the saddle onto Glo.

"How are we both going to fit on this little thing?" Walt asked. He looked at Grace in her many layers. "I don't think Glo will be happy."

Grace enjoyed being the expert on something for a change. "She'll be fine. If not, we'll ride bareback." They mounted Glo in the aisle and nearly knocked out the barn lights. Grace had to practically sit in front of the saddle on the mare's neck.

Glo scampered to the side and snorted.

"Remove the saddle," Grace said. "We'll ride bareback."

"Okay, dear, whatever you say."

They dismounted, and Walt removed the English saddle and put it back on the rack in the tack room. They walked the horse outside into the biting air. Walt gave Grace a leg up onto Glo and then he mounted as well, sitting behind Grace and wrapping his arms around her bulky figure.

The wind howled.

"Brrrr," Grace mumbled beneath her scarf.

She kicked her heels into Glo's sides, but the horse refused to budge.

Grace clucked. "C'mon, Glo!"

After some gentle nudging, Grace got Glo to walk.

The snow fell in silent, peaceful streams as it transformed the cold, dry ground into a glistening white. Steamy puffs of breath escaped the horse and riders.

"Let's trot," Grace said beneath her scarf. She gently put pressure on Glo's sides and clicked. Obediently, Glo trotted down the path.

"Let's not," Walt said, his voice getting higher. He held Grace more tightly than before. She sensed his anxiety.

As they ventured through the winter wonderland, Walt pulled Glo's reins to bring her to a halt and dismounted. He marched through the snow, seemingly intent on a task, while Grace sat clutching Glo's reins and shivering. Within a few minutes, she realized he was creating letters in the snow. She watched as they slowly revealed themselves.

I love you Grace was now etched in the snow.

Grace smiled as a tear escaped from her left eye. "I love you too," she whispered.

After an hour of riding, they found their way back to the barn.

"You want to help me water the horses?" Grace asked, brushing snow off Walt's hair.

Walt nodded and grabbed a bag of carrots. As he walked down the aisles chatting to the horses and calling them by name, he tossed an orange treat into each grain bucket.

"I know you'll miss riding," Walt said to Grace, amid the sound of the horses chewing.

"Hmmm." Grace sighed. "I guess that will have to be my last ride. Dr. Hays said I can still muck stalls, feed, groom, and visit the stable. Preferably with you." She winked as she poured grain into the feed buckets.

"Good thing you have heat in this place." She knew he was referring to the feed room where the garbage bins were filled with grain, the hay bales were neatly stacked, and the indoor sink was ready with a hose attachment to fill the water buckets. "Otherwise in this weather, the water would be frozen solid."

Grace handed him the hose. She heard him but didn't respond. "Walt, do you think we can look at wallpaper for the baby's room this weekend?"

"Sure, Grace. You worry about everything. We'll get it all done, I promise." Walt took the hose and started filling the buckets in the aisle. "But until we do, I thought we might spend a little more time out here." He put down the hose and pushed himself against her, brushing his lips over her damp hair. His hand found its way under all the layers of clothing to her skin. "Just you and me," he whispered into her ear.

The smell of Walt's aftershave was intoxicating. "Walter!" Her breath quickened. She reached up to kiss his mouth. "Hmmm," Grace moaned. "Isn't it kind of cold for, you know, that?"

"Don't worry," he reassured her. Small puffs of steam escaped his beautiful mouth. "I will surely warm you up."

"Sounds good to me," she giggled. "I hope Mr. Mathis doesn't come out. Or one of the horse owners," she added, not wanting to consider anything other than the fun they were about to have.

"We'll close the tack door. And the large barn door squeaks."

Grace gently took Walt's hand and led him up the ladder into the loft. They removed only the essentials and fell into the rhythm of each other's bodies. They lay for a while enjoying their time together.

"Glad it's not a weekday," Grace commented.

"Gracie," Walt said, suddenly serious. "I hope this doesn't hurt the baby. The riding and the lifting and then…this." He lay on her tummy and patted her slightly rounded shape.

"I think we are expanding," he said, referring to the growing mound in Gracie's middle. He now used her tummy as a resting place after making love or while snuggling.

"Isn't Mommy expanding?" Walt spoke to her middle.

"I don't think the baby understands yet. You talk to him like he can hear you!"

"Well, if he can't then I don't care. I love him anyway." He traced his finger up and down Grace's pregnant body. "Or her," he added.

"I love you, Walter Allen Moore. Now, let's go find somewhere to eat! I'm starving!"

EIGHT

The sound of the chainsaw cut through the quiet tree-lined neighborhood at the edge of Sand Beach. One resident preferred labor to whiling away the perfect lazy warm afternoon with a glass of lemonade or a good book. The noisy lumberjack was cutting a large elm in his front yard fully engaged in the task. Sweat poured down his handsome face and found a way onto his white t-shirt creating a wet jagged stain, a badge of hard work. He removed his goggles and wiped his brow with his sweaty hand, as he turned to see his daughter and son-in-law pull up in the drive.

"Hi, Dad!" Grace called out as she maneuvered herself over to give father a hug. She was now eight months along. "We tried to call the house, but you didn't answer. I thought you might be out in the yard."

"Gray, no hugs," he said, pulling away. "I'm too sweaty." He stretched to plant a kiss on her cheek. "Looks like it won't be too long before I am officially a grandfather."

He put down the chainsaw and extended his work-worn hand to Walt.

"Yeah," Walt replied. "I don't think you'd be able to get your arms around her anyway. I know I can't," he added, playfully attempting to hug Grace.

"Four more weeks and that should change." Grace responded. "Hopefully."

"You two arrived just in time to help." Her dad nodded toward the elm that was halfway sawed through.

"I hope you don't plan to work all day," Grace said. "We brought a ton of food. Maybe we can fire up that gas grill we got you for Christmas. Have you used it yet, Dad?"

"Not yet. I was hoping you would join me for the honors. You know I never have company."

It was true. Charles Walker stayed mostly to himself. He discovered that time alone was the safest way to avoid the pain that love could bring. For the past six years, he had found solace in fixing up the house, remodeling, and painting each room, and the end result showed every bit of the labor he had put into Grace's childhood home. Work was his means to sanity. The wood piled next to his four-bedroom brick house in the tidy little neighborhood was a visual testament to the months he'd spent chopping, trimming, and stacking the many trees in the yard. His muscled arms and youthful face belied his fifty-two years. Had Caroline still been alive, he was sure she would still look as young as the day they had met. At least in his eyes. Every time she entered his mind, he felt a twinge of sadness. Even after six very long years.

Walt and Grace took their grocery bags out of the Jeep and brought them into the house. Grace stayed in the house to put the food away, but Walt came back outside.

"Looks like the Yankees are going to have another good season," Charles said to him.

"Yep, doing better than the Tigers. They're 2-6 this year. Grace and I were hoping to catch a game, but I hate to go see a losing team. What's the point?"

"Well, if I could catch a Yankees game, I wouldn't care if they lost every time," Charles said. "I would give anything for one afternoon in Yankee Stadium with a ballpark hotdog. Just one afternoon. If I could do that, life would be sweet." He reached for a cold Pepsi in the small ice-filled chest on the porch.

"Well, why don't you, Dad?" He liked it when Walt occasionally referred to him as Dad.

"I was going to go with Grace's mom. But we never got to. It wouldn't be the same without her." He stared into space. It was time to change the subject. "Bought me another chainsaw." He nodded toward the 4.0 Craftsman lying next to the one he was working with. "Thought I might have you help me sometime."

"Of course, that's what I'm here for." Walt smiled. "I was thinking I'd help you today. That is, if you'd like me to."

Charles thought how he'd always wanted a son. He decided to ask Walt a question that had been hounding him. "What about the Middle East? It seems as though that crazy Saddam is always trying to take over something, that oil-hungry bastard. Will that affect you?"

"Nah, I don't think so. Things are always unstable over there. They never call up the Guard for stuff like that. Which is a good thing because Grace needs me." Walt's expression turned serious.

"She's lucky to have you, Walt."

"Well, enough of that. Want some help?" The half-cut tree looked like it might take the rest of the day and then some to be cut and stacked on the woodpile.

After a little while, Grace joined them outside. "You men," Grace said. "Always working or playing."

"Well, at least we're not always eating and sleeping, oh pregnant one," Walt said, eyeing her prominent belly.

Grace found a shady spot under one of the few trees and sat on a blanket she had taken from the Jeep. She read a magazine while the two men worked.

"How can you stand that hard ground?" Charles asked as he eyed Grace. "My land, girl, get yourself a chair why don't you?"

"Don't worry, Dad, I've got lots of padding."

The men put on their goggles and revved up the chainsaws. Charles let his mind wander with the rhythmic whirring of the saws and thought back to the first time Grace had brought Walt home. He and Caroline had been discerning when it came to suitors for their daughters. Caroline wanted the best for both girls, and together they had scrutinized every boy, raked them over with questions suitable only for someone taking the state boards. They knew from their own union the importance of choosing an appropriate mate, one who would be there through thick and thin, til death do us part.

When Grace brought Walt home on Thanksgiving weekend from the University of Michigan where they both studied, they knew he might be a good catch for her. Walt seemed genuine, sturdy, sincere. He was an intelligent man with plans for a stable future as a journalist and writer. And the fact that he was also in the Army National Guard just made him seem all that more strong and reliable. Yes, Charles had to admit that he and Caroline had been a little hard on suitors, but the end result had been worth it. At least for Grace. He wasn't sure how Becky had managed with men. He hadn't seen Becky since just after the funeral, when his youngest daughter fled with a sparsely packed suitcase and a chip on her shoulder. No letters, not even a Christmas card. He couldn't even say for sure whether she was still alive. It was another one of those things he didn't talk about with anyone.

As the saw cut into the flesh of the elm, neatly trimming its branches, Charles pushed back the raw emotions that emerged whenever his thoughts wandered to the women he had lost.

"Whew, it's getting hot." He tripped the switch on the saw and wiped his brow again." I think we ought to take a break, huh, Walt? How about a Bud?"

"Sounds like a winner. Where's Grace?"

Charles now noticed that Grace had left her spot under the tree.

"Find a seat, Walt," Charles said, nodding toward the lawn chair. "I'll be right back. We might need to fire up the grill soon."

Charles entered the kitchen through the carport, calling Grace's name. The house was silent except for the sound of the fridge defrosting. Then he heard a quiet sob coming from Grace's old bedroom.

He made his way to the room, as a knot formed in the pit of his stomach. He peeked through the door to see Grace curled up in a fetal position on the plaid comforter, looking very small for someone so pregnant. Photos from a familiar shoebox were scattered across the bed. A picture of the four of them at Grace's high school graduation lay next to her hand. He'd forgotten about that one, and the memories made him nauseous. Dizzy, he toddled into the kitchen and found two Buds in the fridge. He cracked one open and took a large swig as he made his way outside to join Walt.

Walt was waiting at the picnic table on the screened-in porch that Charles had built the year before. He had installed a ceiling fan and had decorated with wicker furniture, a glass wicker edged table and a nice area rug.

Before long, Charles had the new grill that sat under the carport sizzling with Jumbo Bryan hot dogs. Charles rolled the shucked corn in real butter and wrapped it in foil and added it to the virgin grill.

"C'mon out Grace," Charles greeted as he noticed the tear-stained face of his daughter stepping out to join them. "You need to eat!" He finished up the meal and carefully set the food on the paper plates, buffet style. The three sat down to eat and Charles watched as Grace picked at a hamburger. She didn't touch the potato salad or the chips or the freshly buttered corn that she usually loved. The men had no problem eating her portions.

"Grace," Walt whispered, observing her meager appetite and swollen red eyes. "You okay?" He looked at her closely as Dad left to get another beer.

"Shhh, she hissed. I'll tell you later. Just my pregnant emotions *again*." A tear welled up in the outside corner of her eye.

Dad returned with two more beers and a Pepsi for Grace.

"I've been thinking I don't like retirement so much," Dad said. "I've about run out of projects around here. You two need any work done on your place?"

Walt responded. "I hate to do too much work on a place I hope to get out of. We're going to need more space soon. I'm feeling kinda stifled with my office where the living room should be." He winked at Grace.

Grace choked. "What do you mean hope to get out of! Are you trying to tell me we're moving?!"

"Maybe I am, sweetie."

"We're moving?" She looked at him with surprise. "You haven't mentioned that to *me*, Walt!"

Dad commented. "It's about time you moved out of that little closet. You need more space. Have you looked at anything?"

"No. But I think I'm tired of throwing away rent. Might as well put our money into something that will be ours."

"Sounds like this has been more than just a passing thought," Grace responded as the news sunk in. She seemed to have regained her appetite and pulled the apple pie toward her, cutting a large chunk. Anybody want some ice cream?"

Grace jumped up from the table to go in to get the half gallon of vanilla bean ice cream that she and Walt had brought.

"That cheered her up," Charles commented as he watched his eldest daughter go into the house.

"Yes, I'm glad I went ahead and told her. I've been thinking about it, and now is a good a time as any to break the news."

"I'm glad you did," Charles replied. "If there is anything I really can't stand, it's an unhappy female."

"Gotcha, Dad" I agree 100%." What a difference a conversation could make.

An hour later, Grace and Walt packed up the Jeep for the drive home.

"You two coming back? How about tomorrow?"

"Soon, Dad, soon. And before you know it you will be saying you *three* coming back when we have your little grandchild with us."

"I can't wait Gray." He watched as the two drove off down the driveway. This leaving thing always tugged at Charles' heart.

NINE

Though the distance was short, it allowed Grace a few minutes to comment.

"Wow, Walt!" Her insides were doing somersaults. "I didn't know you were thinking about us moving!"

"I wasn't going to say anything, Grace, but you looked so darn sad when you got up from your nap, that I thought this might be as good a time as any. I don't want my girl unhappy. What was wrong, anyway?"

"Oh, that," she responded, the previous emotion now a distant memory. "I got into my old bedroom closet where Dad keeps the family pictures and I thought I'd reminisce. When I sorted through them, I didn't realize how much I missed Mom and my sister. It's been six years since I've heard from Becky!"

"Has it really been six years?" Walt put his hand on Grace's knee.

"Six years. And then some. I lose my mom and then my sister. Life isn't fair. It's like half my family doesn't even exist."

"Beck's probably fine, Grace. Probably straightened up and has a family of her own."

"Yeah, but she's my sister. And I really don't know whether she's fine or not. Sisters don't just up and leave and never call again. I'm the only sister she has. Even if she's jealous of me, that shouldn't mean she can't call me. People work things like this out every day. The problem is I don't know if she's dead or alive. I don't know if she's still drinking or with some loser, or what! We used to be so close! I could be an aunt and not even know it!"

"Okay, Grace, I didn't want to make you sad again. I just wanted to make sure that if it was something I could help you with, that I'm here for you."

"You're always here for me, Walt." Grace leaned across the Jeep to try to lean against her husband's side. It was impossible so she grabbed his hand instead.

"I guess the saddest thing for me," Grace continued, "is that our baby will never know his grandmother, and may never see his aunt. There's just something wrong about that."

"The baby will have us, Grace. And that's the important thing. And your Dad. And my parents and Pete. And he will be loved."

"You always know what to say, Walt! Especially the news about the house. What good news! When can we start looking?"

"After the baby, okay?" He grinned at Grace. "We just need to do a little more figuring, and I'd like to have him here first. At least now that you know, we can plan together."

Grace sighed and thanked her lucky stars for all of her blessings, including the rumbling gymnast inside her.

TEN

On a hot, hazy July morning, Grace went outside with a glass of iced tea to find a surprise lily blooming in front of the duplex. This particular lily had not bloomed in several years, but now it opened its bud, displaying pink and yellow petals. It seemed to Grace like nature announcing that something glorious was about to happen.

She was regarding the flower with amazement, when Walt opened the screen door and stepped onto the porch.

"Walt, look," she said. "I've been waiting for that lily to bloom for the past three years. Maybe that's a sign the baby's coming."

Walt stepped off the porch with his coffee mug. He bent over to examine the lily, caressing the delicate petals.

"Remember the last time they bloomed, Gracie? You thought it was a sign I was getting a promotion."

"Well, you did! Two weeks later you got a raise."

"Grace, it was time for my annual review. I was *expecting* a raise." He stepped back onto the porch and found his seat next to Grace. He set his coffee cup on the plastic table and turned to catch her gaze. "And, he added, you are due any day."

"You think I'm silly." Grace pouted.

"Not silly, Grace. But you are always looking for some cosmic sign that something has happened or is about to happen." He leaned over to stroke her hair. "Don't worry, Pumpkin, I love that about you, the way you see the world. When you see some kind of a sign about something, it is so *you*."

Grace took a swig of tea and gasped.

"Walt, I think something just happened."

Walt watched as a thin stream of water trickled down Grace's blue cotton maternity pants.

"What's that?"

"My water broke." Grace sat in the chair, breathless and excited.

Walt bolted towards the kitchen. "I'll get the towels, honey."

"Where are you going, Walt?"

"I'm going to clean up."

"And then what are you going to do?"

He answered from the kitchen. "Call the doctor?"

"Walt, I think this is it. Dr. Hays will just tell us to hightail it to the hospital."

Grace winced as a jolt of pain ripped through her.

Walt returned to the porch. He stood in front of Grace, paper towels his only offering. He fumbled to pull them from the roll.

"Walt, forget cleaning. Just get my packed bag by the door and help me to the car. *Please*."

She waited on the porch until Walt came back outside with her bag and marched right out to the Jeep without her. He threw the bag in the back seat, hopped in the driver's seat and started the engine.

"Walter!" Grace shouted out to Walt as he backed out of the drive, a man on a mission. "Aren't you forgetting something?" She managed a laugh between the contractions, which were already occurring more frequently.

They made it to Sand Beach Hospital just in time. Grace delivered quickly. No camcorders to tape the event. No relatives to flock to the little family. No buddies to pace the floor with Walt. Just Walt and Grace and the tiny newborn.

The eight-pound, eight-ounce infant made his way into the world, flinging his arms and legs, a lone warrior in the bright hospital room. His cries pierced the sterile air.

Grace looked up at Walt, her eyes filled with tears. "It looks like he has all his fingers and toes."

"Yep," Walt said, his voice cracking. "And he's handsome. Just like his father."

"He's *perfect* Walt. Travis is *perfect*!"

Walt beamed at Grace, love for his little family warming the room. He brushed a wisp of damp hair from Grace's cheek. "Yes, he echoed, Travis *Walter* Moore is perfect."

ELEVEN

Some babies coo and giggle during their waking hours and then sleep through the night. Not Travis. From day one, he cried. He didn't just whimper and moan with a tear or two trickling down his cheek. He let out large red-faced wails throughout the day and into the wee hours of the night.

"What's wrong with him?" Walt asked on the day Travis turned two months as he and Grace sat at the kitchen table. He swallowed a mouthful of the grilled cheese sandwich Grace had prepared in between feedings and washed it down with tomato soup. The meals she now prepared for him were wedged in between feedings, changings, burpings, and baths.

"I don't know, Walt. He's been doing this all day." She lifted the baby from the swing, sat on the sofa, and unbuttoned her shirt.

Walt came over to join his son and exhausted wife. "Gracie, Travis seems to be hungry all the time. Do you think he gets enough to eat? You know how they say that breast-feeding might not be enough."

"No, I'm sure that's not it. He's two months old and he has gained three pounds in the past month. He eats like a horse. He just cries *all* day." Grace's voice quivered. "I can't do *anything* right!"

Walt put his arm around her shoulder and whispered. "You're a wonderful mother, Grace. Some babies just cry."

"Yeah, babies cry because something's wrong. And I don't know what it is. Obviously." Her throat tightened and she squeezed her eyes to hold back a flood of emotion. "I feel so cooped up. What happened to my life? I feed the baby and I change the baby. Then I walk with him. Then I put him to bed and he cries. I feel so inadequate!"

"I'm sorry you feel that way Grace. But Dr. Hays says he's doing just fine. I don't see a thing you are doing wrong, other than being hard on yourself." Walt put his head on Grace's shoulder.

"I miss the horses. I miss hanging out with Fran, going to the beach. I want time with you! I miss my old body." Grace wept, big tears forming a river along her pale cheeks. She pulled her shirt closed and handed Travis to Walt. "You feed him! I've got to get out of here!"

She stomped into the bedroom, sobbing all the way. For the first time in a long time, she felt angry. The baby responded in kind, joining his mother's cries. Together they turned the tiny duplex into a loud, wailing asylum.

Grace ran out to the Jeep.

"Where are you going?" she heard Walt shout as she pulled out of the driveway.

Grace asked herself the same question as she sped through town. Suddenly, she realized she had run a stop sign. It was lucky she hadn't hit anyone. Breathing heavily, she pulled into the parking lot at Raymond's. She saw through her rearview mirror that a police car with a flashing red and blue light had followed her into the lot.

"Crap!" Her hands shook as she fumbled for her purse. She located her Michigan driver's license just in time to turn to the large shadow hovering by her open window.

"Ma'am," the husky voice addressed her. "Happen to know why I'm stopping you?"

Grace handed him her license. "You knew I was having a bad day?"

"No, ma'am." He studied the license for a moment and then looked into her eyes. "You related to Walt Moore?"

"Yes, sir." Maybe she'd wiggle out of this one. "I'm his wife." She wore the statement like a badge.

"No kidding," he said, now addressing Grace like an old high-school friend. "Walt's a great guy. I read his articles all the time. He always tells the truth."

Grace didn't know what the officer meant and didn't care. Right now she was just glad to be related to someone who might get her out of this mess.

"Mrs. Moore, you ran a stop sign," the officer said, tipping his hat. He handed her a citation. "What you did was very dangerous. If there had been other cars around, you could have gotten in a wreck. You do realize that, don't you?"

"Yes, sir." Grace sighed.

After the officer left, she sat for a moment. The streets were empty, and stores and businesses were closed except for the convenience store and the Laundromat. She considered driving through Detroit, maybe south. Florida would be nice.

Instead, she drove to the parking lot at Sand Beach Park and faced the lighthouse. She sat for several minutes in the dark Jeep and then stepped into the night air, shoved her hands into her jeans pockets, and walked toward the pier. The waves splashed gently against the rocks, and the moon cast a glow on the barges. She climbed onto the pier, careful not to slip into the deep crevices between the rocks.

Her heart raced. She had never run off on Walt before. What would he do?

Maybe motherhood wasn't for Grace. She loved Travis, but nothing she did made him happy.

She found a flat spot on one of the rocks and sat down. She fell into a trance as her thoughts drifted with the splash of the waves. The full moon inched across the sky. For what seemed like hours, Grace stared into the lake, calm for the first time in months. She felt like she could sit there forever—without demands, without failure.

She awoke from her reverie when she heard a distant siren. "Oh, no." Grace looked at her watch. She panicked as she jumped from her seat on the pier. She leapt over the spaces in the rocks as she rushed to the Jeep.

"Crap," she blurted for the second time that night, as she slipped into a crevice. Her ankle hurt as she tried to pull herself from between the rocks. Her Nikes were firmly wedged. "Why did I have to tie my shoes so tight?" she asked aloud, fuming and shaking.

"Need some help?"

Grace startled at the sound of a deep baritone voice. She squinted and peered into the night air. It sounded like the pharmacist at Sampson's.

"Grace Moore!" the voice said again. "You stuck? What happened ?"

"Don't ask," Grace said. "Let's just say I'm an idiot. My shoe is stuck."

"You hurt?"

Her voice shook and her body trembled. "Not physically."

"Not physically, huh?" Mr. Sampson set aside his fishing pole. He deftly bent down between the rocks and untied the laces. At last. Grace glanced at her watch. Eleven o'clock.

"It's so late. Walt will kill me!"

"He doesn't know you're here?" Mr. Sampson studied Grace. "With Walt, you're lucky he doesn't have the entire police department after you."

Grace's stomach did a double flip. *I already met one of them,* she thought.

"He agreed to watch the baby while I came down here to get some air. But I'm sure he didn't think I'd be gone this long."

"I'm surprised he hasn't come to check on you."

"He probably fell asleep."

"Excuse the pun, Mrs. Moore, but something's fishy about all of this. Are you okay?"

"Mr. Sampson," Grace said as she limped along with him toward the Jeep. "You and Mrs. Sampson have six children. Was it, uh, difficult?"

He was silent for a minute before answering. "Having children has been difficult, yes. You worry all the time. Always think you've done something wrong."

"Did it hurt your relationship?" Grace was eager for knowledge.

Mr. Sampson didn't seem to mind the personal questions. "Our first child was rough. Bessie cried a lot. And she didn't want me to touch her. I think they call it postpartum depression nowadays. Then we called it 'female moods.'"

He smiled as he looked at Grace. "It'll get better, Grace. Is that what this is all about?"

The conversation was now too deep to deny the truth.

"Yes, I hate to admit it, but I'm a wreck. My whole life feels different. I feel guilty and worried almost all the time. All I can ever think is Poor Travis. Poor Walt. Poor me."

The two chatted by the Jeep for a minute longer. Grace never pictured having an intimate conversation with the pharmacist. He now felt like an old friend and confidante.

"Thank you, Mr. Sampson. You saved me!"

"Nothing, dear girl. Just get home where you belong. Walt needs you."

Grace got in the Jeep and pushed the pedal to the floor. She didn't care if the sheriff or the policeman or God saw her. Forget Florida. She headed toward Oak Street.

Her legs wobbled as she stepped onto the front porch. What if Walt was furious? For the third time in one night, Grace was terrified.

She knocked. Glancing at her watch, she saw it was eleven-forty-five. What time had she left the duplex?

She rang the doorbell. The minutes felt like hours. The door slowly opened. Walt looked terrible. His hair was a mess.

"Where were you?" Walt looked like he'd seen a ghost.

"Walt, I needed to get away, get some fresh air."

"For five hours? Fresh air? I *almost* called the police."

"Great. Two offenses in one night," Grace muttered.

"But I knew you needed time to yourself and decided I had to trust that you would be okay. I did call your father. And he is out looking for you."

Grace looked down at the floor. "Walt, I feel like such an idiot. I'm sorry! I've been so scared and overwhelmed. I feel like I live in a shoebox."

"A shoebox! Why didn't you tell me you felt that way?"

"Because I want you to *think* I'm a great mom and a great wife. And I didn't want you to worry."

"You thought I wouldn't worry when you ran off into the night and left me with the baby? You didn't tell me where you were going. For all I knew you were leaving me forever." He trembled and tears welled. "Grace, don't ever leave me, okay? I need you."

"I won't, Walt." She meant it. "I need you too." She nuzzled against his broad chest.

There was a loud knock at the door, and Grace spun around. As the door edged open, she saw her dad peeking in.

"What a relief to see the Jeep out front. You're safe! Grace don't *ever* do that again. You had us ready to call the police! We figured you might be at Fran's but she didn't answer her phone and your car wasn't at her house. Where *were* you?"

"Sand Beach Park. I got stuck." She shared her story.

"And if Mr. Sampson hadn't come, you might have been out there all night. Alone."

Grace felt nine years old. She was young and foolish and causing trouble.

"I've got a big day tomorrow." Her dad frowned as he placed a kiss on Grace's forehead. "Look after her, will you, Walt?"

"Sure thing," Walt answered. The clock struck one.

"Where's Travis?"

"Asleep."

"See. I leave the house and he stops crying. Sleeps. What does that tell you?"

"That his mom's unhappiness is affecting him?"

"Oh, great, more guilt!" She crossed her arms tightly across her chest.

"I think that just means we need to help Grace get happy again."

Walt led Grace to Travis's room. They stood above the crib and watched him sleep. Travis lay peacefully as the nightlight illuminated his flawless skin. Grace collapsed in the rocking chair and began rocking while Walt knelt by her side.

TWELVE

That first year with Travis had been challenging and in what seemed like the blink of an eye, it was the following May. On Memorial Day, the air was as heavy as water. The smell of fish from the lake rose steadily and expanded, threading its way through the residential area of town.

After locating a parking spot among the dozen or so cars parked in front of the Bakers, Walt and Grace walked onto the porch of Fran's white bungalow with blue shutters. Grace removed her light jacket and handed it to Walt.

"I hope Fran doesn't mind that I'm bringing fruit," Grace stated, referring to the large crystal bowl filled with grapes, cantaloupe, and honeydew melon and sealed with Saran Wrap. Walt carried a bottle of wine. They knocked on the door.

Fran opened the door and gave them a welcoming smile. She wore a sparkly gold shirt that accented her recent weight loss and had just gotten her hair cut and styled. She looked radiant as she accepted the fresh fruit.

"Oh, thank you for coming, Grace and Walt!" I don't know what I would do without you guys here. Were you able to find a sitter?"

Grace and Walt followed Fran into the small kitchen. "Yes, thank goodness! Sally agreed to watch Travis. She has been great and I can trust her with him. She loves children."

"Now, Grace, you know if you need a sitter I don't mind watching Travis. He's adorable! All that chatting and gurgling. I bet he's almost ready to walk!"

"Yea, crawling and chatting and putting everything in his mouth," said Grace.

Walt handed Fran the wine and she placed it in the fridge.

"Thanks for bringing the goodies, you two." Fran swirled around and beamed at both of them. "I'm glad you could come."

"Where's Michael?" Walt asked, peering through the dining area at the new screened-in porch, where a dozen or so guests were talking, eating, and laughing.

"He's out at the lake with Paul."

"They fishing?" Walt asked.

'They left the house this afternoon with poles and a tackle box, so I think that's what they're doing." Her voice shook slightly and her face paled. As if on cue, Fran's mom came in.

"Grace and Walt, I'm so glad you could come to little Frannie's get together. How is that baby of yours?"

"Growing like a weed. I think he's about to start walking. He's pulling up on the table and making his way around it."

"He'll be a year old soon, won't he?"

"Yes," Grace replied. "I don't know where the time goes."

"Well, before you know it, you'll have a one-year-old grandchild." Fran's mom looked just like Fran as she spoke, or maybe it was Fran that looked like her mom. "And then before long you'll be in the nursing home."

"Mom, please." Fran rolled her eyes. "Not that again."

"Well, it's true. You raise your kids and then what? An empty life, I say. You'll see, Fran, one day Paul will be gone and out of the house, and you'll just have the four blank walls to stare at day after day."

"Mom, can you help me put out some more shrimp?"

"I can, but where is that helpful husband of yours? Why isn't he helping you with this party? I hope he doesn't have my grandson out at some bar, hootin' on some floozy."

Grace excused herself and found her way to the long table in the corner. She took a plate and filled it with cheese chunks and peanuts, poured herself a glass of wine, and found a seat on a wicker chair. She put full attention to her food, grateful for something to focus on. Fran's mom was Fran's mom and, for some reason, Fran never complained about her. She just kept her in her life. She did have a point: the years were already flying by and this Pamper stage was just a blink of an eye in the cosmic scheme of things. She didn't want to think ahead to when she would be a grandma. This day was enough—a day away from the baby, a night out with her husband and a party at Fran's.

Fran had been inviting them over for a long time and there always seemed to be a reason they couldn't make it. Now Fran had decided that since she had slimmed down to a size eight, she would have half the town over. And Michael wasn't there with her.

"Hey, Grace."

Grace looked up to see Shelly, a stylist at Glamour Clips who was meaner than a snake and a big gossip.

"Hi, Shelly," Grace mumbled as she ate a piece of cheese. She looked away and out onto the screened porch in the hope that Shelly might move on to talk to someone else.

It didn't work. Shelly plopped down into the seat next to Grace as she placed a jumbo shrimp into her large mouth. After she swallowed it, she licked her fingers.

"So what's up with Michael?" she asked Grace, looking at her intently.

"What do you mean?"

"Well, like, Michael, *hello.* It's Fran's big weekend. She's lost all this weight. And she wants to show off her house. So, like, where is he?"

Grace wanted this nosy prima donna to disappear. "He's fishing."

"Yeah, right. He always has an excuse. If he were my husband, I think I would conveniently push him and his rod into the lake."

Grace grimaced. "Well, you know, he just wants time with his son on a three-day weekend, right?" But she was actually thinking that Shelly was probably right, that Michael belonged in the lake. She looked over at Walt and his little group on the porch, yearning to join him, even if he was with the pharmacist and his wife.

"Well c'mon, he's like never there for her. Did he come to her birthday party? Did he come to the recognition event at the hair shop? What about Paul's soccer game? He's never there for her. Or for Paul, except when Paul gives him a convenient excuse to not be at his own party."

Was Shelly sticking up for Fran?

"I know," Grace said. "I was hoping he would be here. I know Walt wanted to talk to him about installing some new faucets in the bathrooms."

"Well, good luck, I don't think he is very reliable." Her piercing blue eyes narrowed and her thin lips were pursed. She seemed content to have spoken her venomous comments.

Grace knew Shelly was right. Ever since the day she and Fran had found his car parked at Mavis's house, she had felt Michael was a jerk. But Fran loved him so much, and Grace could not bear to tell her what she really thought of her cheating husband. And for just a flash, she realized that Shelly, even though she was a nosy, loud-mouthed gossip, had spoken a truth. A teensy bit of admiration rose in Grace for this bold red-haired hairdresser who had addressed the elephant in the room.

"I hope you and Fran are staying busy at the shop."

"Of course, everyone wants shorter hair and painted toenails in the summer."

Grace looked toward the screened-in porch and saw that Walt was laughing at something.

"Excuse me, Shelly, I think I better spend a little time with my husband."

Grace stood up from the chair with her empty plate and made her way to the group outside. She hoped that Mr. Sampson wouldn't ask about the post-partum depression. On some days she felt that the depression oozed out of her and into Walt, settling deep into his bones and making him weary.

"And then," Walt said as he jiggled his wine glass. "Travis pointed right at me and said 'newspaper.'"

"Sure." Ben Sampson snorted. "That is a fine first word. Bessie, remember Abe's first word? Fork! And he hasn't put the fork down yet. He loves to eat."

"Well," Walt replied, "it just shows, that my son is going to be a great vocabularian. Skip the simple words and go right into the big ones, the complex ones. I don't even know how a little guy his age can come up with a word like that. Maybe he will one day be a famous writer."

Grace laughed as she interjected. "You think so honey? I thought he was going to be a famous baseball player!"

Walt turned and when he saw her standing next to him, he smiled, pulled her into the circle, and relieved her of her empty plate. "Motherhood looks good on Grace. Doesn't she look great?"

Bessie smiled. "You do look great, Grace. And having said that, Travis must be sleeping through the night?"

"Well, not all the time. Some nights he is up a lot. I think he must be teething. But overall, compared to those first few months, I must say, yes, things are better."

She blushed when she realized that Bessie had probably heard from Ben Sampson about the late night at the lake the previous fall. She was surprised that the word hadn't gotten out more than it did, at least not that she was aware of. It was very hard to keep a secret in Sand Beach.

"Grace, can we talk for a minute?" Bessie whispered.

"Sure."

Grace followed Bessie into the front yard. The now-cooler air was still damp and held the smell of the lake. The two found a couple of chairs beneath the oak tree and sat facing the house.

"Beautiful night."

"Yes, it is, I am so glad that Fran decided to do this. She really has a cute place."

"She does. And she is a great gal. Grace, are you really okay?"

"Well, yes, why?" She hoped that Bessie Sampson was not going to finally let her know that her husband had told her about the postpartum escape at the lake.

"Because, well, you know sometimes having children can take a toll on you. And I know you and Walt don't have a lot of family here. And isn't Walt in the Guard? Isn't he gone a weekend a month?" Bessie pulled up a spare weed by the side of the chair and started peeling it back.

Grace felt the blood drain from her face. "I know, but we're okay. I'm not going to tell you that parenting hasn't been a challenge though. And the Guard has been good for us! It helped to pay for Walt's education and has supplemented our income."

She gazed out toward the lake and sighed. "The first time I met Walt he told me that that he didn't want his parents to foot his school bill and he didn't want to go into debt with student loans. He said that a National Guard recruiter came to his high school in Cleveland one day and a week later he was signed up. He told me it was a great way to get extra money while being of service. And he always tells me now that it was better than signing up for the Marines."

"He's a great guy. He loves you, Grace."

Grace heard a boat horn blare in the distance and a few stray cars drive by the house, then a car door slamming shut. The party-goers were still loud and animated in the house, and with the lights on and the curtains drawn, you could clearly see Fran, her mom, Shelly, Walt, Linda, and all the other stylists and their spouses from Glamour Clips.

Suddenly, she saw Michael step onto the porch with Paul in tow. So he had finally returned, hours into the party. She slapped at a mosquito on her bare leg.

"Everyone says that Walt loves me. Is it that obvious? And in a way he probably enjoys a little time away when he does the Guard. A change of pace." The wine that earlier had made her relaxed now started to give Grace a headache.

"I don't know, Grace, but I think about young mothers a lot. And I know you don't have your mom to help you. And, of course, as you are probably learning, being a mother can make *worry* your middle name."

Grace didn't know Bessie all that well, but it occurred to her that from this brief conversation that maybe Bessie worried about everything. Worried and prayed. Maybe that was what women with children did. Grace was starting to think that all of her worrying had started with that blue test strip. And apparently it wasn't going to end anytime soon, at least not in the foreseeable future anyway.

Bessie pulled a sweater over her shoulders and crossed her arms over her chest. She looked directly into Grace's eyes. The light in Fran's house seemed far away as the two women huddled under the protective oak with its hovering branches, surrounded by twinkling lightning bugs.

"How is Walt handling being a father? Is he good about talking about things? Or does he brood?"

How does Bessie know that Walt has been brooding? Please change the subject, thought Grace. "No he really doesn't talk too much about anything. He is more of a listener than a talker."

"Well, I know when Ben has something on his mind, he broods, he stays away from me and finds other ways to spend his time."

Grace suddenly saw Walt's behavior in a new light. Maybe he had been brooding. He had been staying at work later, talking less, and sometimes left their bed in the middle of the night to go to his desk in the corner of the living room to write. He would sometimes still be there when she got up in the morning, ready to sleep by that time, but instead had to run off to work.

"Sometimes he doesn't sleep so well," Grace replied. "But I figure that is just because our sleep schedules are off because of Travis."

"Can I pray for you and your family?"

Oh, please, thought Grace, *I don't need this person I really don't know all that well to start thinking and praying about me.* "Sure," she said. "If you think it will help, but really, Bessie, I don't see anything happening with us. We are doing great! And it feels so good to get out of the house and have a night free, without Travis."

"I'll pray for you. Why don't you come to the Methodist church with us?"

Going to church was the last thing in the world that Grace wanted to do. "We'll see, Bessie. I haven't gone to church in a long time."

"Well, think about it, Grace. We would love to have you there."

Grace was so glad that Bessie didn't talk about her mishap at the lake, but the thought of attending church and the idea of her husband brooding had combined to put a damper on her mood.

"Bessie, thanks for your concern. I hope there is nothing wrong and we are just going through a phase."

"Me, too, Grace. Me, too. But here." Bessie fidgeted in her handbag and pulled out a card from Sampson's with Ben's work number on it. She pulled out a pen and scratched in their home number. "Here is our number, in case you need anything. And I mean anything…to talk, babysitter, whatever, okay?" She handed the card to Grace, and Grace tucked it neatly away in her small woven bag.

Bessie swatted at a mosquito. Grace scratched a spot that was freshly bitten, and the two sat quietly until the sound of a loud, drunken Michael Baker inside the house interrupted their repose.

THIRTEEN

The following day was hot and muggy. Dust rose as the Jeep traveled through the dirt and gravel leading to the stable. Fran had phoned Grace hours earlier, sounding desperate, to ask her if she would be willing to get together for lunch at Gloria's and to let her know that her mom had offered to watch the children. Grace couldn't refuse but said she would meet her at the stable instead. Mr. Mathis had given her the freedom to come and go as she pleased to groom, feed, muck stalls, clean saddles, and exercise the horses as needed.

Entering the barn, Grace drank in the familiar smells of hay and fresh grain. When Fran arrived a few minutes later, Grace noticed that her face was swollen and tear-stained and there was a faint fingertip-sized bruise on her upper arm. She handed Grace a canvas bag filled with carrots, apples, and dog biscuits before following her into the tack room. Macie Mae, the stable dog, waddled over to the two visitors and gazed imploringly at Grace until she found a biscuit in her duffle bag and bent down and patted Macie's smooth tan head.

"I'm glad you agreed to meet me *here*," Grace said to Fran. "I'm sorry. I know you would've preferred lunch," Grace breathed in the barn air, stretched, and sighed. "And I really appreciate your mom watching Travis. I'm gonna get spoiled—all this free time to play."

Since Sally was out with Silver Glo, Grace chose her second favorite horse to groom and ride. She slid open the stall door and approached Sparky with a carrot. The large bay gelding grabbed the treat and crunched with his powerful jaws as he peered at Grace from behind his long tangled forelock.

"Hey, boo-boo, you need a brushing. Wanna good brushing?" She snapped the lead on the red halter that accented Sparky's dark coloring and led him to the door.

"Grace, you know what you said about Michael? I'm afraid you might be right. But what am I gonna do? When he finally came home, it was awful." She was referring to the previous night's party and the dark ending to what was supposed to be a happy evening. Fran choked and swallowed hard as a new tear appeared at the corners of her brown eyes, causing her mascara to run. She wiped them away and then took out a tissue from the pocket of her cutoff shorts and blew her nose.

Grace was silent as she led the large horse through the door. She stood in the aisle with him for a minute before pulling out another carrot from the bag and letting him seize it.

"Grace, did you hear me?" Fran tried again. "What would *you* do?"

"What would I do? Fran, you know what *I* would do." Grace thought she would grab him by the testicles, lead him out to the lake, find him a boat with a hole in its hull, and invite him to take a long ride in it.

"Yeah, I know you would have left him after the second date or at least the first time he yelled at you, right?"

Fran uncrossed her legs and stood to let Grace and the large horse pass through the narrow aisle. Grace led Sparky to the cross ties and snapped the buckle on his halter.

"What can I do to help?" Fran asked.

Grace pointed to the large bucket on the floor. "Could you grab that for me?"

Fran lifted the red plastic pail filled with brushes, combs, and liniment and handed it to Grace.

"Gray, I can't stand it! I want to throw up! I was soooo embarrassed last night. He had been drinking. I know it!" Fran scrunched up her face and tightened her fists. She spat out her words. "He was such an asshole! An asshole! He told Mom to shut the hell up when she asked if he had been drinking, and he pinched my arm so hard, I could have screamed!" She began to sob. "He scared me!"

"I don't blame you, Fran. I'd be scared too. If Walt ever even thought about hitting me or pinching me or scaring me, I don't know what I would do." Grace paused. "What about Paul?"

"I don't know, Grace, I just keep thinking that things will get better. You know, I think he really loves me deep down. And some of the time, he can be a good guy. Mom told me she would keep Paul for a while if I want…til the dust settles."

"Does the dust ever settle?"

Grace reached under Sparky's mane and began scratching him, working her way down his long neck to his withers. His lips curled in enjoyment.

"Sometimes it does, Grace. Sometimes things are great. Remember last summer? I was sure he was going to be the man I met ten years ago." She was referring to the previous summer when Michael had tried to win his family back.

Fran sighed. "For three straight months, I thought I was in heaven. He cooked, he cleaned, bought me roses. And our trip to Mackinac Island was fantastic. You know I never even thought about Mavis, I was just glad I had my husband back. I thought we were having a second honeymoon. And the best part of all of that was I was sure he could finally beat the drinking."

Grace wiped sweat from her forehead with the back of her arm. "I know, I was right with you, girl. I thought he was gonna quit too. And I thought he had given up on Mavis. He tried, didn't he? I really thought that things had taken a turn for the better. That took a lot of effort from him."

"It did. And it reminded me of when we met. He was so, well, comforting and protective. He doted on me, and I used to feel safe with him. And he was so handsome, he sometimes took my breath away. Sometimes, he still does take my breath away."

Michael was great-looking, and his years of manual labor had left him muscled and fit. His sculpted body, thick brown hair, and chiseled features managed to turn many heads.

"He's still pretty hot, Fran."

But Grace thought that *hot* was just a term. To know Michael was to know that hot could turn to horrible in a heartbeat when he became a drunk, mean, two-timing bastard. And his actions could make a person hot—hot enough to wring his neck.

Grace began using the hard brush on the horse, whisking the dirt she had loosened out of his coat and onto the soft dirt floor. She continued to alternate using the stiff bristled dandy brush with the curry that she worked in small little circles, pushing Sparky's thick black mane to the other side of his neck. She massaged the curry deep into his skin causing him to tilt his head pushing his weight into the comb while his upper lip twitched.

"Michael didn't have the best childhood, you know. His dad was a drinker and whipped the tar out of him. All the time. And his mom and his sister just took it all in. I think his mom tried to leave his dad once, but it didn't happen, they stayed with him. It was pretty awful. I know he felt a lot of guilt when his dad died. I don't think he has ever forgiven him."

Sparky snorted and pawed at the ground and stomped as he pulled his weight against the cross ties. Grace turned her attention to the horse, glad for the momentary distraction. "Sorry, Spark, I just need to finish cleaning out your hooves and we'll get ready to ride. I know you want to ride, don't you?"

She looked at Fran from underneath the horse's neck. "A bad childhood doesn't make his behavior okay."

"He's not always bad, you know. In fact when he's good, he is very good. But I must admit that when he is nice and affectionate to me, it usually only lasts for a minute or two and then he starts again. He criticizes me *all* the time, and you know it seems like everything I do is wrong. I hang up the bath towels wrong or I put too much milk on his cereal. I try to be perfect for him. I thought when I lost thirty pounds he would be happy. But now he just has other things to complain about."

"He should have nothing to complain about, Fran. You worship the ground he walks on."

Fran looked at Sparky, who patiently allowed her to stroke his lean side, his coat now glistening from the vigorous grooming.

"Well, I admit that maybe I shouldn't have had the party last night, you know? I mean he harrumphed when I told him I wanted to have everyone over. But I thought he was okay with it! He even helped me get some of the groceries and ran the vacuum. But then, as it turned out, he really didn't want company. He told me last night that I embarrassed him—that he just wanted a quiet day to fish with his son and I had to have half the town over and that when he came home tired, he should not have had to smile at people. And he said that he felt shamed, that he thought that people probably judged him for being out at the lake doing what *he* considers fun rather than spending time with them. But he knew about this for weeks! He could have convinced me to cancel rather than just moping around! The way he cleaned up, I thought for sure in the last minute he would be there. But he made an excuse saying that he needed time with his son and time alone. I even invited Ralph. Ralph asked about him all night and had left by the time Michael came home. It was such a scene! Such a scene! I'm so embarrassed! What will I ever do when I go back to work and have to face Shelly and the girls? Shelly will tell me that she knew all along that this would be a disaster. Why didn't she tell me ahead of time?"

"It's all about him you know, Fran."

"Yeah, but some of the time he works hard. He fixes things— the toilet and the gutters and the washer—and helps pay the bills. And, you know, he actually checked out the local Boy Scout office and requested information for Paul."

"Now you are making excuses for him." Like she always does, Grace thought.

"Well, what would you do? I mean, he does do something!"

"Yeah, he keeps his family on edge, and when his beautiful wife loses thirty pounds and is a fantastic hostess and friend he has to go and complain about something stupid. Something that doesn't matter. Like stupid bath towels and too much milk on his cornflakes. Haven't you figured it out yet, that it's not you? That he's just looking for an excuse to be an idiot? I guarantee you, Fran, if it wasn't you, it would be someone else. If he were with Mavis, for instance, he would be the same way."

"I don't know, Gray, I keep thinking that he needs help!"

"He does need help, Fran, and so do you!"

"Yeah, but he is the one who drinks, he had a terrible childhood, and he never had the opportunity to go to college."

"Neither did you, Fran, and from what you have told me, your childhood wasn't so fantastic either. And you aren't a raging maniac alcoholic." These were words Grace had held back for years, and she was shocked that she had let them come spurting out.

"Yeah, but it's different for women. We have more outlets. More friends. You know, more support in general. Michael only has me!"

Yes, Grace thought, and the affair of the moment.

"Well, I love you, Fran and I don't want you hurt."

Grace stepped back from Sparky to look for areas she might have missed while brushing his now-glistening coat. She lifted a heavy hoof and dug into the center with her pick. Horse manure and dirt flew onto the ground as she cleaned out the impacted manure, hay, and occasional stone. Fran's sad story brought back a fleeting memory of a dorm mate back in college who had hooked up with some jerk one night and had come back to their room with a black eye and a bleeding mouth. What the hell were women thinking when they hooked up with such men? What was the attraction? Well, it didn't matter what the attraction was. Fran was in pain and was obviously struggling.

"I believe you, Grace, and I don't know why I always ask you what you would do, when I know full well that you would leave. You are much classier than me. You would have left a long time ago. If I knew what was good for me, I would leave too. Both you and Mom think I should leave and both of you put up with me. Mom has offered to keep Paul while I try to work things out with Michael.

But I swear I never want to be divorced. The thought of being single terrifies me. I don't think I'm up to the challenge of that!" Fran continued to pet Sparky and occasionally Macie Mae, who now stood next to her. "Macie, you are a nice dog." The canine's tail wagged in appreciation.

Grace knew from the beginning of the conversation that it would end this way. It didn't seem that Fran could stand to be alone. It didn't matter how many heartaches she had to endure, Fran always came back to the fact that she didn't want to be alone. She would tough it out. She would make things work. Michael would be the man she always wanted him to be. It was a lucky thing that she had her mother to smooth things over and to support her and Paul.

The women became quiet as Grace went into the tack room and put away the brushes and searched for a saddle. Grace thought about her own mom and swallowed hard. She was present in a whisper, in a tear, and sometimes took the form of a hard lump in Grace's throat. Although at times her family had been less than perfect, now that Mom was gone, Grace remembered only the good times. She remembered the mom who was comforting. She remembered the times Dad and Mom took her and Beck on picnics down by the lake and to the amusement park in Detroit. She clutched at those memories with an intensity that scared her sometimes, replaying them in her head like a well-worn tape. She rejoiced at the thought of her mother's laugh as she held her head back and the sun shone on a pretty face surrounded by soft, flowing curls. The way she would pack a school lunch—a bag of chips and a bologna sandwich accompanied by a little note that said things like "Smile Grace!" or "I'm so proud of you!" The way she used to cluck when they had done something she approved of. The way she sang when she did the dishes. The way she made Dad happy.

And now, the only evidence that Mom had been alive were the pictures tucked away in a box at the home in which she and Beck had grown up. A box that had been untouched by a father who had renovated everything in his life except for the closet filled with memories. She might not have visible bruises like Fran, but she did have a wounded heart.

Bit by bit, Walt had helped her repair her heart. Now that she knew how short life could be, she felt impatient with people who couldn't get along. Fran was great and needed help, but sometimes Fran's inability to cut the cord with an abusive husband was hard to witness. And for the life of her, Grace did not know how to help. Except to listen.

"Grace, you know I wouldn't be good alone. Remember when I lived with Mom before Michael and I got married? I was a mess. If I leave Michael, I'll have to stay with Mom, and I don't think I can do that. Maybe it's better to just stay with what I have."

"Well, maybe you wouldn't have to stay with your mom. What about getting your own place?"

Fran reached across Sparky for the plaid wool saddle blanket that Grace lifted onto the horse's back, and together they pulled it into place. Then Grace hoisted the heavy saddle onto Sparky's back. Fran knew just enough to be able to pull the girth from on top of the saddle and guide it down under the horse so that Grace could grab and fasten it.

"I thought about getting a place, you know, but I'm not good at being alone—have never been alone. Geez, before Michael, I hated dating! It was so depressing! And what would Michael do without me? He needs me. And Mom says she doesn't mind watching Paul, and you know maybe it will just be for a while. And Paul needs two parents, not a divorced family! You think he drinks now? What would he do if I left?"

A new wave of tears erupted from Fran as her small shoulders hunched over and she reached for a wadded-up tissue in her pocket. Macie Mae looked up at her and whimpered. She put her hand down to rub her soft yellow fur.

"Fran, I'm so sorry, but I don't know what to do for you. Are you gonna be okay? I really need to ride for a while. We'll have to head back home before you know it. I'm sorry."

"It's okay, Grace, you need to ride." She wiped another set of fresh tears from her worn face, this time with the back of her hand as she found a place along the fence in the hot sun.

As Grace mounted Sparky, she felt a little weak. She had only been on a horse a few times since Travis was born. Her thigh muscles felt like jello as she worked to grip the saddle. She gathered the reins and walked around the ring for several minutes as her mind wandered and her eyes took in the familiar flat green cornfields, the Sand Beach water tower, and the large oak trees filled with noisy blackbirds. The earth was silent except for the birds and the steady click of Sparky's shod hooves. His head bobbed up and down and Grace thought that a horse neck was an odd bit of anatomy—so long and gangly, carrying that heavy head. She patted Sparky's side and asked him to trot.

As Sparky obeyed and fell into a slow steady trot, Grace let her thoughts flow. She thought that it was inevitable that one day Fran would have to leave Michael. He wasn't getting any better—in fact, it seemed that every time he made a scene or Fran came crying to her, things were actually getting a little worse. It had to be difficult for Fran to consider being alone. She knew that she would have a very hard time if she had to live without Walt. She guessed that all lives had tradeoffs— some people had sick children, some people had sick mothers, some people had alcoholic husbands. Even the most famous, beautiful people who seemed to have it all encountered death and illness and lawsuits. Grace had lost Mom and Beck, but she had a wonderful husband and father. Fran had lost her dad and now struggled with a sick husband, but she had a healthy son and a mother who didn't mind doting on her. And she could do a kick-ass job on hair, enjoyed it and got paid well for it. Yep, Grace believed that all people had a deck of cards and each hand was different, and sometimes it just seemed like the luck of the draw. If that were the case, Grace thought, as she shifted Sparky into a canter, then the thing that mattered was what you did with the cards you were dealt. His canter was smooth and rhythmic as she worked him into figure eights; her riding confidence returned. As Grace rode back toward Fran, she noticed she was motioning to her.

"Grace, the phone is ringing." Fran pointed toward the barn.

Grace pulled back the reins and came to an immediate halt.

"What?"

"The phone, it's ringing."

"Well, go ahead. Answer it. Just make sure you say 'Sand Beach Stables.'"

When Fran came back out again, she said, "Grace, can you come to the phone? It's Walt."

"Hi, Sweetie!" Grace hollered toward the barn as though her voice would carry right through the line. She stopped by the fence with Sparky who was panting heavily from the workout. Grace was sweaty too and needed to rest.

"Walt wants you to know that he picked up Travis from my mom's. And he says your dad has called him twice today and has another house for you to look at."

"And," she continued, "my mom gave Travis a set of stacking blocks." Fran smiled. "Walt wants to know when you're coming home!"

"Tell him that I'm going to jump the fence and gallop home and swoop up Travis and him and gallop around the town. You'll do that for me, won't ya', Spark? I wonder if Sparky minds a car seat on his back for Travis."

Fran laughed. "Wouldn't that that be a horse seat?"

"Maybe we'll hook a carriage up to him."

Grace leaned over and sprawled onto the large gelding's neck as she breathed in his dusty horsey smell. Happiness settled into her being.

"Fran, tell him I love him and I'll be home as soon as Sparky will drag me into the barn."

"Grace, you tell him that!"

A minute later, Fran said, "Grace, your husband is laughing! He says not to rush, that he and Travis are going to sit down and eat some ice cream and check out the blocks."

Fran hung up the phone and looked at Grace.

"Hmmm. Ice cream sounds good! Chocolate chip!"

Fran's tears had dried.

FOURTEEN

The following days turned into weeks, and before long it was August. Every morning, the sun rose majestically over Lake Huron announcing the start of another day filled with the hum of bees and the sound of gulls and the occasional ice cream truck that wound its way through the streets. Though the days seemed lazy and predictable, there was a tension in the air, the cause of which Grace could not quite put her finger on. It was as though a storm were brewing. Yes, in this hot, hazy summer of 1990, a subtle shift in mood had woven itself into the fabric of Grace Moore's life and the lives of those around her.

You couldn't see it in the streets, all was pretty much the same. Sampson's Pharmacy still stood on the corner of Main and First as it had for the last ninety years. Mrs. Givens still walked out of her house at six-forty-five every morning to bend down to pick up the latest copy of the *Sand Beach Times*. And Bill and Janice Duerr at the State Street Inn still had patriotic swags hanging on their wrap-around porch awaiting summer guests. Linda still went to work at six a.m. to serve the regulars at Gloria's. Fran still started her day with sanitized combs and brushes at Glamour Clips. You couldn't see any change in the weather, as each day started out hot and dry, and most afternoons there was a brief downpour of rain.

Travis was growing like a weed. At a year old, he had found his way along the floor, crawling through the duplex, pulling himself up on anything he could hold on to. He fell a lot. He tasted everything and made his way through the day by putting things in his mouth—car keys, pens, sunglasses. He ate little jars of carrots and pureed prunes. He drank more formula now and less breast milk.

Before Travis—the era that Walt and Grace now referred to as BT—Walt had been able to go straight to his writing at night. Back then, he could choose to drink a glass of wine with Grace and gaze at the stars from the front yard. Now, every evening the both of them tended to Travis, making sure he didn't open the door to the kitchen cabinet that was filled with cleaners. They read to him and woke with him in the middle of the night when he cried. They talked to him, calmed him, and cooed to him. Now they had to avert their gaze from one another and toward the round, blond giggling toddler they had created.

At the corner of town, Grace's father still had an immaculate home, and the garden he had planted earlier in the season summer was now lush with hues of red, orange and purple. He had added a little pond by the gazebo in the sprawling green yard as well as a trellis by the side of the large brick home.

One day, out of the blue, Grace's dad showed up at the duplex with boxes and boxes of photos.

"Grace, I finally got to those closets. Thought you might like these."

Grace opened her arms and accepted one by one the dozen or so matching striped cardboard boxes filled with photos. She and Dad brought them into the living room and set them on the coffee table.

"Gee, Dad, there sure are a lot of them."

"Yes, Gracie, I thought you might like having them."

After he left, Walt looked at Grace. "What was that all about?"

"I have no idea." She looked puzzled. "Was he wearing Aramis?"

"What?"

"Aramis, you know cologne. He smelled good. I just don't remember him wearing any ever, even when Mom was alive. He always smelled either like sweat or just plain soap. Not cologne."

"Oh, Grace, you women, always concerned with how we look or smell."

So her dad had finally gotten to cleaning out the closet and dealing with the boxes of photos of their family in better times. He had also started paying extra attention to both his appearance and his scent. This man who had worked his fingers to the bone had apparently finished most of his projects and was now working on himself.

He also found time to occasionally go with Grace to look at houses, as Walt was often busy working long hours. Sometimes they brought Travis along. Since most of the homes that they looked at were empty, he could move around easily and open cupboards and attempt to climb carpeted stairs. He would take Grace's hand and stand quietly behind her to hide from the real estate agent as he shyly held his sippy cup.

Despite looking at dozens of homes, Grace had yet to find a house with a horse barn that was also fairly close to town.

One afternoon, after Grace had come back frustrated and tired of not finding a house that they would both like, she told Walt that it was exhausting and that it just didn't seem that anything was going to work.

"I think we need to give up the house hunt for now, Grace. Obviously, this is not the right time to buy."

"But, Walt, you promised. We have been looking for a whole year, do you realize that?"

"Yeah, well, a year and we haven't found anything yet. We don't even know if we are going to have a larger family. And since you really want a home with a barn, it'll be almost impossible to find the perfect place."

"There was that old house on County Highway."

"Yeah, and you could have sneezed and the place would have caved in. And I don't have the kind of time or the expertise that your father has to fix up a home like that."

"Well, I think we should keep looking. What if I stopped looking and then the perfect place became available? I keep thinking that the Jones home will come up for sale. From the outside it looks perfect."

"Oh, Gracie, you never give up do you? Maybe you're right. I guess it's not hurting anything."

"Yeah, it gives me something different to do. And it gives Dad a new project and gives Travis lots of new territory to discover. Dad seems to really enjoy it. He has taken to calling me every day to let me know the current mortgage rate and to tell me if anything has sold and for how much and is the first to let me know of a new listing."

Meanwhile, as part of his obligation to the National Guard, Walt spent one weekend a month at Harbor Bay Army Base. These weekends now took on meaning with the invasion of Kuwait by Saddam Hussein. Walt's unit was put on alert, meaning they had to be prepared to leave at any time on short notice. He had not told Grace this fact yet and tried to keep his worries to himself. Most nights he tossed and turned into the wee hours of the morning.

And the days were no better. Many days he found himself slumped at his desk, exhausted, staring at his diploma on the wall along with the expanding array of pictures of Travis and Grace. He shared his fears with no one. No one, that is, outside of his work buddy, Jim.

"Jim," he said one afternoon. "Want to join me at Sammy's after work? I need to chill."

When they arrived at Sammy's, the place was empty except for an old drunk slumped in the corner by the bathroom. They found a seat at the bar and ordered.

"Two Millers on draft, please Joe." After ordering the beer and two bags of chips, Walt could contain himself no longer. "Have you been keeping up with that Kuwait invasion?"

"A little." Jim pulled out a chip, examined it, and deposited it into his bearded mouth. "Why?"

"Well, you know I *am* in the National Guard." Walt swirled his beer glass as the music played in the background and the bartender read a hunting magazine.

Jim set the chips aside and gave Walt his full attention. Jim was the friend who Walt could confide in. Jim was the friend who would shoot the bull after work and was always there if he needed him. Jim was the friend that confided in Walt when his wife had left him. Jim had once told him that he thought that Walt wrote the best damn articles in Sand Beach and would, if given the opportunity, write the best damn articles for the *New York Times* too.

"Walt, cut the crap, no lead-ins, okay? What the hell is going on with you? Spill."

"Well, for the first time in years, my unit has issued an alert, a warning order. That means that a decision has been made that the Guard may be called over to Saudi to deal with that invasion of Kuwait." Walt gulped some beer. "Not certain that our unit will go yet, but it looks possible. And the term warning makes it feel *very* possible." He avoided looking at Jim as the words poured out.

"When will ya know?"

"Soon, I'm sure. Don't tell anyone though, okay? I haven't even told my wife."

"Wow, Walt." Jim picked up the bag of chips again and resumed crunching. He looked his friend square in the eye. "Ah, heck, it'll be fine, Walt. I'm sure of it. Go. Get it over with. I'm sure it will be more exciting than this small-town crap. You'll finally get to really see the world. Maybe you'll find that something missing you've told me about. Maybe it will be your chance to escape for a while. And just think of the experience! The writing. Think of all the journalists who would give their eye teeth to cover something like that. It will be a once-in-a-lifetime deal. And think of all the shit you'll bring home with you. Stories. You will have tons of fodder for your stories. Make your town proud."

Jim went on and on while Walt sat quietly. In a rare event, they ordered a second beer.

And so this particular summer Dad had started to wear cologne; Fran had Paul staying with her mother while she tried to fix her marriage; Grace continued to try to find the perfect home; Travis was growing like a weed. And Walter Allen Moore, a member of the Army National Guard, had been issued a warning order that he might be called up to fight in the Middle East.

And if that happened, he needed to be prepared.

FIFTEEN

A few days later, Walt and Grace packed a few suitcases with toys and a week's supply of diapers into the Jeep and headed for Cleveland. Walt's parents, Lou and Molly, had been eagerly awaiting the couple's visit for months, Travis was their first and only grandchild.

"I can't believe you told Jim before you told me." Grace turned away from Walt as she buckled Travis into the car seat. Travis started crying. Grace handed him an animal cracker.

"Grace, it's a five-hour drive. Can we please make it enjoyable rather than tense? I can hardly stand it."

Grace swung around to catch Walt's gaze. His steel blue eyes melted her. With a catch in her throat, she apologized. "I'm sorry. I'm just freaking out!"

Walt put his arms around Grace and held her. She felt his beating heart underneath his t-shirt and breathed in his saltiness. She exhaled.

"I just don't think I can do this, Walt."

"And what is it you don't think you can do?"

"If you get called up, I don't think I can let you go! We're just getting started here. Travis. The house hunt." She looked up at him and smoothed the back of her hand along his face. "Your writing."

Walt released her. "Well, at this point, it's just a warning. It's not a full blown deployment. We'll just live like we do every day, and if the time comes we'll deal with it. And Grace, if you can't handle it, what am I supposed to do? I'm the one who, if it happens, will have to go to some god-forsaken desert and put my life on the line."

He hurried to the other side of the car, hopped in, started the engine, and leaned over to speak to Grace, who was still outside, stunned, looking away.

"C'mon, sweetie, the air conditioning is running."

"Okay, then, let's go." Sighing, she straightened her t-shirt and settled into the seat next to Walt.

When she turned to check on Travis, she saw he was sucking on a soggy giraffe cracker and had crumbs all over his cheek and hands and was about to run his sticky fingers into his hair. Grace grabbed a wipe, twisted her body around, and began to clean up his face and fingers.

"Let's just enjoy the trip if we can." She leaned over to plant a kiss on Walt's freshly shaven cheek. "It will be good to get away."

Walt pulled onto Highway 25 South and accelerated. For the next five hours, it was just miles and miles of farmland and a sapphire sky. Grace pushed the seat back and stretched her legs. Maybe if she just relaxed and enjoyed the ride, maybe, just maybe it would last. The moment. The day. The trip. Maybe she and Walt and Travis could just continue driving away to avoid the fact that at some point, in the not too distant future, Walt might be gone. Maybe if they just drove into the future, and didn't stop driving things would be okay. She held on tight to the moment.

"What do you think your folks will say?"

"I don't know, Grace, I haven't thought much about it. I told them over the phone and made it clear it wasn't a sure thing and that we could talk about it during our visit."

"I bet they are worrying." She rubbed her forefinger along a hangnail that had started on her thumb, then grabbed it between her teeth and bit.

"Yeah, Mom, probably is. But isn't that a mom's job?" He glanced over at Grace and winked, his strong hands clutching the steering wheel. He paused. "But Dad might just think that I joined the ranks of the few, the proud, and…" He paused to let Grace finish his sentence.

"The crazed. And he will probably bring out his medals from World War II."

"And Mom. Mom will bring out the tissues."

He continued. "I always thought that if I ever went to the Middle East I would be going as a journalist, not a friggin' soldier. They haven't deployed the Guard since Korea. If I'd known this might happen, I would've been a lot more cautious about getting married and having a family."

Grace didn't like the sound of that. She turned to her husband. "Thanks, Walt! You wish you never married me?"

"I didn't say that. I said I would have been more cautious. I didn't say I would not have married you."

"You did, you said that since you might be going overseas, you wish you didn't have a family."

Walt clenched his jaw. "You are absolutely wrong. I am crazy about my family and wouldn't have it any other way. I just can't stand the thought of leaving you alone with Travis. Give me an orange slice, please. You did bring the orange slices didn't you?"

Grace reached down into the snack sack and pulled out a piece of orange candy in the shape of a slice of orange and handed it to Walt.

"You think I can't take care of Travis?"

"I didn't say that."

"Yeah, but you thought it, and you said you didn't want me alone with Travis. And all the time I've had him, I only went crazy once. But I only did that because I knew you would stay with him. You always stay with him. I never did that again. And I never will. It was just a fluke."

"Yes, Gray. I understand. I know how you felt. I know you just needed a break." He opened his hand and put it in front of Grace and waited on another sugar feed.

"I'm sorry, Walt, I'm just so frightened. I'm scared for you. For us." She gave him another piece of candy. "But you know Trav and me, we'll be fine. We have Dad and Fran and Fran's mom. I know they'll look after us. But you. You are the one who, as you put it, might have to travel to some god-forsaken desert to put your life on the line. I *still* can't believe it."

"Exactly, Grace, so please go easy on me, okay? No moaning that I never wanted a family. No accusations that I think you are a dreadful mom. I don't want to argue. It gives me a headache."

As if on cue, Travis let out a scream. Grace whipped around to find him red-faced and pounding his fists on the front of the car seat.

"Do you think he can eat candy, Walt?"

"Why not? He eats animal crackers, doesn't he?"

"Yeah, but sugar-coated jelly seems like junk food. At least animal crackers don't have so much sugar."

"Go ahead, spoil him. How can we say he can't have one if we are chowing them down?"

Grace grabbed an orange slice and gave Travis his first taste of candy.

"Honey, I'm used to having you help me make decisions. I love that about you. You take my calls during the day and you always give me an answer that makes sense. If you go overseas, I'll go nuts when I can't just pick up the phone and ask you if I can give the baby an orange slice. I can't just call you every time I have a silly question like what brand of drain cleaner I should use, or whether I should even use a drain cleaner when we have a clog."

"But I trust that you will know the answer when the time comes, Grace. And you can always call your dad."

"And then there's the house. What if I find the house of our dreams while you're gone? How in the world would I make *that* decision?" She swallowed hard and stared out the window at the cornfields whizzing by.

"You've got your dad, and he's totally into the whole thing. You two will actually probably do better without me. Just make sure, Grace Ann, that you find a nice office for me. Make it overlook the riding ring. I want bookshelves and a spot for a corner desk." He gave Grace a sidelong glance and patted her bare thigh. "A place where I can finally write my version of the great American novel."

Grace rolled down the window and closed her eyes as the wind met her cheeks and tousled her hair. "Your office will be perfect! I will make sure that it has room for all of your books and your awards and your diploma. Ah, I can see it now," She smiled and let the wind wash over her face and shoulders. "I can see it now..... plants in the corner, that antique smoking stand you love. Oh, yes, Walt, that makes me feel good! I will get us a grand house with a special office for you!" She smiled and giggled. Then, pointing to an oncoming car, she shouted, "Wisconsin!"

"I already saw that plate, Grace, no fair."

"Yeah, but I called it first!"

"That's only because I was listening to you."

She pulled out her yellow legal pad and wrote down Wisconsin. "We have Michigan, Ohio, Utah, Illinois, Florida, Rhode Island, Kentucky, North Carolina, Iowa, New York, New Jersey, Washington, New Hampshire and Tennessee. Fifteen down and thirty-five to go."

"Ma-Ma!" Grace whirled around to see that Travis, whose face and hands were covered with orange sugar, was reaching out to her clearly asking for another treat.

"Walt, look what I started, I can see years of a—"

Walt interrupted her. "Grace, just a minute."

"Don't tell me you are going to stop for that car up ahead."

"If I don't, some nut might and then I'll read about it in the paper." He slowed the Jeep and flicked on the emergency blinkers.

"What if it's a mad raving lunatic?"

"What if it's a mom with a baby?" He smiled at Grace.

Walt pulled onto the easement and stopped just behind a small blue sedan. She and Walt both got out of their car to find a sixty-something woman in the front seat with a terrier on her lap. A piece of paper with the word HELP on it was attached to the side of her car facing the road. She smiled weakly as she turned to greet her rescuers.

"Hello, Ma'am, no fun to have a flat tire in this heat," Walt said. "How bout I change that for you?"

"I didn't think I could last another minute out here, I was hoping someone would come along. Yes, please if you would change the tire, I would be so grateful. She turned to the terrier. Isn't that nice Tiffy? There are still some nice people in the world."

Noticing the sweat pouring down the woman's face, Grace went back to the car to get a root beer from the cooler in the back seat for her.

For the next half hour, Grace and the woman chatted while Walt changed the flat. Grace told her about Walt's service in the National Guard, among other things. She pulled Travis out of the back seat and kept him occupied by rocking him back and forth and pouring some root beer into his cup.

"Okay, you are all set," Walt told the woman as he put the flat tire into the trunk of her car. "Now, get Tiffy home and enjoy your day."

Just as Grace and Walt were turning away to head back to their car, the woman said, "I can't thank you enough!" and extended a hand clutching a twenty-dollar bill. But Walt shook his head.

"Pay it forward, ma'am," he said. "Always. Pay it forward."

As she pulled the HELP sign off the car, she said, "Angels, I tell you. God always sends angels. I'll pray for you, Mr. Moore. Thank you for serving our country. And you, Mrs. Moore, thank you too for supporting men like him. The world needs more young people like you." And then she drove off.

Walt turned to Grace. "I'm starved. Let's have lunch. I think I saw a sign for the service plaza back there."

When they got to the plaza, Grace lifted her sleepy child out of his car seat. It felt wonderful to once again leave the car and stretch her cramped, sticky legs. When she went to use the Ladies room, she noticed it contained a dispenser for condoms and paused to contemplate who would need to stop along the highway for condoms.

After changing Travis's diaper, rejoined Walt by the car, where together they pulled out the cooler and the paper sack filled with a table cloth, napkins and plastic utensils. She had packed ham sandwiches, corn chips, root beer and fresh sliced strawberries. The sun beat down as they found a spot in the shade, stretched and watched the dozens of cars driving into the parking lot. Grace boosted Travis up to table height by sitting him on the cooler. She watched Walt as he bit off a small corner of his sandwich.

"Remember our first picnic?" Grace asked.

"Of course I do. Out on the grass of the University of Michigan. We couldn't afford ham then. It was PB and J all the time, and when we cooked it was mac and cheese." He swallowed. "Can you hand me a napkin?"

Grace wiped her greasy fingers before handing over a napkin. The salt tasted good on her lips as she finished off her small pile of corn chips.

"Candy, mama!" Travis had added a new word to his vocabulary.

Walt paused for a second and looked serious. "Parochial school."

"What?"

"Parochial school. I want Travis in parochial school." He bit into a corn chip. "When he gets to school age, I want him to go to St. Matthias."

"St. Matthias? Isn't that school expensive?"

"I think a private parochial school will be good for him. Teach him some values."

"But we don't even go to church."

"Doesn't matter, I bet half the kids that go to those schools don't attend church on Sunday. I just think it's important to have discipline. Discipline and small class size. Especially nowadays."

"Yeah, but what about the nuns? I've heard they are mean."

"I went to Catholic school and it worked for me."

"Yes, and I remember you telling me about spending a day cleaning out the rectory for passing a note in class. And that was after you had to stand in the corner like a dunce for half an hour."

She sipped her root beer and smiled. "Okay, sweetie, Catholic school it is. But the first time a nun smacks him with a ruler…"

"And we need to make sure that he doesn't watch too much television. I mean the kid needs to build something, blocks or whatever. He doesn't need to grow up in front of the idiot box."

"I'll probably teach him to ride, you know." She reached over and smoothed the toddler's fine blond hair and protectively put her arms around him. A middle-aged woman with a poodle walked by and some children tossed a Frisbee on the grass.

"Of course you will. But please not before he's five years old, okay? I don't want him tossed about before he is even big enough to wrap his legs around a one-thousand-pound animal."

For the tenth time or so in the last few days, Grace felt that they were planning their life. It was the first time, when discussing such things, that there was the smallest hint of doubt. Doubt about everything. It was true that Walt had only been issued a warning order that was not in fact a true order yet, but the word *warning* was ominous and tainted everything. If he were called up he had been informed that he could be gone for three months, maybe even up to a year. The longest they had ever been apart was for a week when Walt needed time to think—a week he had taken to be by himself before he made the decision to ask Grace to be his wife.

This idea of a National Guard call-up was throwing a wrench into everything. Planning where Travis would go to elementary school seemed premature. He hadn't even been potty trained yet! They had years to make decisions like this.

"Grace? You with me?"

"Just thinking."

He reached out to grab her salty hand above the cement table. "Let's say a quick prayer, okay?"

"Of course, sweetie." Grace reached out to hold Travis's small fist. They closed their eyes.

"Dear Heavenly Father, thank you for this day. Thank you for our baby and the sunshine and the food we are blessed with. Thank you for my wife and my parents and the time off from work and the opportunity to be with family. Please stay with us as we travel and visit and in the few weeks to come as we prepare for the possibility that I may be deployed. Please help us to accept this event in our lives and to use this opportunity to learn more about ourselves and to serve others. Please have us do your will in all things. And if our unit is called up to serve in Saudi Arabia, please bring us all home safely. And while I'm gone, please guide Grace in raising the son you have blessed us with. Amen."

"Amen," Grace said.

Walt squeezed her hand. "Time to hit the road again. I bet my Mom has a tray of fresh cookies and a strong cup of coffee awaiting us!"

SIXTEEN

Grace could never understand why Walt's parents remained in Cleveland. The large metropolis was smoggy. Regional transit buses squeaked and squealed and blew diesel as they traveled the Shoreway, the road along Lake Erie. At night, smokestacks spewed plumes of black exhaust and lit the industrial areas of the city a twinkly orange. Winters were brutal with snow that arrived early in the season and lingered well into late March and even April.

Despite the long, relentless winters and the unsightly factories, there were Cleveland enthusiasts who showed pride in their hometown. In recent decades, the Flats area, which historically housed factories and warehouses and contained massive steel drawbridges, had been renovated as a fashionable restaurant and bar district. Supporters bragged about the Flats, the Westside Market, the Cleveland Orchestra, and the Art Museum.

Some had been born in the city and never left. Others, like Walt's parents, had come from elsewhere and had found reasons to stay. Originally from Philadelphia, Lou Moore had traveled to the suburb of Shaker Heights on the east side to accept a job as a principal of a small private school before Walt and Pete were born. Over the years, he and Molly had fixed up a seventy-year-old colonial home and entertained friends they had made through the theater. Walt's younger brother continued to find refuge from becoming an adult in the detached garage on the property.

About three months after they first met, Walt had shyly invited Grace to his hometown. He had told her stories about growing up there, the snowball fights in the winter and the early morning stops for a twenty-five cent chocolate iced doughnut on the long walk to St. James, his Catholic grade school. He had told her tales of his boys-only club out in the garage and fishing on Lake Erie on Saturday mornings with his dad. Before that first visit, Walt had brought Cleveland to life in her imagination and she had fallen in love not only with the man, but also with the stories of his childhood. His stories seemed more magical than hers. When they first drove into the hazy city, she was disappointed. The town didn't seem nearly as magical in reality as it did in Walt's stories about it.

Her disappointment must have showed on her face because Walt said, "You better not tell my parents what you think of Cleveland."

Over the years, she had every now and again caught a glimpse of the magic Walt had seen in the smoggy city. Its main redeeming quality was that its shoreline was similar to that of Sand Beach. It offered places to boat or fish or watch the same sunrise or sunset.

Although Grace was not a Cleveland fan, there was something about a vacation, even a relatively short trip to the in-laws, that offered a fresh perspective—a time to relax and let someone else do the cooking, pay attention to Travis, mow the lawn, that made Grace appreciate time away.

It was mid-afternoon, when they finally arrived at the familiar, wide, tree-lined street where Walt had spent his childhood, playing hide and seek and riding his bicycle. They stepped onto the porch of his childhood home, and rang the bell. Molly opened the red oak door about three seconds later.

"Travis!" she exclaimed as she reached down to lift up the sticky toddler. Tears immediately filled her eyes.

Travis wrinkled his nose and stuck a thumb in his mouth.

"Omigosh, I can't believe what a few months can do to a baby! I missed you, Travvy." She nuzzled his round red cheek.

Lou appeared behind her, grinning.

"It's been a long trip, Gramma." Grace greeted her mother-in-law. It was nice to be able to call someone Gramma.

Before they even made it into the foyer, Lou grabbed their bags and whisked them off to the guest room.

"Why don't you two ladies stay cool in the kitchen while Walt and I run over to the West Side Market?"

Walt seemed to like that idea. "Yeah, sweetie, you and Mom and Travis stay cool in the kitchen. I'll get us some of that whole grain bread from Stehlmans. And don't wait on us. We might be a while in case we stop at Andy's for a beer."

Molly gave her daughter-in-law a hug and led Travis by the hand to the kitchen, which over the years had been the site of numerous daily pleasantries and heated arguments. It had accommodated Molly's quilting club and Lou's meetings with football coaches. Back when Walt's younger brother Pete was still in the house, it had been a place for drunkenness. The kitchen was where he would stagger in after missing dinner to burn bacon, eggs, and toast in the wee hours of the night while the rest of the house had to listen to the sounds of him dropping pots and pans on the kitchen floor. Occasionally, a half-asleep Molly or Lou would come in and make him a cup of coffee and finish the breakfast. In those days, they weren't quite aware just how intoxicated he was and wanted to make sure that he didn't burn the house down. They wanted to just be done with it and get back to bed. They were enablers, loving their two children equally, both the underachiever and the summa cum laude grad. It didn't matter.

In the days before Walt had met Grace, the kitchen was the place in which he wrote term papers, worked on algebra, and wrote poetry while sipping hot chocolate. In the days before Walt and Grace were married, the kitchen offered a place for Grace and her future mother-in-law to plan the wedding, complete the invitations, and search through bridal catalogs. Currently, it was the venue for the latest Moore obsession with crockpot cooking.

"Did you want some coffee Grace? I wasn't sure if you'd want it this time of day, it being so hot and all." Molly wiped her brow. She seemed pensive, uptight.

Grace pondered the idea of freshly brewed coffee. "Are you kidding? You know I'd love a cup of your coffee." Grace had learned early that you did not say no to a cup of coffee at the Moores for it was comparable to failing to shake a hand at the end of an interview. Though a tall glass of lemonade was what she would have preferred, she put her arm around Molly's shoulder.

"Even when I go to Gloria's, the coffee is never as good as you make it here. It's watered down or something." She half smiled. She was not going to let her in-laws know that sometimes she resorted to a cup of instant that had no flavor at all, a cup of crystal dirt that transformed to mud when hot water was added.

"The secret is in the beans." Molly peeled open the bag of Colombian coffee beans, tossed three scoops into the canister and turned the switch. Travis held his ears and made a face at the loud noise.

"So, Grace how have you been managing with the possibility the Guard will be deployed?" Molly said without looking at her as she poured filtered water into the coffee maker.

Grace, who had picked up Travis, began to rock him. She felt a trickle of sweat start at her temple, trickle down her neck and past the soft crevice between her breasts. Molly, like Grace, was also in the category of those that might be left behind when that big aircraft carried their loved one over the ocean into a place that was foreign, diabolical, misunderstood.

"Not well, I'm afraid." Grace wiped the sweat with the back of her hand as she nuzzled Travis. "It seems like a bad dream. I just can't understand how one day things are so normal, your kid is growing, your husband is going to work, and you're picking out drapes. The most important thing I've had to think about lately is how I'm going to clean the mold out of the bathtub." Grace managed a weak smile as she pulled Travis closer to her. "Now, since the news, everything has changed. How come no one ever told me life could be like this?"

But she knew. She had known that life could be like this starting the day her mother had received the news that there was a lump in her breast. And that it had metastasized. She knew when she saw the blue color on the test strip that life could, and did, change in a heartbeat.

Molly poured cream into a flowered creamer and bit her lip. "I've been saving every last page of the *Plain Dealer*, and I now have a pile of articles about this *invasion.*" She shuddered and pointed to the neat stack of newspapers on the table by the window. "I used to just pull out the crosswords and the comics and the food section. Now I go straight to the international news."

Molly took the scones out of a paper bag and arranged them on a crystal platter. "I really didn't care before, you know. Overseas, it's a different world. But now everything has changed." She went to the sink and began to wash her hands.

She continued. "I keep hoping this is a joke. Or maybe a dream. Or maybe I just thought last week that Walt had called and said he might be deployed. But *no*, it's a fact! I hate it! You don't know how many times I've crept down to the living room and sat in the dark with the cat on my lap over the past week! Every night. I keep wondering why we didn't pay for Walt's school. We could have afforded it. We take care of Pete, why Pete hardly pays rent. We could have done the same for Walt. But *noooo*. Walt always had to be the best—always had to take care of himself. He was putting together his own peanut butter sandwiches and placing a bag of chips and a cookie in a paper bag when he was in kindergarten. He paid for his first car with his paper route. He paid for school. He scrimped and saved, and I am so *proud* of that *boy*." She dried her hands and turned to face Grace.

At that moment, Grace noticed the dark circles under her eyes and knew that Molly was really concerned.

"I know that he wants to buy you two a nice home someday. He said so! And I know that the two of you have been looking! What now?" She ran her fingers through her thinning white hair. "Grace. Sweetie." She looked straight into Grace's eyes as her tears formed. "I can't begin to tell you how sorry I am that he had to join the Guard to pay for school. I felt at the time that it was okay, you know it was just one of those weekend away things, but now it seems rather overwhelming."

Grace swallowed hard and looked away.

She reached for Travis and picked some lint off his shirt. She patted his hair. "How about some of Gramma's yummy scones?"

"Cones, Mommy!"

The two women carried trays of coffee and scones to the living room. As soon as they had settled themselves on the velvet sofa, the front door opened and in strode Pete, wearing cut-off shorts and an Indians baseball cap. He was unshaven and the hair that was visible from beneath his cap looked unwashed and greasy.

"Hey, sis. What's goin on?"

She stood to greet him.

"How's that nephew o' mine?"

He turned to Travis and bent down to give him a high-five. Travis grimaced and whimpered.

"Hey, boy. You are growing, aren't you? What are you now—two years old?"

"He's fourteen months." Grace looked down at Travis as she couldn't bear to look at Pete. Why couldn't it be Pete who was going overseas? He didn't have a baby or a wife. He didn't have anything much to take care of beyond his daily hangover.

"We were just going to look at some photos before your dad and brother get home," Molly said, nodding toward the coffee table that was stacked a foot high with photo albums. It was something they often started the visit with to get reacquainted. And Grace always loved seeing pictures of Walt as a child: Walt when he was missing his two front teeth; Walt and Pete dressed in red, white, and blue and seated in a wagon for the Fourth of July parade; Walt dressed in a suit and tie in front of the house just before his First Communion.

"Coffee, son?"

"Don't mind if I do." Pete leaned over to grab a mug and poured from the silver urn. So what's this I hear about my brother?"

"Not right now, Pete. Grace doesn't want to talk about it." She gave Pete a look. "Can't it wait? They will be here a week. We all will have plenty of time to talk and to catch up on the latest news. Right now, Grace and I are going to look at some pictures."

Pete poured cream into his mug. "Okay, I get the picture. Ha, *'picture'!* I made a joke! What would a visit be without photo time?" He pulled off his cap, revealing thick black hair that was either damp or greasy, and combed it back with his fingers as he took a sip of the coffee. Finding a spot next to Molly, he propped up his legs on the velvet ottoman, grabbed the album at the top of the pile, and handed it to his mother.

The three settled onto the velvet cushions and combed through the worn leather albums pointing, laughing, and reminiscing as Travis played in the corner with a new shiny red fire truck. They looked at photos of Walt and Pete when they were children; in the tree house, Pete's broken arm, Walt's toothless grin. They poured over black and white images that detailed the beginnings of Molly and Lou's life together. Grace stared especially hard at the faded sepia pictures of Lou in his military attire standing next to Molly up in Philadelphia before he was shipped off.

Grace became more comfortable and once again felt a part of the Moore family, as the clock ticked off the afternoon. It was the first time that Grace could remember feeling relaxed around Pete. Maybe he wasn't such an idiot after all. When the coffee pot was empty and the sun had made its way into the west, the room fell quiet. Despite the caffeine, Grace felt sleepy. She yawned.

Molly noticed and said, "Grace, why don't you take a nap before the men get home? I'll take Travis for a little walk in the neighborhood. And Pete needs to get ready for work, don't you, son?"

Pete nodded, picked up the tray and carried it to the kitchen.

A nap sounded wonderful, luxurious. Grace excused herself and went to the familiar guest room. The antique bed was topped with the Amish quilt Grace and Walt had purchased for the Moores' thirtieth anniversary a few years earlier on a day trip to

Millersburg, one of Ohio's Amish areas. Vanilla candles sat atop the walnut dresser. The guest bathroom sparkled and smelled of lemon-scented soap, and Egyptian towels hung on the wall rack. Grace brushed her teeth and then removed her jeans and changed into a clean t-shirt. As she peeled off the silver ring that had been her mother's, she wondered what her mom would have thought of all that was happening. She slipped between the crisp white percale sheets, stretched, curled into a fetal position, and gazed at the filmy curtains waving in the light breeze that came through the window. A cardinal sang outside the window, and the late-afternoon sun flickered and danced on the dresser. Her eyes became heavy, her thoughts blurred, and she drifted into a deep sleep. And she slept, really slept, for the first time in a week.

Three days later, the Moores took Walt, Grace, Travis, and Pete to an Indians game. Downtown Cleveland bustled with honking cars, busses, sirens, and pedestrians. The Moores carried plastic seat cushions, rain ponchos, and a diaper bag as they stepped into the steady throng of baseball enthusiasts that formed a walking locomotive headed toward Cleveland Stadium. Grace pushed the stroller. Walt, who normally wore t-shirts and cut-offs, now wore his fatigue shirt with khaki shorts. His fatigues were new. Grace noted that he was gradually transforming from civilian to soldier. Grace and Travis both wore blue and red Indians T-shirts and matching baseball caps that Molly had bought for them during a shopping trip the previous day.

Grace began to feel dizzy as she walked along trying to keep pace with the crowd. The sound of baseball music, the smell of hot dogs and sauerkraut from the street vendors, and the blended mumbling of strangers' conversations all combined to overwhelm and nauseate her. She wanted to have fun, to laugh and joke and have a wonderful time. If she pretended hard enough and imagined it was two years ago, pre-Travis, pre-news that there might be a deployment, then things would be easy. This would be a time to enjoy the game and the in-laws and get into the life of the city.

But it wasn't two years ago, it wasn't ten years ago, it was today. A Tuesday evening in August, damp and distressing in its insistence on calling Grace's attention to this being another of the possible last times before Walt left. This was possibly a last ball game together, at least a last ball game before deployment changed their lives. What would Walt be like if he did make it home? Would he be a paraplegic? Would he suffer from posttraumatic stress disorder? She had heard from some of his buddies at the *Times*—in fact, Jim had written a story about it not long ago— that sometimes men stationed overseas came back just a shell of themselves, depressed and despairing. Sometimes the burden of the war made them suicidal, losing hope for their future and questioning the meaning of life. She gulped, suppressed her thoughts, and put on a happy face, reminding herself that the future was unknown and on this day, at this moment, she had her wonderful Walt, warm and alive.

Four innings into the game, she turned to Walt and said, "I wish we would have done more of this." She nibbled his ear while he munched on popcorn in the nosebleed section of the stadium. He barely looked at her as he stared at the scoreboard: Tigers 4, Indians 2.

"Ohhh….. Way to go!" Walt shouted as he stood up, spilling popcorn all over Grace.

The crowd roared.

"Did you see that, Grace! He took three bases. Whoa! We got a winner. Got a *winner*! Right, Travis?" He grabbed Travis and lifted him over his head. "See that son? That is a *home* run, my man! And someday you are going to pitch Little League, right, Grace?"

He held his son high in the air, making him giggle. Pete whistled for the pin-striped vendor and motioned for him to bring a fresh roll of blue cotton candy. Grace had no appetite for the popcorn or the cotton candy. She noticed Molly staring blankly at the scoreboard and casting frequent glances at Walt. Apparently, the two of them were brooding while the men were lost in the game.

During the remainder of the game, the men shouted out whenever the Indians got hits and went wild when they scored, while the women picked at their nail polish and shuffled to get comfortable in the hard wooden seats. Travis clutched a baseball that Walt had picked up on his way to get the popcorn.

The evening ended a success for the home team with the Indians winning 9–4 against the Tigers.

The next day, Lou and Molly announced they would take Travis to the beach to give Grace and Walt some time alone. When they were ready to go, Grace followed them out onto the front porch and handed Molly a large floral cloth bag filled with beach towels, sunscreen, sandals, and toys. Travis got to wear his first bathing suit—red-and-white-striped trunks—and was given a sand bucket and shovel. Molly held a magazine and a cross-stitch. Lou was lugging a briefcase filled with paperwork.

"Lou, you and your work." Molly rolled her eyes and winked at Grace. "We both married workaholics, didn't we, Gray?" Turning back to her husband, she said, "What will you do if your work gets caught in a good wind and flies into Lake Erie?" She grinned.

"Moll, you worry too much. Always thinking about the what-if," Lou said as he picked up Travis. "Doesn't she worry too much, Travis? Does Grandma worry?"

"Worryyyyyyyyy," Travis cooed as he tweaked his Grandpa's nose. He had really taken to Lou.

"We'll be back around five o'clock or so, kids! After the beach, we've been invited to Dave and Carol's for lunch. I expect that they will have their grandbaby there, so Travis will have someone to play with. You two have a great day!" They waved their goodbyes to Walt and Grace who stood on the porch.

As they drove off, Walt turned to Grace and pulled her toward him with his muscled arms. "Okay, young lady, you are going into the house with me."

"Walter!"

"We have the whole place to ourselves. The whole day."

"But what if Pete comes home?"

"Not gonna happen. He went to Cedar Point this morning."

"And what if your parents come home early?"

"I'll lock the front door. It has the chime on it. And the bedroom has a lock too!"

He grabbed the strap on her thin tank top with his teeth as he carried her to the guest room. He lay her on the bed. She closed her eyes as he unsnapped her shorts, pulled them down, and tossed them on the floor. He came up to kiss her, and she met his kiss, warm, wet, and smiling as her body softened and melted into his familiar touch.

She hummed a low sound of pleasure. "Are you sure we're alone?" He put his hand across her mouth and kissed each eye closed. He pulled off his shirt revealing the results of his many years of working out at the base. His smooth hard skin was tan from his jogs along the lake.

"You, my dear one, are going to get a good shower. I'll do the lathering and rinsing, and then I'm going to take my time with you." He pulled off her thin top and revealed her breasts, which had grown larger from the year of breast-feeding.

She turned to Walt and unzipped his blue jeans, slowly removed them, and playfully tossed them into the pile that included her shorts, panties, and tank top.

"I think we need to forget the shower." He breathed heavily into her blond hair.

"You, do?"

"Oh, yes, I can't mess with that!" He moved along her body, letting her know how much he had missed her after months of tending to the baby instead of to him.

Grace had forgotten about the way her body felt. Before the pregnancy it had been firm, but now it felt soft, mushy, and maternal. Walt looked at her appreciatively as he lay over her, naked and alive.

"You forgot something."

He examined her body in search of something he might have forgotten.

"Okay, turn around."

She dutifully turned so that he could unclasp her silver necklace. He skillfully used a quick thumb movement to undo the latch and then got up to place it on the dresser. He stood in the window and closed the curtains. He returned to his wife, who was now facing him, her arms reaching for him to come to her. She succumbed to his nimble hands, trusting him, letting him explore, caress, and pleasure her.

They spent hours playing, touching, rediscovering things that brought them both delight, their bodies moist and burning with desire. They tumbled and fumbled and worked their way onto the floor, into the shower, and even onto the sink. They lost track of time and place. They interspersed their lovemaking with idle chatter and trips to the kitchen for glasses of water, a few cookies. They giggled. They were back to the days of when they had first married, happy, lustful, and in love. At one point, Walt lay behind her, let his male form curve around her, and whispered into her hair, "Where has this sexy woman been hiding? I need to take you home more often, if this is what it is going to do to you."

"Vatt has become of me, Valter? I have been running around like a nymph in your parents' home! Why, if they were to find me here with my panties on the floor, what would they think of their daughter-in-law?" She looked up at the ceiling and pulled the sheet over her, as though someone might walk through the door at any time.

There were no interruptions, not even a phone ringing, no Pete, no mailman. Nothing invaded the wonder of the four hours they spent blissfully allowing pleasure into their lives. By two o'clock, they were happily exhausted. Grace nestled her head against Walt's familiar chest and purred contentedly.

Walt was quiet.

"Whatcha thinking?"

"I'm wondering what it's like to die."

"Walt!"

"No, really Grace, What happens? I mean, I believe in God, and I want to believe there is a heaven, but do you realize that when you die, you no longer have anything! I mean, you can't see the ocean, or the trees, or the flowers and you can't taste pizza and you can't make love. Basically, all the things you've ever known are gone."

"Walt, you're being morbid."

"I'm sorry. I've just been thinking about dying a lot."

Grace turned toward him and caressed his arms.

"And you know, I don't want to leave you and the baby." He choked. "And if I die, I want you to be okay."

"That is *not* going to happen, Walt. Now let's forget about that."

"But, Grace if something does happen to me, just know. I'll be watching over you! Maybe I'll be a bee buzzing around your ear! Or maybe I'll be the ladybug crawling on your arm. I'll bug you!"

Tears began to flow down her cheeks. "Walt, I love you, you know. I wish we could just stay together. I don't want this to end. Let's run away. Go on an Alaskan cruise. Or…or maybe you can sneak me away in your suitcase if and when you go overseas to fight a nasty war."

She stopped herself, the minute the word escaped. War had no place in the bright sunny afternoon, with the sound of children yelling outside the window and the smooth feel of Walt's skin beneath her hand. The word echoed throughout the bedroom, escaped through the small window opening and into the summer air. Once the word had left the room it was not welcome to come back, not today. They whispered and talked, their bodies entwined.

"I think the only way we'll survive this, honey, is to hope for the possibility that you will not be deployed. I know it seems like it might happen, but you haven't yet gotten the final marching orders."

Their chatter continued for a while, but eventually their eyes closed and they drifted into a shared afternoon nap.

The week went quickly and on Friday, it was time to head back to Sand Beach. After packing, Grace sat on the bed with Travis and gazed out the window, watching Walt perform a last-minute oil change on Lou's van.

Molly entered the room and sat on the bed next to Grace.

"I hope you know, that I will be here for you if you need help. That is, if Walt is deployed, I can come visit and you can come here and well you know we are all in this together." And I'm sure I speak for Lou as well." She put a comforting arm around Grace's shoulder.

"Thank God for that. I am going to need all the help I can get! And Walt needs you too."

Travis went over to the nightstand and reached for the lamp with one hand while he clutched his juice with the other. Grace deftly picked him up, sat him on her lap and bounced him on her knee.

"And the offer for you and Travis to stay with us stands, you know."

Grace was preoccupied with the task of diverting Travis from the lamp. "Travis stop it! That is not a toy. Here. Take the truck." She pulled the fire truck out of the canvas toy bag. Travis grabbed it and waved it in the air. Then she turned to her mother-in-law with a smile. "Thanks, Molly. My dad has made the same offer. I feel very lucky."

"Oh, honey, you are going to be okay. This is all going to be okay." She patted Grace again in the reassuring way she had. Molly let go a deep sigh and continued. "So now you know that if you need anyone, we're here in Cleveland for you, your father is in Sand Beach for you, and please, Grace, know that we are all in this thing together. And together we will get through this. Next year at this time, we will all look back and laugh that we even worried for one minute. This will be easier than we think. Everything is going to turn out just fine." Her voice became stronger as she articulated positive thoughts.

Molly helped Grace lift the suitcases and placed them in the foyer. They proceeded to the kitchen where Molly had filled a picnic basket with snacks. Walt came in the room, washed up quickly at the kitchen sink, whirled around, and lifted Molly right off her feet.

"Walt!"

"Ma." They hugged, locked in a long embrace. Lou walked in

and gave reprieve to the moment.

"Thanks for the oil change, son. I don't know why I never learned to do that."

"No prob, Pop." He released his bear hug.

Lou paused by the refrigerator and gripped the handle. His jaw clenched as he opened the door and reached for a ginger ale.

"If you do get deployed son, you know that your mother and I will look after your girl and Travis. You got my word on that one."

Walt looked up at his father for a moment, thanked him and changed the subject. "Grace, did you get everything?"

After checking the house twice for items that they might have left behind, they were ready to go.

Four back smacks, two short hugs and seven minutes later the Jeep was loaded and carried the little family away from Cleveland and toward Sand Beach.

SEVENTEEN

Early one morning, a week after Walt and Grace returned from Cleveland, Grace answered the phone and was greeted by a gruff voice that requested to speak to Walt. When she told the caller that Walt was at work, he requested that Grace relay his name and number to her husband and ask that he call back as soon as possible. Grace knew in her gut that this was the call that they had anticipated. She jotted the number down and relayed the message to Walt and within a half hour, Walt had phoned her back to confirm that he was in fact being deployed out of the country. Although the announcement was not a surprise, it did erase any hope that it might not happen.

Once the deployment was confirmed, the news spread, weaving its way through town, into the nooks and crannies of homes, businesses and shops. The news had spread at Glamour Clips, while woman sat and gossiped in hushed tones as they were shampooed, trimmed and manicured. It spread at the Laundromat among whirring washing machines and customers folding t-shirts and underwear. It spread in line at the pharmacy and it spread through Gloria's amid the smell of fresh brewed coffee and fried bacon.

When Fran heard of the deployment, she brought over a fresh batch of the peanut butter and walnut fudge that she had been making recently for every occasion. Once the crisis queen, Fran now took on an encouraging role as her best friend faced adversity.

"Oh, Grace, you'll be fine. It's just a short time—what, three months, six max? It'll go fast."

When Grace turned a dark eye on her, Fran softened. "Oh, I didn't mean that Grace. I know three months can be a long time. Three minutes can be a long time. Remember driving by Mavis's house? Now, those three minutes lasted *forever.* I might as well have been in hell." Fran sliced off another piece of fudge. "C'mon, you know my homemade fudge does wonders."

Grace indulged in the sweet treat, allowing Fran to spoil her a little. Nowadays, for at least a few minutes at a time, Fran was able to hide her drama about her relationship with Michael and her relationship with life in general. Grace had taken over the stage while Fran took a seat, front row center. And Fran showered Grace with attention and care. And food.

When Linda from Gloria's learned of the deployment, she spread the news to everyone who would listen. Now, when Walt visited the diner for his daily toast and coffee, eyes turned on him and people would come to his table as though he were a celebrity or stop him by the cash register as he paid his tab. Some people even picked up his tab.

Linda put a date on the restaurant calendar for a sendoff party for Walt and printed up flyers announcing it.

Saturday September 15th

11:00 AM

Please come to Gloria's as we show our support to Walter Moore and Tommy James who are being deployed to serve overseas.

Your presence is requested.

Gloria's will provide the food.

Gifts welcome.

Walt's boss assigned him to write an article explaining the president's decision to deploy the National Guard and Reserves. In the article, Walt explained that for years, the National Guard had been an option for those struggling to pay for college.

Historically, Guardsman expected to serve during natural disasters. They did not expect that they would be called to serve during a war. He noted that the war and the demand for soldiers did not discriminate. Those being deployed came from all walks of life. Among those called were business people, doctors, teachers, and students. They were public servants, Boy Scout leaders, and church members. During this conflict, those being deployed were not career soldiers who had planned or expected to be oversees. These were Americans who were snatched out of civilian life.

At the end of the piece, he revealed that he was being deployed.

And by the way, I speak from experience on this one. I will be packing up and leaving for Saudi Arabia myself at the end of this month. I realize that I am only a writer whose absence may not be as strongly felt as that of a doctor or a mayor. But even so, my respects go out to my employer, Stu Warner, as he works to find a temporary replacement for me here at the Sand Beach Times. I know that this will be a hardship on Mr. Warner and the Times. And my wife Grace will be left the daunting task of holding down the fort, taking care of all the things that are usually my responsibility, while continuing to be the wonderful Mommy that she is and has been to our son, Travis.

Let it be known that I am not the only resident from Sand Beach that will be deployed. Tommy James, a 21-year-old college student who has been working summers at the factory and has been finishing up a degree at the University of Michigan will be deployed as well. And it is my understanding that Tommy just got engaged to Pam Miller from Aston.

I know that while we are gone, there will be support from our neighbors, friends, and families. That is one of the things I've learned about Sand Beach. I know that people care. And I am certain that they will look after my loved ones and the details of my job while I am gone. For this, I will be forever grateful.

Shortly after the article was published, Grace's father came over in the late afternoon on a clear, blue, cloudless day as Grace was hanging sheets and towels on the clothesline in the backyard.

"That was a good article that Walt wrote, Grace. I hung it on the refrigerator."

Grace bent down, reached into the plastic container, retrieved a clothespin, and clamped a wet towel to the thick white cord that was strung between two oak trees. Her tired puffy face was clear of any makeup, other than a coating of Chap Stick to heal her dry and bitten lips.

"Yeah, well, the words were nice, Dad, but don't let the words fool you."

Charles gathered a long sheet, stretched it lengthwise, and clamped it to the clothesline. "I thought he did a nice job. But I'm sure that what he wrote can't possibly describe what you're going through." He turned to face her and placed a hand on her shoulder.

Any touch, any act of kindness was now a trigger for the release of feelings that lurked inside of Grace. She held back her tears and managed to swallow a lump of anxiety that had been hovering in her throat. "You're right, Dad. Walt *seems* to be handling everything well on paper. And I've been thinking about that a lot lately."

"About how Walt handles everything well on paper?"

She avoided his gaze and pulled away from his touch. "I've been thinking about how things are different when you just read about something. When you read about someone's life in the news or you watch a movie, it's someone else's life and even though you care about them, you don't have to wake up next to them. You don't have to hear them brush their teeth or cough in the middle of the night. You don't have to feed them breakfast. Those people that you read about belong to someone else. When you hear that they are suffering, you can disconnect. When you are finished reading about the lives that have been touched by tragedy, you can fold up the newspaper and toss away the evidence that someone is hurting. Or you can choose not to read it in the first place. You can ignore it and go scoop up a big bowl of ice cream and curl up on the couch. Or you can do something you love, play some mini-golf, walk along the shore, take a nice leisurely horse ride along a country road."

As she spoke into the cool breeze, her heart rate accelerated, her teeth clenched. Two large tears unashamedly escaped the corners of her green eyes and rolled down her cheeks. Her father had become speechless, his attention focused on her weeping face, absorbing every word. He had stopped his labor and became her spellbound audience.

She wiped her tears on her sleeve and sighed. "And I am afraid that this time the story is about me. And about my husband. And it affects our baby. And it affects Walt's parents. And you. And everyone who knows him. This article is personal. This article hits home. This article is about us. The Moores. The Moores who live at 1017 Oak Street. And you know what? I can toss the article in the trash when I'm finished, but I cannot escape the fact that this article is about me. And it cannot be discarded. I'm going to have to suck it up."

Grace was discovering she had a whole new appreciation for the tragedies she had been reading about for years. Behind each person's story there was a struggle. People hit by trains usually had a spouse who had to wake up the next morning in an empty bed or a child who had to go to sleep at night without a kiss. The young mothers who lost a child in a summer drowning had to enter a silent room filled with toys. Those in the statistics of the unemployed had to face the fear of an empty cupboard or the fear of losing a home.

Grace now felt as though anything could happen to her at any time. Though adversity had visited her in the past, when she lost her mom and her sister chose to vanish from Sand Beach, she thought she had made a new life with Walt, a start over so to speak. And she treasured the wonderful memories she and Walt had made. The cozy talks, the love making, the joy on their wedding day. Walt resting on her belly to hear the first heartbeat of the life they had created. The day they found and moved into the small duplex and decorated it with things that made a house a home, good cooking, soft words, fresh paint.

It was all still so new. Eight years together was just a beginning. Her parents had been together for twenty-six years. And for twenty-three of those years, Grace had been a witness to what love in a family could do. It was at once intangible and tangible—it brought with it lightness, a joy that material things could not offer.

When there was love in your heart, the world sang. Her mother's love was a gift Grace had taken for granted. She took it for granted until that fateful day in spring when she saw her mother crying in the den, her father looking worried, with his arm around her, his head hung in defeat, and the subsequent announcement to the girls that a doctor had found a lump in their mother's breast. And it was malignant.

The news of the deployment was unwelcome too, like the diagnosis of her mother's cancer. An unwelcome presence had just marched right into their lives. Out of nowhere, uninvited. And now it was casting a dark shadow over everything. It seemed to be in the walls, under the floorboards, in the water coming out of the faucet. It dominated their conversation, thoughts, plans, and dreams, and was the source of their greatest fear.

Grace set down the small bucket of clothespins and sat down on a chair, rocking back and forth, hugging herself, stretching the sweatshirt sleeves around her cool, damp fingers.

"I don't know how in the world I'm going to get through this." She felt the tears rolling down her cheeks as she searched her father's expression for an answer.

"Grace, you *will* be okay. I know it doesn't feel like it. I know you don't believe it." He smiled down at her as he pushed aside a wayward wisp of hair that had fallen from her ponytail. "I know this deployment is a challenge. I also know that this is not your first challenge. And it is probably one of the hardest things you've had to deal with. And I hate to say it, but having lived as long as I have, it probably won't be the last." He paused and rubbed his weathered hand across his plaid flannel jacket. "And you are a strong girl. If your mother were here today, she would be proud of the life you have made. Above all, she wanted you to be happy. And you are.

You have created a life for yourself, one that Mom would be proud of. So, I know you will work through this one too."

"Easier said than done."

Dad continued. "Everything is easier said than done, Gray, you know that. You say you don't know how you are going to get through this, and frankly I don't know either. It is one day at a time. Sometimes, I have learned, it is just one minute at a time. And the thing that I have learned about troubled times, is that sometimes it helps to shift your thinking. Right now, you are thinking as though the worst is about to happen, when in fact you really have no idea. Walt might come back with some great experience. This might be a chance for you to try your hand at independence. It might be a chance for you to find a house and surprise him when he gets back. It might be an opportunity for the paper to realize how important Walt's job is and to realize he can't be replaced. He might get a raise. If you shift to hope for a positive outcome, you will feel better and you just might be right. Make lemonade!"

She knew her Dad was right. When she and Beck were little, Mom and Dad had taught them about making lemonade, both literally and figuratively. In the heat of the summer, Caroline would drive to the Go Mart and pick up a five-pound bag of lemons, and together they would squeeze the bitter fruit. When they added ice, water, and sugar, the bitterness was transformed into sweetness. The girls would then set up a small folding table with a cardboard sign advertising fifteen-cent glasses of lemonade. They typically earned several dollars a day, which they stored in their piggy banks. And with the money they saved up, they would treat themselves to hair bows at the five-and-dime, tootsie rolls, and an occasional matinee at the Sunset Movie theatre.

But Grace's Dad had been making his own sort of lemonade in the years since her mother died. He had found ways to add sweetness to his life. After living for a while in the dark despair of his loneliness, he gradually started moving again. He changed his bitter lemon of resentment into productive activity. He threw away many of the items that had cluttered his home, and carefully stashed away in closets or drawers the ones that carried the most intense memories of his beloved wife. Gradually, the layer of dust that had collected on the shelves was removed and the home was cleaned. New carpets were installed and old pictures were donated to the church. Mom's dresses were donated to Goodwill.

Grace had witnessed her father morph ever so slowly from a man of intense sorrow to a man of hope. She had seen how he had moved past his sadness to create some beauty in the world—a renovated kitchen, a carefully crafted screened-in porch, a small water fountain in the center of his English garden in the backyard. After he was finished with the renewal of his home, he stepped out into the world. He became a strong support for the little family that he had. He started reaching out to his neighbors. He volunteered at the Sand Beach Fire Department.

Now he stepped closer to her and started singing "He's Got the Whole World in His Hands" in a deep baritone voice that resonated throughout the small yard. It caught the attention of the neighbor dog, who stopped yapping, bounded up to the fence, and tilted its head toward the singing. It caught the attention of Travis, who looked up from where he had been sitting near the tree, playing with his small shovel and his Tonka truck. Travis got onto his feet and toddled toward the enchanting sound emanating from his grandpa.

Grace winced, thinking it was a good thing Mrs. Givens was hard of hearing and the Johnsons had gone on vacation. "You know,

Dad," she said, smiling. "I would sing with you, but ever since Walt told me I can't carry a tune, I stopped doing that. But I'm glad you can still belt it out. You are really something."

Her dad smiled. "I am something. What am I? I am a *great* something!" He pounded his chest and lifted his plaid flannel covered arms toward the clouding sky with the dimming daylight. He inhaled a deep satisfied breath as his voice became a part of the landscape. A song of joy in the September air.

"And life don't get me down." His voice deepened even further into a low octave as he ended on the word *down*.

Grace gently set the tufts of braided grass she had been weaving on the ground and stood to lift the last rust-stained towel and hang it on the remaining spot on the line. Giggling, she realized the interaction had done as much to lift her spirits as a strong cup of coffee. "Leave it to my Dad to wake me up and make me feel better." She stretched her arms out and reached around her dad's large frame and squeezed. "My father, the opera star. Remind me to get you over to Sammy's on karaoke night."

After they finished hanging the wash in the fading afternoon light, Grace closed her eyes and took in one last whiff of the clean sheets hanging on the line. The empty laundry basket in one hand, she looked down at her son, who was covered in grass and dirt, his face a light yellow from rubbing his cheek with a limp dandelion, and reached for his little paw with her other hand. "C'mon, Travis."

Dad followed Grace and Travis into the duplex, where the aroma of a thick vegetable soup simmering in the crockpot greeted them.

"I got a card from Beck." Her dad said this in a sober monotone, as they sat down together in the living room. He picked up a magazine and began leafing through it. His face was expressionless.

"What this time?" Grace had become weary of these teases, the occasional letters that told them nothing.

"It was just a birthday card." He avoided her gaze. He had gotten a birthday card two years earlier but nothing since. Grace tried not to get her hopes up. At least a birthday card meant that Becky was alive.

"Well, how is she?" Grace felt a surge of stomach acid wash her insides.

"I don't know. She didn't say."

"But she sent a card."

"Yes. She signed it just 'Becky.' Not 'Love, Becky.' Not 'I am fine.' Nothing." He looked up from the magazine. "Just the same small, scraggly signature she always signs with, the one your mother taught her at the dining room table. That girl used to love making a big B and a curlicue y at the end of her name."

Grace suddenly had a vision of Beck and herself seated at the living room table, coloring and practicing penmanship.

"What about the return address?"

"Didn't have one."

"Where was it postmarked?"

"Tampa."

"Hmmm. At least she has made contact." Grace sighed and turned to hug her father as he placed the magazine back on the table. "It's a step in the right direction, Pop. As long as she sends an occasional birthday card, there is still hope that she'll come back to us."

She mussed her father's hair and went to the kitchen to grab a large paper sack of apples, handed him the bag, and saw him to the door. There was a renewed confidence in her father—an electric energy. He seemed lighter, less serious, able to handle the problems of the world. And able to offer sage advice as well. And that singing. That singing he had comforted her with as a child had reemerged. The same old twinkle in her father's eyes, though they were now lined and topped with graying brows.

As he walked down the step, she noticed that he was still wearing that new cologne. And it looked like Dad might have lost a good ten pounds.

Oh, life, she thought, as she watched her aging father pull away from the curb in his pickup truck. So unpredictable!

EIGHTEEN

During the next few weeks, the days went by in a blur. Walt finished up his work and spent every free moment with Grace and Travis. Nights were hell for Walt, and his sleeplessness took its toll. Each morning he awoke and hugged Grace before doing anything else. He made biscuits and gravy and brewed fresh steamy coffee. When Travis cried, he scooped him up and inhaled his warm, milky essence. He had stopped working on the novel he had started and packed it away in the knapsack he would take overseas. He was now focused on preparing to leave with the hope of a safe return to his small family in the not too distant future, to finish the great American novel and live the quiet, blissful life that he had begun. Grace found excuses to call him at work, and outside of following him to the bathroom, the base, and to the office, she did everything possible to stay connected.

"Walt, can you bring home some sugar? We're out of sugar." And then, thirty minutes later. "Walt, what kind of clothes are you going to need packed? I don't even really know what the weather is like in Saudi Arabia. It is the desert, isn't it, sweetie? I've never been to the desert, but I think I heard somewhere it's cold at night. Did they issue you a packing list?"

One Tuesday she called him eight times. That evening, she sat on the floor of the living room with Travis, the bills neatly stacked in piles, along with birth certificates, insurance papers, and all the other documents that Grace wanted to ask Walt about while he was still home.

"If Dad finds another place for us to look at, can I still house-hunt while you're away?"

"You have asked me that before. And what have I told you?" He rubbed his unshaven chin.

She became quiet. "I'm not a child you know."

"I know, I'm sorry. I'm just tired of thinking about the house when I have so much else on my mind. And I hate the thought that you will find the perfect place and I won't be there to find it with you. But of course you can and of course you should look for our place while I'm gone. It will keep you busy. Not that you aren't going to be busy with Travis."

He found a spot on the floor, folded his long legs, and settled on the carpet as he grabbed Travis and sat him in his lap. He reached over and picked up the cable bill and placed it into the file marked TV. "Don't worry too much about the bills. It's pretty simple, Gray. They come in the mailbox and you write out a check and that's that—the phone, the cable, the rent, the electric. And, of course, you have to write the amounts in the check register so that you know how much is left in the account."

Oh, boy, Grace thought, my husband thinks I'm a dimwit. He must have forgotten that I lived for two years on my own before we married. She looked up at him and gave a weak smile. And silently forgave him.

Travis wrapped his little arms around his father's neck. The toddler's body was growing rapidly. So rapidly, Grace had observed, that if you were to stop and focus and listen to her son, you might hear his small bones lengthening. You might actually see the skin stretching, the tiny teeth erupting from his gums, causing him to whimper and whine. They couldn't keep him in his new outfits long before he stretched into another size. His vocabulary, fine motor skills, speed, and dexterity were all improving as well. Watching him became an obsession to make sure he didn't stick a finger into a light socket or drink a bit of bleach. Cabinets were locked and dresser drawers were guarded.

Walt lifted the giggling boy up over his head and then swung him down between his legs. Travis's round chubby miniature body was relaxed and limp. Walt tossed the little bundle into the air, counting to ten as he tossed. Then he pulled Travis close and rubbed his stubbly chin into the boy's cheek.

"Don't worry about doing too much. You know we are acting like it's going to be years, but it's only going to be months! Silly! A few months! You aren't going to have that much time to find a place for us. Why don't you just take it easy? If I'm going to be over there in the desert fighting, I don't want you over here fighting. Relax and let your dad and Fran and my parents look after you. Go to Cleveland and spend a few weeks. Go to the barn. Please, I want to be able to imagine that you are having it easy."

"Oh, c'mon, sweetie, having it easy? I'll try, but I will only be doing it for you. At this point, I will do anything for you. I will sing down at the beach every day. I will paint the entire house. I will buy us a home and have it all fixed up and awaiting your return. I will type up all of your notes on the novel you are planning to write. I will come oversees and make sure they are feeding you and the bad guys aren't messing with you. How's that sound? What if you could have whatever you want?"

Walt laughed. "If I could have whatever I want? I'll tell you what I want! I want a million dollars. And a million years to live. And how about twenty-seven novels published by the time I'm sixty. And I'd like to see old Mr. Hodge fix up his rundown shack that has a million newspapers and twenty-four rats. And I'd like to see him get his health back." He thought for a moment. "And I'd like to see Pete grow up and find something he is good at and find a nice wife, like I have. I wish I could have whatever I want! I would not be leaving here."

He winked at her and set Travis down in his playpen, handing him an octagon-shaped puzzle. "But you know. What I *really* want, since I have to be realistic?" He drew her toward him and gazed out the window into the moonlit yard. "What I *really* want is that when I'm in some makeshift tent to know that you will be looking at the same moon that I am looking at every night and that you will be looking at the same sun rising every morning. The only difference, my girl, is that your moon and sun will be shining over the cool of Lake Huron and mine will be hovering over the dry heat of the desert. I want to be able to think of you and still be with you somehow." He squeezed her shoulder. "But I don't want to be worrying about you. I want to be thinking of you and Travis enjoying yourselves. I want to imagine Christmas with the tree and the colored twinkly lights that you pull out of the red plastic storage box every year. I want you to put up that illuminated reindeer in the front yard. And I want to imagine you with your little green apron and Santa hat, bending over to pour red sprinkles on freshly baked sugar cookies. I want to imagine eating them on that Santa plate you bought at the after-Christmas Sale at Marshalls last year. And I want to imagine enjoying them with a glass of ice cold milk. And I want to imagine that I will be here with you to enjoy every minute of my son's second Christmas."

Grace wiped the back of her hand across her forehead, feigning a swoon. "You have such an imagination. No wonder you are a writer."

He pulled her hand toward him and kissed it as his voice lowered. "And," he added. "One final request. Please, please sing in your Grace voice. Sing so loudly that I can hear you belt out a Christmas carol across the sea. I want to hear you. Can you do that for me please? 'I'm Dreaming of a White Christmas' would be nice."

"What about the fact that you think I can't hold a tune?"

He leaned in to breathe in the smell of her soft hair. "Hmmm," he whispered into her ear, his warm breath causing her to shudder. She looked up at him to see that his jaw was clenching like it did when he was worried, and the corner of his eye twitched ever so slightly. He dropped his arm from around her and turned away, reaching to pick up his shoes and socks, and stood in the center of the living room clutching them.

"If you find us a house while I'm gone, you know I'll trust you with it." He turned and walked away and closed the bedroom door behind him.

NINETEEN

In early November, Walt was sent to Harbor Bay Army Base in the town of Harbor Bay, ninety miles from Sand Beach to prepare for deployment. Grace quickly followed with Travis, holing up in a nearby Days Inn. Walt was not able to spend much time with them due to the intensity of the training, but she wanted to at least be near him and available should he catch a minute to join her.

The town was filled with visitors as families and friends traveled from afar to be with their Weekend-Warriors-turned-full-time-soldiers. Traffic was heavy on the two-lane roads and drivers were tense, more likely to jerk up their middle fingers than to let another driver cut in front of them. The area did not have the streets to accommodate the crowds. Horns blared continually. The temporary residents invaded nearby hotels and created a community among themselves, but it was not a festive one. There was tension in the air that brought quick tempers and exasperated sighs.

Grace chose to stay at the Days Inn for the duration and the hotel room became a temporary fortress. Grace would wake each morning and even if she didn't shower or put on makeup, she somehow managed to pull out the day's clothing from the suitcase. She would take Travis down to the breakfast area, pick up a complimentary copy of the *Detroit News*, and glance through it as she noshed on bran flakes, grapefruit juice, and English muffins smothered in butter and jelly. She would tell herself this was a vacation—after all they were away from home and staying at a hotel. She had stayed in hotels while vacationing at Niagara Falls, the Grand Canyon, Miami and Vancouver. It was easy to deceive herself for a moment or two, to believe, as she sipped the rich coffee from Starbucks that was not available back home, that she was simply enjoying some time away from her routine.

She shopped at the little stores and boutiques on the square, bought a pale gray wool sweater for Dad, a winter jumpsuit for Travis, a makeup bag for Fran, and searched for small packable items that Walt could stow away in his baggage—a book of crossword puzzles, a new leather-bound journal.

Each afternoon, Grace bundled Travis up in warm layers and a knit cap and pushed him in his stroller, sometimes walking for hours at a time. She would soak in the autumn sun and admire the shimmering colors as she shuffled through the dry crunchy leaves, the scent of decay permeating the cool, crisp air of the waning days. Grace put in the miles as though walking would end the countless questions she had about the future, the next few months in particular, which she really didn't want to think about. She couldn't change the fact that Walt was leaving her for who knows how long and putting himself in danger, but what she could do was make a choice in how she reacted to it. So she had decided that she would hide her fear as her own contribution to making the situation better and would busy herself with learning to take on the responsibilities that Walt usually managed—paying the bills, taking the Jeep in for servicing, and making sure that Travis got his inoculations and checkups with the pediatrician. She had already marked it on the calendar to have the air filter changed on the heat pump every three months.

In the final four days before Walt's departure, Molly, Lou, and Pete drove to the base and stayed at Super 8 motel up the street. Grace welcomed the company—it saved her from her gloomy thoughts. It was nice to have help with Travis, someone to change his diaper, play with him, and give her a minute to step inside a store with breakables and places that did not welcome small children. She enjoyed having other adults to talk to and found Lou to be quite entertaining as he spouted knowledge of Cleveland history and art. He always had some morsel of information about the city and its past that was interesting, like the history of the shipping industry or of the old Bond or Allerton Hotels.

They dined at the Amish Buffet and China Palace in the evenings. Grace and Molly went purse shopping on the small town square. When Walt had a few hours free, the five of them played a chilly round of miniature golf. One afternoon, they went to an art gallery so that Molly could pick out an oil painting for the guest room.

Since their summer visit to Cleveland, Grace noticed that Pete had added a new word to his speech. Pete, the son with the narrow vocabulary, usually kept his conversation limited to talk about playing gigs at the bar around the corner or spouting out the Indian's scores like a statistician. Pete who would talk about his latest job as a dishwasher that he held for two weeks before being fired for calling in sick one too many times. Yes, it was apparent, that Pete had added a new word to his vocabulary. And he used this new word with a frequency akin to announcing the latest dark brew he had sampled, the latest decision to try to find a place on his own.

Susan.

Yes, Susan was the new word that Pete rolled off of his tongue in between shouts and back slaps and bragging. The name Susan now peppered his conversation and after the first day of its use, Grace had come to expect to hear more about Susan. How he had managed, in just a few short months, to find so much to say about a girl was beyond Grace. She expected that Pete Moore, a playboy at best, for the first time in his long adolescence, had perhaps fallen in love.

The word *Susan,* like the word *deployment,* had become a frequent part of the family conversation. Grace soon learned that since the summer visit, Pete had met and pursued Susan, and somehow she had found her brother-in-law interesting enough to spend time with him.

"Susan even enjoys fishing," Pete added when Lou had asked about the fishing at Sand Beach and whether Grace's dad had done much.

"Susan loves Chinese takeout," he said when one evening when they went out to eat. Grace could not imagine how he had managed to pull himself away from Susan for four days to spend time without her. He had brought along pictures of the petite redhead. His favorite was one of the two of them that had been taken in a photo booth, with Susan looking up at him as he playfully nibbled at the rim of her baseball cap. In another, the two of them stood smiling in front of a roller coaster at Cedar Point.

The final day was drizzly and cloudy. The tension in the air was thick, and the mood among the family had become funereal. Fran and Dad had come up the day before, and now the entire group spent the day at the departure gate. Travis followed the adults around and played peek-a-boo relentlessly with anyone who would engage him. Molly and Fran entertained him, handed him animal crackers, changed him in the bathroom and pushed his stroller on mini-walks around the waiting area. Grace's every muscle ached with tension and her head split with a migraine as she paced the room, her heart fluttering, and her palms sweaty. Observing the many other families in the same predicament, she saw that their actions and facial expressions mirrored her own. She wondered how many of the couples were married, how many engaged, how many relationships would endure the time away.

"Grace Ann Moore, what are you doing?" Walt motioned to Grace to come sit next to him on the padded airport seat. He lifted Travis onto his knee and then reached for Grace's hand. He traced her name repeatedly with his finger across her skin, up the back of her arm, as he had done when they were dating. The smooth, loving touch that had a way of sending shivers down her spine now caused her a feeling of dread. She recognized the clenching of his jaw, which he reserved for times such as this, the stressful ones, the same clenching that she remembered from their arrival at Sand Beach Hospital, the day that Travis was born. Although the family was all around them, it seemed as though there wasn't another soul in the room.

They sat together this way until the last minute before he had to board the 747 to leave the United States—on his first trek oversees. At that moment, Grace stopped Walt's soothing movements and clutched his hand tightly, so tightly as to cut off circulation of her white-knuckled hand, now tingling as she bit her lip and leaned in to his chest. Travis fidgeted, as he gnawed on his fingers and played with a button on Grace's blouse.

The soldiers formed a crooked line. Walt stood tall in his fatigues, squeezed Travis, and kissed his son's forehead, breathing in his baby smell. He handed him to Molly and hugged her. She patted him and told him to be safe.

Lou, silent and withdrawn, stood to the side, sipping strong coffee from a paper cup. He was able to eke out only a few words "I'm proud of you, son. Hope this conflict doesn't last long."

Pete had little to say as he hugged his brother.

When Fran got her chance for a hug, she said, "Okay, handsome soldier, I'll try to bake you some cookies and send them along."

Finally, Walt took Grace's sweaty hand, and they stood weak-kneed and teary in the somber now-empty room with the sterile chairs lined up. A large wall clock ominously counted off the minutes as the soldiers squeezed and patted and wept with their loved ones, trying to forestall the inevitable.

Walt's steel blue eyes were penetrating as he gazed at her. His expression was serious and spoke a thousand words. His gruff voice cracked.

"Take care of yourself. You."

She choked in response. "You too."

A hot seething volcano formed in Grace's chest, and the only thing holding back eruption was her firm resolve to not fall to pieces, just yet. She felt her blood race and her chest fill with pain and fear. Her mouth felt dry as she attempted to smile.

Travis seemed to sense her distress and scrunched up his face. She held him close for a minute, then gave him a cracker and carefully lowered him to the floor. He clung to her leg as she stretched her arms up to embrace her clean-shaven, boot-wearing soldier. She felt the cool harshness of the stiff fatigues and the warmth of his skin against her cheek. She clung to him for a long moment, feeling her heart beat against her thin blouse, and imagined his skin against hers, skin that was now covered in army gear and inaccessible to her. She clung for as long as she could until her tears sprung loose. She felt him stiffen in her arms and felt his wet tears in her hair.

"I love you, Walter Moore. Travis and I will be fine. You make sure you write and call every chance you get, you hear?"

She studied his face as though studying for final exams,

paying close attention to his watery blue eyes, his broad nose, high cheekbones, Adam's apple, and dimpled chin. She hoped that every feature was now etched in her memory. It was inevitable that she couldn't hold him now, couldn't change the mind of the commander-in-chief, couldn't change the events that led to this moment and the necessity that her husband, one of many, had to face the next step, had to go to fight the unknown and keep her, her family her town and her nation safe.

He turned his back to her and joined the line of brave men in large boots and brown uniforms carrying rucksacks. The jagged line moved too quickly as he disappeared behind the gate and then for a brief second reappeared as he stepped outside, his back still to her as he climbed the steps onto the large imposing aircraft. He never looked back. She waved goodbye as he disappeared.

Molly and Fran took their places next to Grace by the window as Pete and Lou stood silently nearby. After the last soldier boarded the plane, its doors closed and it soon began moving across the tarmac. Quickly, it gathered speed, turned, and then rose up into the wild blue yonder. Dazed, Grace saw with her eyes a sight that did not register with her heart as the wheels were swallowed into the plane and the aircraft diminished until it became a speck in the distance. Its white tail receded into the fluffy, clouded, drizzly day until it was no longer visible.

"Bye-bye, Daddy." Travis clutched Grace as he smiled and waved at the sky where the airplane had disappeared. His lower lip then jutted into a moist pout.

TWENTY

When Walt stepped into the plane, he had the sensation that he had stepped into something more significant than a mere aircraft. He felt himself stepping into a commitment. As he found his way down the narrow aisle to an empty seat, he entered another world that was much bigger than himself—one that he shared with innumerable men before him who had done just as he was doing, protecting their families and freedom. He felt a sense of responsibility, and though it was a heavy one, he could not help but feel the honor in it.

Once the wheels were swallowed into the large cavity of the plane and he left the solid earth behind, the world that had been his ceased to exist. He was now afloat and adrift, being whisked off to a foreign land where no one was going to be waiting on the other side with a hot meal or open arms. Except to his fellow soldiers, he would be a nameless face. His primary identity would be that of American soldier. He was transforming from an average U.S. citizen into a foreigner in an unfamiliar land. His new focus in life was to do the task before him and to come back to American soil alive and uninjured. He had to turn off his sensitive, caring side and turn on the machine. This transformation was necessary for himself, his family, his country and his survival. In appreciation of this challenge, Walt made a private imaginary sign of the cross over his chest and found a seat.

Noble as that transformation was, the Walt he was leaving behind was still in some ways the Walt he was taking with him. The Walt he was taking with him could not stand flying and avoided it whenever he could. He had flown to training with the Guard by necessity and only twice had he flown by choice outside of the military—once to the Grand Canyon on a hot Sunday in June for his honeymoon and once to Chicago for a job interview. He much preferred a rental car, a train, a boat, or a bus.

Removing his heavy gun belt, he settled into the stiff, narrow seat and clasped his seatbelt. He reached into his breast pocket for a fresh packet of Juicy Fruit. He undressed the striped piece of sugarless gum, curled it and pushed it into his mouth and began working it between his molars forming an occasional bubble. Chewing gum kept his ears from popping and allowed him to work out tension.

He leaned towards the window and peered out over the wing, half wishing he could see Grace and Travis pressed against the window waving or something and half dreading it. Not seeing anyone he recognized, he stretched out his long legs, cracked his knuckles, and put his hands in his lap. Twenty seconds later he was restless and flipped through a magazine that was stuffed into the seat beside him. He turned the pages which had nothing of interest and then tossed the magazine aside and opened his small rucksack that had no place in the cramped seats other than on his lap.

A slow feeling of panic rose in his chest, as he suddenly became aware that he might have left something behind, something of importance, something he could not retrieve once he had risen to five hundred feet above the clouds. He opened his bag and started reviewing the things he had packed days earlier, going through his supply list in his mind. Gun belt, licorice, canteen, dry socks, identification, magazine, shaving supplies, toothbrush and toothpaste, comb, patrol cap, picture of Grace and himself, latest picture of Travis, Motrin, Twizzlers, pistachios, pen, notebook, journal, and a paperback. If he forgot anything, it was already too late. And a missing nail file wasn't worth the worry right now. He could trim his nails with his pocket knife. He pulled out a scratchy wool blanket and placed it on his lap. After sampling a few salty pistachios, he got out his journal and scribbled seven goals.

1. Come home safe.

2. Learn from this experience, learn about war, learn about the desert, and take this information and jot it down for my novel.

3. Make friends with at least one other soldier and learn about him.

4. Practice the skills I have learned in training and perfect them.

5. Have five minutes of meditation and prayer when I wake and before I go to bed.

6. Read one Bible passage a day.

7. When I feel like giving up, if I feel that way, think of home, think of my goals.

Walt's thoughts were invaded by a large, round-faced lieutenant who was seated directly across from him.

"Hey, man, where you from?"

He turned to face the intruder.

"Mind if I join you?" Not waiting for an answer, the guy parked his oversized body in the empty seat next to Walt.

"I'm from Alpena." The man had a broad, lopsided grin that made him look simple and friendly.

"Technical name is Ralph, but some folks call me Boots."

Walt glanced down at the man's large feet dressed in military-issued boots. He didn't want to ask Boots how he'd gotten his name. People with nicknames usually had a story, and he preferred a little quiet. But since it was likely this would be someone he'd be spending the next twelve hours with—or maybe even the next twelve months with—he responded and offered his hand.

"Walt." Walt nodded. "Walter Moore," he added. "From Sand Beach."

"Boots McCall." Boots eyed Walt's ring finger. "Ah, got a misses, eh? Kids?"

"Yep, a little one, almost a year and a half. Just one. A wife I already miss." He pulled out a worn photo of Travis and Grace that he had in his jacket.

In turn, Boots showed him a picture of his basset hound. "This is Oh, which is short for Ohio, where we picked him up… or *Oooohhhhh,* for the howl he likes to make. Oh is staying with my girlfriend, Sharon, while I'm gone." He popped the lid on some Copenhagen snuff, pulled out a sizeable chunk, and tucked it neatly into the side of his mouth, which made him look like a squirrel. He held the can out to Walt.

"No, thanks, Boots."

"Your son looks just like ya. Bet he'll be a great ball player one day."

Walt laughed. "I think he might look more like my father, but don't all men want someone to be just like them? If he wants to be a ball player, I'm good with that. I'm a proud papa any way you cut it. But if he does join a team, it better be the Tigers or the Yankees. The Tigers are my team."

A captive audience, Walt learned a lot about Boots on the twelve-hour flight to Saudi Arabia. Boots had been raised in Oregon and had moved to Flint in his junior year after his father lost his job as a logger and Flint offered work in the auto industry.

"My senior year really sucked."

Walt listened half-heartedly until the interviewer inside him took over. If he was going to be stuck with Boots McCall, it might help to know a little something about him. He figured Boots might have to save his life one day or vice a versa. That was an intimate deal. So he might as well get to know the person who had such an obligation.

"What made your senior year so bad?"

Boots stared out the window beyond Walt into the blue sky. "The bad thing, the really crappy thing aside from being a new kid in town and not very popular at that, was that my parents, both of them died within a few months of each other. My mom died in a car wreck and my dad died of a broken heart. And me, I was left to carry on."

"Oh." Walt felt a little guilty for not really wanting to listen to this large, clumsy stranger. "Sorry to hear that." Walt did not want to hear sad, heavy news right then. He preferred guy talk, something light. *Please* something light.

"And when they died, I promised myself and my little brother that I would make sure he was okay."

"Where is your brother now?"

"He stays with my grandparents in Oregon. He has cerebral palsy. I pay for him to fly out for a few months in the summer. And probably when my grandparents can't take care of him anymore, I suppose he'll come to Alpena and live with me or near me. Sharon is okay with him. And that is real important to me. Anyone that cares about me needs to care about my little brother. I'm a package deal of sorts. Me and my brother and Oh. But Sharon is a good girl. I think she cares a lot. She seems to anyway. She cares about me and she cares about Oh and she cares about Marc. In fact, she helps me a lot with him when he comes for the summer. She takes him to the beach and sometimes to the mall near Detroit. She even got him signed up and participating in the Special Olympics. He plays a pretty mean game of table tennis."

He continued. "So I don't know about you, Mr. Moore, but I saw the National Guard as a great way to boost my income. I would have joined the army full-time, but I really like cars and wanted to work in a body shop. My parents left me some money, so I went to mechanic school, and the Weekend Warrior stint has helped me pay the rent. And the mechanic job, well, it has paid the bills. I bought me a little house on the edge of Alpena about a year ago. And that is where Sharon is now, looking after the dog. I hope she waits for me. I plan to ask her to marry me when I get back."

Over the course of the next few hours, the information Walt gathered was enough to write a sizeable biography of Boots McCall. He learned specifics about his life, not only from what Boots said but also from his own observations. Boots was a talker and not a listener. He learned that Boots was messy. He learned that Boots snored when he napped and although there were some qualities that he could admire in the man, he hoped that Boots would not be in the cot next to him when they landed. Boots slurped when he drank through a straw. Boots loved machine guns and military history. Boots drooled literally and figuratively at the prospect of tearing someone up. Though he had never killed a man, he thought he might just like to do that because, "when you are protecting your country, Mr. Moore, you do whatever it takes, even if it means taking a life."

He droned on about politics and oil and Bush's policies and gave Walt little time to respond. He talked about fixing up BMWs and Sharon moving in with him two months earlier. There were no pictures of Sharon. But he did have a picture of his brother, Marc, in his wheelchair with a big grin and a number 77 on his chest for the Special Olympics.

"Yeah, I'm glad she'll be looking after the fort. Don't know what I would've done if I'd had to leave the place empty." After a pause, he added, "Hope she don't find anybody while I'm gone."

After about two hours, Boots finally ran out of steam and went quiet. Walt closed his eyes and made a mental inventory once again of the items in his pack. His thoughts drifted to Travis and Grace, realizing he had never once had the idea that Grace would even look at anybody while he was gone. He really had not fully considered what time away would be like at all. Not until this minute. He had been in denial.

At 10:45 a.m. Saudi time, Lieutenant Walter Allen Moore stepped out of the 747 and was greeted by grains of sand assaulting his face. He grabbed his bag and stepped down onto the runway with the deafening hum of airplanes all around him. The dimly lit, chaotic airport had no welcoming family. No smiling faces. Welcome to Desert Shield, he thought. With a mixture of adrenaline and dread he hoisted up his bags and found his way to the armored vehicle that would take him to his destiny—his new life as an unknown soldier and a pawn in the game of war.

TWENTY-ONE

A few weeks after Walt left, the washer stopped spinning.

"Travis, get your sippy cup! We have to go to the laundry."

"Lawn-dee." Travis said, trying to repeat the word. "Lawn-dee, Mommy!"

"I'm not messing around now. Help Mommy get things together."

While she was certain that if she showed up at Dad's or Fran's with her dirty laundry, they would have willingly shared their washing machine; Grace already felt she was a burden. So she counted out her quarters from the large popcorn tin, gathered up Travis and his diaper bag, and loaded piles of blankets, towels, blue jeans, socks, and toddler clothes into the Jeep and hauled them over to the Soap Box. Grace pulled up to the curb and opened her trunk in the cold, damp air and dragged load after load inside. She backed into the door carrying her ten-pound basket as she tried to keep her eyes on Travis in the back seat. She was keenly aware that if she failed to supervise her son, something could happen—a choking on something, a kidnapper, a vehicle slamming into the car. Any assortment of evils could befall the helpless youngster, and it was her job to protect him. It was her job to keep him alive.

When she finally brought Travis inside the dimly lit Laundromat, she set him on a chair near the window with his teddy bear. After loading up four machines using all the quarters she had in her pocket, she took a deep breath and settled into the seat beside her son. As she began to flip through the latest issue of *Horse and Rider*, she kept one eye on the page and the other on Travis.

After only a few minutes, Travis started whining, so she dug in his bag looking for something to console him. She offered him a cloth book. He shoved it away. She pulled out a teething ring. He shoved again. She offered a half-empty bottle of Welch's juice. He took a sip and sent it flying.

Grace considered giving him run of the place, allowing him to wander up and down the aisles. She had assumed they were alone in the Soap Box, but out of the corner of her eye, she noticed that since she had arrived a stranger had somehow managed to enter the building and was now sitting quietly, unobtrusively in the corner. The man now made eye contact. He knew she was there. And he smiled at her. He had rotten, crooked teeth and there was something in his eyes that looked very sad, empty, like he was missing a part of his soul. He was dirty and unshaven.

When had he gotten there? Had he been there all along? And why didn't she notice earlier that it was after 8:00 at night and he was the only other person in there? Why would a man like that be doing laundry? He should be searching for shelter. Maybe he was planning to sleep in the corner on the stiff chair. Was there someone she needed to notify? Maybe she needed to call the owner of the Soap Box. She looked for a phone number on the wall. There was no phone and no number.

The clothes the man was wearing were tattered and soiled. And he didn't look like he had money in his pockets to pay for the wash. But she wasn't going to hand him any money. She did not want to get close enough to him to do that.

Grace judged the distance between her chair and the door. She clutched her keys and leaned toward Travis to pick him up. She estimated that she could smoothly pull off a getaway.

"Howdy, ma'am." He nodded.

She acted like she hadn't heard. She stood and walked over to where Travis sat and lifted him.

"Aren't you Walt's wife?"

Oh, no, the stranger knew her! He better not know her address.

"Fine thing he's doing for our country, Mrs. Moore."

Just then the glass door opened and in walked Linda from Gloria's Café.

"Hi, Grace, what are you doing here?"

"My washer broke."

"Hi, Linda." The vagrant smiled and offered a little wave.

"Hi, Hank, what's going on?"

Grace looked from Linda to the stranger and back to Linda.

"Just washin' up some clothes. And saying hello to Mrs. Moore. I just wanted to let Mrs. Moore here know that I appreciate Walter serving our country. Seems like every generation has to do it. I served in Vietnam, you know."

"I did know that, Hank, and we appreciate your service to our nation." Linda gave him a generous smile.

Hank looked one hundred years old. But Vietnam wasn't that long ago. What happened to him? If Walt were there he would have wanted to know his story. If Walt were there he would have been over in the corner with the man, asking him where he was from and what year he graduated. Walt would ask about his work history, he would find out if he had a family. Walt would have dismissed the soiled clothes, the lack of hygiene, and would have gone straight to the heart of the matter—who was the man, what made him tick. In no time, the man's story would have been out there, spoken into the dingy Laundromat, into the stale air. Walt would have recognized that this unfortunate man was alive…and had a story.

Linda turned to Grace and lowered her voice. "I just saw your Jeep out there and wanted to know you were okay. Why don't I help you finish up your clothes and then why don't you and Travis come over to our place for some hot cocoa?"

An angel had come to rescue her from an uncomfortable situation and was offering hot chocolate. She accepted the invitation. Linda helped her dry and fold, and the two chatted as they worked. Hank and Linda chatted the entire time. Grace's heart rate finally slowed as she became convinced that this vagrant, who now had a name, was harmless.

"Bye, Hank. Stop by Gloria's, why don't you? We have our ninety-nine-cent special this month. Eggs, coffee, and toast with jelly."

"I'll be there," Hank said. He held up his weathered hand in a half salute and tilted his cap as the women went out the door and loaded up the Jeep with the freshly washed and folded clothes. Grace followed Linda to her house.

When they arrived at the two-story home on Elm, Linda welcomed her and Travis into the warm foyer, took their jackets, and walked Travis into the living room to join Linda's kids who were piled in front of the television with her husband. After a friendly hello to Bob and the children, Grace followed Linda into the bright, clean kitchen.

"So what happened to that man, Linda, that man at the Soap Box? I don't remember ever seeing him."

"You mean Hank? He comes in to Gloria's sometimes. I know what you mean about him. He seems depressed, doesn't he?"

"Linda, he looks a little more than depressed! He looks like a street person. An alcoholic. I don't know him or anything, and I don't mean to judge, but frankly, he scared the crap out of me!"

Linda smiled and went about making the hot chocolate.

"I've seen Walt buy him breakfast and I've listened to Hank talk about 'Nam. I've overheard them discussing PTSD—post-traumatic stress disorder—so I kind of figure that Hank may have that. It seems as though Hank was damaged mentally when he served. When he was in high school, he seemed to be doing pretty well. He was on the track team and didn't seem like a misfit or anything. And then right at graduation he joined the Army. I guess that was probably the turning point for him, the choice he made that changed every—." Linda put her hand over her mouth and apologized with her eyes.

Grace wasn't quite sure why she had stopped midsentence.

"Oh, Grace, forget I said that, okay? I mean that doesn't happen to everyone! Think of all the World War II vets. Those men went over and fought, came back to their sweethearts, and started families. They had children and successful careers. They were a strong generation. Maybe if Hank had married, he would have had the support he needed. Maybe then things would have been better. And maybe he would have had mental problems anyway, even if he didn't go fight in that war. I'm sure there are lots of men who have come back just fine. "

"Yes, but he is not the first person I have ever heard about from Vietnam having problems. It seems like an epidemic. Walt wrote an article about it once. Gee, for all I know, he had Hank in the article. But really, despite all that, I am not anticipating that Walt will come home with PTSD or anything. However, having said that, I suppose it could happen. Lord, I hope not! What in the world would I do then? He's the one who keeps me going. I don't think I'm very good at helping people in a crisis. I tend to fall apart. He is the glue that holds *me* together." Grace felt a little dizzy. "I sure miss him though. I got a letter from him yesterday." She patted her purse where she had tucked the letter away.

"Oh, Grace, I wondered how long a letter would take to get here. What a way to communicate. It must drive you crazy that you can't just pick up the phone and call. But in a way, it's kind of romantic too, don't you think? Kind of like our parents in World War II writing love letters and promising forever."

"Yes, it is so old-fashioned, relying on letters. He must have written this one on the plane. He said the flight was long and he met some guy from Oregon. The agony of waiting to hear from him is just about all I can take. And it hasn't even been that long yet."

"Stay busy and the time will fly by. He'll be back before you know it, and this will just be a jump on the page. A moment in time."

"It's just that I can't stop thinking about him. I wonder what his days are like, what the other men are like. I wonder about the little things, what kind of food they serve, what they talk about. I can only imagine the climate and think about the pictures I've seen of the desert. I imagine the bearded religious fanatics in long white robes and the camels crossing over the desert. What if Walt gets bitten by a scorpion? I wonder if he is working on his book or if he is just sweating it out till his days over there are done."

"You know, I never thought about all that! I just think about him protecting our freedom," Linda replied.

"My imagination runs wild. The only way I know for sure what is going on is when I get a letter like this one that gives me details. Otherwise, I just can't track him. I don't know if he's in trouble or fighting or bored or what. It drives me nuts. I miss picking up the phone just to chat."

Grace opened her purse, pulled out the already worn letter and clutched it while she rocked back and forth in the chair. "And then I can't sleep and everything around me seems to be falling apart. The washing machine broke and the toilet has been running non-stop. And everywhere I go, I have to bring Travis with me. Walt was *so* good about watching him and letting me run errands."

"You poor thing. I can't imagine not having Bob around to help me with repairs and stuff like that. And homework. Bob always helps the kids with homework. Oh, I'm pretty sure I could hold the fort up for a day or two, and I have on occasion. The time he went on that fishing expedition a few years back, I sure did count the minutes till he would return. A week felt like a long time, and I knew he was coming back at the end of it. But I think I would probably have some issues if I had to do the whole thing every day. And then not to mention having to work on top of caring for the house and the kids! I could do that for a day, but not every day, not without help. Even for a few weeks. It would be crazy! And as for missing Walt, I bet you do. We miss him too! When someone else sits at his regular table, I almost feel like telling them that the seat is reserved. I keep expecting Walt to enter the restaurant, like clockwork at 7:05 every morning to find his spot by the window. I keep expecting he will be sitting there ordering his whole wheat toast, holding out his coffee cup for a refill, reading his paper, or starting a conversation with someone or other in the place, or at least saying his hellos. I still keep the strawberry jam dish filled for him. And customers ask about him all the time. There is not a day go by that I don't hear his name come up in a conversation."

Linda poured the steamy water over the thick cocoa powder at the bottom of the mug. She stirred and added a layer of mini marshmallows and handed the warm brew to Grace.

She continued. "But you know if we stay busy, the time will pass and then things will be back to normal. Vietnam was just a crazy war. I think this one is probably different."

Linda didn't explain why she thought this war was different. How could you know anything about a situation until it was over, until you could see it in the rearview mirror?

"Linda, I'll never understand war. What does it really accomplish? I mean killing? How does it help? Walt doesn't believe in killing, but he does strongly believe in protecting our freedoms and the freedoms of those around the world." Grace tucked the letter back into her purse and blew gently on the drink to cool it.

"It's hard to believe once you have taken part in creating a life that ending a life is ever okay. Even though the people that he is fighting might be a threat to us or our freedom, if you end up putting a bullet into flesh and kill someone, you have killed someone's child. Or some child's parent. Someone, somewhere will be grieving because of something you did. That bothered him before and I'm sure it still bothers him."

When the cocoa was finished, Linda took the cups and rinsed them. "Would you like to see the work that Bob did on the bathroom?"

"Of course!" Bob had just updated the bathroom with vanity lights and a new oak cabinet. When she entered the bathroom,

Grace was reminded of her running toilet. She told Linda about it.

"Bob can come over on Saturday if you like. You probably just need a new flapper. Ten minutes and less than ten bucks, no problem."

Grace felt needy. She shouldn't have to accept help from a family with four children and two jobs. But she did.

"Thanks, Linda! I'll take the kids out to the barn sometime, if you would be okay with that. Or I can make you something. Maybe I can make some lasagna."

"You don't have to do a thing, Grace, just take care of yourself and let us help you."

Grace went to get Travis in the living room, where he was watching television with Linda's kids, one of his small hands petting the family dog and the other busy digging into a large bowl of potato chips. Linda's boys looked so natural together—laughing, throwing dirty socks at each other, and then acting like they didn't know who did it. Bob didn't seem to mind. Travis looked like he belonged there amid the other children.

"So, Grace, don't worry, we are all keeping an eye on you. Don't hesitate to call anytime, even if it is the middle of the night. And please let us know if you or Travis get sick. He can come play with the kids anytime I am home. One more won't mess up the mix. And you need to come have lunch at Gloria's, when I'm working."

She handed Grace her jacket and saw her to the door. "I don't want you to leave here empty-handed, so please go through this bag and see if any of these clothes will fit Travis. If he can't use them, you can send them to Goodwill. It never ceases to amaze me how fast the boys grow out of things."

"Oh, Linda, you are too good! Thank you!"

"And wait, I almost forgot, take a batch of these pumpkin walnut muffins. I made a ton for the bake sale, and we'll never sell them all, and the kids have been stuffing on them all day. And when you write a letter to our hero, make sure that you tell him that Gloria's is not the same without him. You tell him that his spot by the window is his spot, no matter what, and that he can have free breakfast for a year when he gets back."

Grace reached for Travis's small, salty hand. She felt blessed to have a friend who invited her for hot cocoa, rescued her from the Laundromat, and offered to save her from a life that seemed to be unraveling without Walt.

TWENTY-TWO

When Grace arrived for her appointment with Fran at Glamour Clips the day after Thanksgiving, it seemed the Christmas season was already in full swing. Joyce, the new stylist, was in the corner of the salon, hanging ornaments on a tree. Four red felt embroidered stockings with the names Mary, Shelly, Fran, and Joyce hung from the front glass counter. Christmas music was coming from out of a boombox at Fran's station, piping out goodwill and glad tidings.

Shelly, who was rolling out a permanent, nodded to Grace in the mirror. The smell of the perm solution was strong and pungent in the chilly salon air.

"Geez, Fran, must be all of ten degrees outside today. Did you see that it's already snowing out there? Won't be long before the lake freezes and becomes a skating rink."

"No kidding. Winter comes early and stays late around here." Fran lowered the volume on the music and used a broom to clean up the previous client's hair from the floor. When she was finished, she gestured to Grace to take a seat.

"So what's it gonna be my friend? If I've checked my calendar correctly, you are way overdue for a makeover."

— 161 —

"Thanks a lot, Fran."

"No, I mean, I am so glad you finally are going to let me put some highlights in that dull hair of yours."

"Yeah, well, we'll see. You promise I won't look bad? I don't want to end up looking like a zebra with those stripes."

"I promise, Grace! For god's sake, I'm not dying your hair red or green or anything. Highlights will soften your features. And bring out that pretty emerald shade to your eyes."

"If you say so, Fran. You're the expert. My beauty is in your hands."

Grace settled into the orange chair amidst the sound of the music, hair dryers and chatter. Snippets of conversations about gall bladder operations, sweet potato casserole recipes, and an upcoming wedding for a niece drifted in and out of her awareness as Fran fastened a clean dry cape around her shoulders and pulled Grace's hair back behind her ears.

"How about I take a few inches off of the side?"

"Oh, why not? Go crazy on me then." She closed her eyes, while Fran wet her hair and snipped an inch or two. Grace watched her blond locks fall in clumps onto the floor.

"Grace," Fran whispered. "I've decided to go to Al-Anon. I went to my first class on Thursday over at the Methodist church. I really need it. I hope it helps!"

Grace made eye contact with Fran in the mirror. She smiled and whispered back. "Fran, that is fantastic! I know it is going to help you. If you can't change Michael, at least you can take care of yourself."

"Oh, you know." Her voice raised an octave. "The first step is admitting you're powerless. I think I kind of get that one, but it is strange. I can't seem to really grasp it. It hardly makes sense. Why would anyone *want* to be powerless? I'm already powerless, and it doesn't feel so great. How does admitting it change anything? And then there is supposed to be this greater power. Where is that greater power when I need it? If there is a greater power, why isn't it helping me? Why hasn't this greater power helped Michael? Why hasn't it kept him from drinking?" Fran lowered her voice. "And why in the world hasn't the greater power kept my husband from cheating on me?" She raised her eyebrows and looked in the mirror like she expected the answer to jump out of it.

Shelly chimed in. "Fran, I think you got the first step all wrong. The first step is admitting that Michael is an ass. The first step is admitting that you need to get rid of the man. That is where you are powerless. Get rid of that man and you will be one powerful woman."

Idle chatter in the salon had ceased and all eyes were now on Shelly. The only sound in the room was the music of the song "O Holy Night" emanating from the speakers, which helped ease the tension.

Gazing at her reflection, Grace noticed that her face and neck had turned beet red. She was embarrassed for Fran and irritated by Shelly's insensitive statements about something that was not her business to begin with.

In a voice loud enough for Shelly to hear, she said, "Fran, I am proud of you. You are doing great. And I know you will get past the first step, and I'm sure through the twelfth. *I* think you have already worked the first and second steps. And I'm certain you are well on your way through the third. I'm proud of you for not giving up. You stand by Michael through thick and thin. You honor your vows. And I think, for sure, there is something to be said for that."

Shelly clenched her teeth. "We'll see about that. Me? I'd get rid of the bum. What purpose does he serve?"

Grace noticed the flushed face of the woman held imprisoned in Shelly's chair. She wished for a second she could free her from her captivity. Free them all. "Well for one thing, *Shelly*." Grace was seething. "He *is* Paul's father."

"Yeah, and he's the father of a half a dozen or so other kids around town, if I have my facts straight." Shelly lowered her voice and spoke to the customer getting the perm. "I bet if you looked real close at Mavis's kids, you just might see that a few of them look like Michael."

All conversation stopped, and this time the dryers had shut off and the CD had finished playing. You could have heard a curler drop.

Shelly continued. "Alcoholism can be real strong in a small town like Sand Beach. Just look at the regulars at Sammy's. A lot of them are there before lunch and stay until they can't even get up from their stools without falling."

Shelly didn't seem to notice that the room had gotten quiet.

"What I'm trying to say is that alcoholism can be real strong in a small town due to the boredom, the gossip, the lack of purpose, and the pressure to be just like everyone else."

Though Fran seemed embarrassed, she completed the haircut and began working on Grace's highlights. When she finished the first strand, she went to the sink to wash her hands. Then she removed the Christmas CD and popped in some Frank Sinatra.

"Anyways, Grace. Not to change the *subject.*" She saturated a thin slice of hair with highlighter, wrapped it in tin foil and rolled it, repeating the process in sections as she spoke.

"I've been thinking…and wondering if you might like to get a part-time job. There are always a few extra positions around town, especially at Christmas. You know we could use a shampoo girl, and I heard that Art's needs a weekend waitress. The tips this time of year can be great."

Grace was silent for a moment as she pondered this idea. It would be nice to get out more. Especially now that the duplex was so lonely without Walt.

"And just who would watch Travis?" She thought about the invitation Linda had recently made about keeping him.

"I could. And then if you came home tired, you could spend the night."

Spending the night at Fran's, complete with an alcoholic philandering husband was not on Grace's list of things she wanted to do.

"Thank you, Fran, we'll see. I'm not eager to add anything to my plate. Maybe after the holidays."

"Well, think about it."

Fran carefully unwrapped each piece of tinfoil, revealing the strands of softly highlighted hair. After she finished combing, gelling, drying, and spraying, the results were stunning. Grace smiled at Fran in the mirror as she admired the final product. Fran had managed to sculpt soft feminine layers that framed Grace's flushed face, and the layers now were streaked with shades of blond and brown. Fran was right. Her eyes did look brighter. They sparkled.

The dismay in the room that had been a result of Shelly's harsh comments had dissipated. The room came back to life, the conversations had returned to normal, and Frank Sinatra was singing as though nothing had happened.

"Thanks, Fran. What would I do without you?" She stood and left a twenty-dollar tip by Fran's station. "I feel like a million bucks. You are the greatest."

She hugged her friend and leaned in to whisper in her ear. "And I am so sorry that you have to spend the rest of the day with *her*." She tilted her head toward Shelly.

Fran whispered back. "Oh, Grace, it's part of my day! I don't know how I'd have a normal day without her. Sometimes I like Shelly. Sometimes I hate her. But most of the time, I just tolerate her."

"If you say so, Fran, but she doesn't seem so normal or nice to me!"

Grace donned her winter jacket and gloves and stepped out into the snow. An inch had accumulated in the time it had taken for her to get a fresh look. Maybe next time she would get some new mascara and eye shadow. She was glad that she had chosen to walk. The light snow, especially this time of year, was invigorating. It gave her a fresh perspective on the scenery and on the day. She hurried off to retrieve Travis from her father's house, hoping that he was enjoying the visit and that all was well.

TWENTY-THREE

Three weeks before Christmas, her father phoned.

"Meet me over at Crescent Real Estate. The Jones home has just gone on the market. Apparently, Mrs. Jones went to the nursing home and needs to sell the place."

Twenty-eight minutes later, Grace and Travis arrived at the small office that was wedged between Arnold's Bakery and Tyson Insurance. Its storefront, displaying photos of homes for sale all over Huron County, was adorned with pretty white Christmas lights. With Travis on her hip, Grace took a deep breath, pulled open the door, and stepped into the lobby. Dad waved them into a large pine-scented office with built-in bookshelves. Charles was beaming.

"Grace, I want you to meet Janice Nielson." He sounded ecstatic. "She has been working with me to find the right house for my dear daughter."

"Hello, Grace." The petite brunette with friendly brown eyes and dimples smiled and extended a hand.

She must color her hair, Grace thought. Probably in her fifties.

"I have heard a lot about you Grace. About you and Travis and Walt."

It discomfited Grace to hear this. It put her on guard. She pulled Travis closer to her and removed his red stocking cap. She peered at the brunette.

"I think you will be excited by this property. Your father told me that you wanted land on the outskirts of town—a few acres so that you could have some horses. And he mentioned that you and Walt had always joked about the Jones place, knowing full well it hadn't changed hands in the sixty years it's been standing. So somehow this seems like it just might be meant to happen. Who knows, you may not like it, but for some reason, I think this is a match made in heaven." Janice pushed back a wisp of thick hair to reveal a silver star-shaped earring that accented her delicate ears and slender neck.

"We thought this would be a great time, just before Christmas, to find a house," Dad added. He and Janice exchanged glances.

Janice continued. "So let me tell you about it! It has four bedrooms, wood floors, a fireplace, a wraparound porch. It also has two and a half baths, a six-horse barn in the back of the home, and it sits on five acres." Looking at Charles, she added, "And the place is within three miles of your father's home."

"Whoa," Grace said. She felt lightheaded. Everything was happening so quickly. Walt was six thousand miles away on Travis's second Christmas, and the house she had dreamed about for years was suddenly on the market. And now she was having this strange sensation that Dad might be spending time with this woman. A realtor. A realtor she never knew existed.

Despite the dizzy sensation, there was a feeling of excitement in the air. A buzz. Newness, promise. A place that might just be what they were looking for.

"Let's go." Grace led the way out of the building and then followed her father and Janice to a small gray minivan. Janice opened the front passenger-side door for her, while her dad and Travis sat in the back, which was equipped with a child seat.

Janice put the vehicle in drive and soon they were heading to the outskirts of town.

Dad tapped Grace on the shoulder from the back seat. "I think you will love it, Grace. I haven't seen the inside yet, but I have a good feeling about this one."

Grace clutched the handle on the inside of the door. "I can't believe it. I wish Walt was here. I wish I could call him. Maybe I won't like it. Do you think I'll like it? It seemed like my dream place, our dream place, but what if I don't like the inside? What if Walt wouldn't like it? How will I know if Walt wouldn't like it? How can I make such a decision without Walt? Maybe the loan won't go through. Maybe it will have problems that I can't detect. Maybe I will like the inside and he won't. Maybe he'll come home and not have the energy to work on the outside. Maybe it will be too far from his work. Maybe he won't like having to drive to work. Maybe we'll never get any horses and we'll just have a big cumbersome barn to take care of."

Grace turned around to look at her dad and saw that he was looking up at the rearview mirror, probably exchanging glances with Janice.

"That's a lot of maybes, sweetheart. Relax, Grace. Maybe, just maybe, it will be perfect."

Janice looked straight ahead as she clutched the wheel. Grace noted that she wore a pale pink shade of lipstick. "This is the first time I've shown the place, Grace. It just went on the market this morning. I've been watching it like a hawk. As far as the horses go, I think the barn has been empty. I understand that Mrs. Jones stopped taking boarders several years ago. But don't quote me on that." She glanced up at her mirror.

The Jones place was less than three miles past Dad's house on Old Huron Road. Grace and Walt had joked about buying if it ever came on the market, but she never really believed that it would. She expected Mrs. Jones would pass the place along to her children. But then Grace really knew nothing about Mrs. Jones, other than that she kept to herself. Years ago there had been a Mr. Jones. The Joneses had not really mingled much with the folks from Sand Beach. When they did come to town, they didn't linger.

They pulled up the gravel driveway and parked near the pale green house with white shutters and a wraparound porch on which was affixed a wooden sign etched with the letters J-O-N-E-S. To the right of the house were a small horse barn and a riding ring. Grace was the first one to step onto the porch, with Travis by her side.

"Look Travvy. A big house!"

"House, Mommy." She reached for his hand, and together they went to the side of the porch and stood by the railing to study the view. Miles of flat fields interspersed with homes dotted the landscape. A fence, now covered with two inches of snow, surrounded the house. There were neighbors on either side of the property—to the left, a newer brick home with a shoveled drive and a brand new silver Lexus parked by the garage; to the right, a home similar to the Jones house, with a white Chevy pickup parked at the end of a long gravel drive. The neighborhood was quiet except for an occasional car driving by and the squeak of a barn door moving slightly in the cold wind.

"Travvy, want to buy a house?"

"House, Mommy," Travis said.

Janice opened the large oak door and beckoned them inside. They entered the modest foyer that led to a large room with glass windows overlooking the outdoor riding ring. Grace's mouth went dry. In her dreams, in her mind, this room was the place that she had daydreamed about when she thought of Walt writing in the office, a room that overlooked the riding ring so he could watch her out lunging a horse or giving a lesson.

He would love it, wouldn't he? Wasn't this just the kind of a place they had talked about when planning out their lives, sharing their dreams? Walt would write the great American novel and she would build a horse business complete with lessons, boarding, and trail rides and the occasional horse show. He would love it! She was sure. In her mind, she knew that if he were here he would be twirling her around and giving Travis a high-five. She admired the built-in bookshelf near the fireplace, and closing her eyes, smiled and imagined her dear, sweet husband in deep thought, biting the tip of his pen as he wrote his stories. Whenever he took a break, he would wave to her out in the riding ring.

"Come see the bedrooms, Grace."

Like Walt might have done if he were here, her dad moved through the house, turning on the water spigots, checking the electrical outlets and light fixtures, and examining the carpet. She followed him through the rooms and admired the fine old-fashioned craftsmanship in the details of the window frames and the molding on the ceiling and the doorways. She liked the fact that the place had four bedrooms—the master bedroom with the fireplace would be for her and Walt, the one nearby would be for Travis, and the third might be a bedroom for another child if they were so blessed, and the fourth would be a guestroom, bright and airy with a bath nearby.

The home smelled musty, like an old person, but Grace was certain that could be corrected with a few open windows, a fresh coat of paint, and some air freshener or scented candles. Before long she could have it smelling like homemade bread and fresh flowers. Yes, this house could be whipped into shape in no time and ready for Walt's return.

The foursome wandered outside to the barn. Dad opened the creaky door to reveal a dimly lit stable containing wisps of moldy hay. It hinted of yesterday, of the horses that had once lived there. Two of the stall doors had the names Trojan and Camelot neatly stenciled on them, and there were scattered old buckets stacked against the walls and down a concrete aisle that led to the indoor riding ring. Grace pictured riding lessons, jumping and small horse shows. She imagined a few boarders, a horse of her own, a pony for Travis!

"A nice tack room," Dad said as they stepped into the small room near the end of the barn. He opened up the storage bins under the saddle racks and inhaled. "Still smells like leather."

Standing in the cold, dusty room, her hand on Travis's shoulder, Grace felt herself blush as she remembered making love with Walt up in the hayloft at Sand Beach Stables. It was hard to believe that was only two years ago. It felt like a lifetime. She longed for Walt's breath on her neck, his arms around her waist, his strong heart beating against her back. His tender smile. He should be there with her, with them. He would love the place!

She left the tack room and walked down the dusty aisle, Travis shadowing her as he picked up dirt and sifted it in his small hands. If Walt had been there, he would have put Travis on his shoulders and pointed out the little details of their surroundings to him. Her heart called out to Walt. Could he hear it? She couldn't even pick up the phone to let him know about the house. She would have to write everything down in a letter and send pictures. She would suggest that they find some time to "christen" this barn in the same way they did the last one. Now *that* was something to look forward to!

"What do the electric bills run?"

Janice thumbed through her small notebook. "Let's see. From what I can make out here, last winter the electric bills ran anywhere from ninety-five to one-hundred-thirty dollars. You can keep some of those costs down if you use the wood-burning fireplace. Don't know if you noticed, but there is a wood-burning stove as well. Now, the barn is a different story. I think that Mrs. Jones used space heaters out there."

"Janice, I have to say that I love those fireplaces, especially the one in the bedroom. It's so rustic!" She visualized Walt and her father chopping wood in the late autumn while and she and Travis worked on art projects or cooked a hearty batch of chili. She removed a glove to bite at a fingernail.

"I don't know, Janice, I love the place, but there is a lot to think about. I have no idea how we'll afford it. And no way to know for sure if my husband would agree."

"It is a big decision, isn't it, dear?" Dad put his hand on Grace's arm and steered her toward the van. "Janice, why don't you drive us back to the office? Grace and I are going to take a little time to talk about it. Meanwhile, please don't show the place to anyone else!"

Janice winked at her father. "As far as I know, if someone asks, there is a contract."

They swapped vehicles in the parking lot behind the realty office, and Dad brought Grace over to Art's for lunch. Grace ordered a side salad and tea and Dad had the lunch special.

"I know you've already made a decision, Grace. I saw that look in your eye as we went through the house." Peering over his bifocals, Dad smiled at her and stirred a packet of sugar into his iced tea.

Grace took a small bite of her salad and lowered her fork. "Yeah, no kidding! Can you tell? I can't believe that place came up for sale now. Why now? Why not last summer? I just can't figure out how things like this happen. I mean, just after Walt leaves, one of the biggest decisions of our lives comes up. How in the world do things like that happen? I love it and all, and I'm pretty sure that Walt is going to love it too, but what if there is something about the contract or the decision that he won't like? What if I decide to sign on the dotted line and use the power of attorney he gave me, and what if after all that he comes home and isn't happy with my decision? What then? We'll be stuck with a huge debt and an obligation that he didn't agree to. What if he actually hates the place and wanted something easier to take care of? If I sign on that dotted line, it will be final. Finito."

Dad dipped a french fry in ketchup. "Okay, my dear, I'm going to counteract that negative thinking. What if he gets back and loves the place, what if you don't buy it and he gets back and wishes you had. He did tell you he would trust you with the decision, did he not?"

"He did, but it's a lot of money."

"And as you told me, he has squirreled away a lot."

"Yes, but…"

"And, I want you to know that the Moores informed me when we saw Walt off at the airport that said they planned to contribute when you two finally found your first home. They wanted to wait till you found something because, as they said, Walt has always been so good with money and since they didn't help him pay for college, they wanted to at least help with his first home."

Grace turned over this information in her mind. They were going to help pay? Really? How could people keep such news from her?

"Really, that is amazing! Oh, Dad, this would *not* be a starter home for us! This is definitely a finisher home. I can see living out the rest of our lives in that place. I can see growing old there, just like Mrs. Jones, and I can see raising our kids and having this be the place where we will have the time of our lives! It's no wonder she couldn't part with that place and stayed there for sixty years! I feel like this could be a dream come true for all of us. And, you know, Dad, having said that, I am pretty sure that husband of mine will love it." She pushed away the salad and gave an affirmative nod. "Let's do it!"

"And, my dear," Dad said as he pushed aside his own finished plate. "Your old wonderful wise Dad, wants to chip in too. I have a good feeling about this, Grace. I get the feeling this is a once in a lifetime opportunity for you. And when a window of opportunity opens, you need to climb through it before it slams shut again. That is one of the things I've learned as an old man. Besides, if you buy this place, you will be nice and close to me, and I kind of like the idea of having a few barn projects to work on. And lots of wood to chop!"

"Oh, Dad, you and your projects," Grace said, tears of joy now welling up in her eyes. "That's what this is all about. You're done with your house and you want to start on mine."

"I think some of those saddle racks might need replacing. And I would love to do some woodworking on those signs for the stalls."

Her head was swimming. She was overwhelmed with the idea that something so magnificent could actually be hers. She had never done such a big thing by herself.

"Oh, my gosh, Dad," she squealed. "Let's do it!" She planted a big kiss on Travis's sticky cheek and pulled at the edge of his cap. She held him close. "Travis! Mommy and Daddy and Travis are going to have a house."

"Oh, Dad, I love you!" She put her arms around both Travis and her father for an enthusiastic group hug. With Christmas coming up and it appearing that she and Walt could actually afford their dream house, it looked as though it would be her best Christmas yet. Or scratch that. It *could* have been her best Christmas yet, if Walt had been there and if she knew there was never going to be another deployment. Ever.

The first thing on her list, after they barreled back to Crescent Realty to sign the contract, was to sit down and dash a letter off to Walt. The pictures could come later.

After doing that, she would have to pick up some pizza and bring it over to her father's house and thank him again. And over pizza, she just might have to ask him more about Janice Nielson.

TWENTY-FOUR

Walt's temporary home was a large makeshift tent with a small amount of personal space for his cot, clothing, weapons, and journal. His new "family" consisted of thirteen men, all young and scared, many of them away from home for the first time.

Walt was especially conscious of the sounds around him: blowing sand, gunfire, cussing, whistling, farting. The most profound was the lonesome melody played on the trumpet at dusk. The sunset took on new meaning, as the fall of night was a time of fear of the darkness. It was hard to believe that the same beautiful, calming sun that used to disappear into the cool of Lake Huron, was here a hazy, dusty sun that settled into the desert at dusk amidst smoke and gunfire.

It was a Monday, weeks into the deployment and Walt huddled over his journal under the dim light above his cot in the cool pre-dawn hour. His journal had become his oasis in the storm, a place where he could vent his feelings, thoughts, fears, and observations. A place to examine the novelty of this deployment and render this situation temporary and stow it away for use someday in a book that would give him a purpose.

After scrawling a few dozen paragraphs on the lined yellow legal pad, he looked around at the sleeping men and was struck by the idea that he was very fortunate to have met such interesting men. This was a mismatched family, brought together by a common goal, yet their personalities and the backgrounds that had shaped them were as different as salt and pepper.

As the early morning hours progressed, the men rose, one by one, some alert and ready to start the day, others groggy, silent, gruff. Walt's time to write had elapsed and he now switched gears from writer to soldier. He smoothed his palm over his closely cropped hair, laced up his running shoes, donned his sweatshirt and shorts, and gulped down a tepid bottle of water. He stretched and practiced his breathing exercises as he waited for the men to gather to join him for forty laps around the perimeter before their breakfast of a Meal Ready to Eat; the soldiers daily pre-made meal, and grainy coffee in a tin cup. Then there was time for cleaning and checking weapons, performing drills, guarding the fuel tanks in shifts, trench digging, and debriefings. Finally, in the late afternoon there was time for the guys to hang out and chat, read, play cards, listen to the radio, and write letters home.

Walt never went anywhere, not even to the latrine, without his gun and his gas mask. On day one, he and the other men in his platoon had been trained to use the mask and warned of the possibility of an attack involving chemical weapons. Without the mask, they were extremely vulnerable.

That afternoon, during BS time, which is what the guys had started calling their afternoons, Walt opened up a large box that was mailed from home. The return address was THE TOWN OF SAND BEACH c/o 140 Palmer Street, which was the physical address of the Sand Beach Times.

"Whitman, what did you do, let everyone in the world know you were coming over here, just so they could send you something? Did they send any *Playboy*s? You got any jelly beans in there? Cigarettes?"

Walt still cringed slightly at the sound of his nickname. At least, it was a name associated with literature. They had at first tried to name him Hemingway, but the name Walt and Whitman went together "like peanut and butter," Boots had remarked one day while cleaning his gun.

"You have got to be kidding, man, like Mrs. Jordan's third-grade class is going to send us some *Playboy*s. Here, I think this Christmas card is for you. From a grade-schooler, you idiot." Walt tossed a card that had pictures of hands all over the envelope and in the center was the blue scrawled words TO A HERO.

"You ought to be ashamed."

"Well, you know one thing I have learned is you can't have what you don't ask for."

"Yeah, jerk-off, and you can't have any *Playboy*s from out of this box, 'cuz there aren't any in here. But there are a few packs of gum and some socks. So for now, keep your fantasies to yourself, because I ain't interested in hearing about them."

After grabbing a few items, Walt tossed the contents of the box—puzzles, books, socks, Chap Stick, and cookies—onto his cot.

"Okay you guys, choose what you want."

Within seconds the items were picked through. Good thing Walt had already gotten what he most wanted—another journal, a six-pack of yellow legal pads, a few pens, several packs of Twizzlers, and a disposable camera.

Sitting nearby on his own cot, holding a sewing needle, Rob Matusik, a nineteen-year-old from Hoboken, grinned from ear to ear, his scrawny face lighting up like Christmas. "Thanks, Mr. Whitman! Apparently, my clan didn't think enough of me to send *me* a box like that. Is there any Skoal in there?"

"C'mon, don't you get enough from the PX?"

"Yeah, I get enough, but not enough of the right brand. I want the good stuff."

"How 'bout a nice pair of socks?" Walt grabbed a new pair of gray wool socks from the pile and tossed one to Boots. And since he already had a dozen or so pairs, he pulled out another and tossed it to Rob.

"Thanks, Mr. Whitman. I probably could use a new pair of socks. I had no idea when I came over here that I would be so obsessed with my feet." Rob, nicknamed Eagle Eye, for his ability to spot a camel from miles away as it poked across the desert, pulled the tag from the new pair of socks and set them down next to him. He was at that moment concentrating on using the needle to poke a large red blister that had formed on the bottom of his foot.

"Don't get any sand in there. This is no place to have a blood infection."

"Well, you need good socks and you need to have clean skin. If you don't stop picking at those blisters, you will get a raging infection. You have no idea what kind of germs that damn needle has sitting on the end of it."

"Oh, come on, you are exaggerating, Whitman. A little germ never hurt anyone."

"Oh, yeah, well then apparently you never heard of AIDS, hepatitis, the Spanish American flu. How about the bubonic plague? A little germ, my friend, should be feared above all else. It's the things you can't see that sometimes cause the most trouble."

Boots agreed. "Yes, really Eagle, you are going to need those feet, why not go over to the med tent and let them clean that blister?"

"I want to save the medics for when I pass out from the heat."

"Oh, come on, that is what they're there for. And you don't want to save them for a raging blood infection or a foot amputation, do you? You won't get a chance to pass out from the heat if you don't make it till the heat of day. You need those feet for running."

"You worry too much, Whitman."

"Well, I'm just being cautious."

"Is that what being a Daddy does to you?"

Walt thought that might be the case. He did worry more, ever since the blue stick had made its way into his life. Travis was his responsibility. He felt like it was important to stay alive, so germs and wars and stuff like that were to be avoided.

"Well, if you're lucky, you'll find out someday," Trump shouted from one corner of the tent. He had earned his nickname, short for Trumpet, after he had established a daily ritual of stepping outside the tent, pulling out a worn trumpet, and performing a medley of popular jazz and mournful melodies. Out of respect, he did not attempt to play "Taps" there in the desert. Trump was a quiet, thoughtful man, and when he opened his mouth, others listened as he usually had something notable to say.

Boots howled. "Yeah, if the dude ever gets a girlfriend!"

Rob tossed aside the needle. "I got a girlfriend, you idiot. Not like I seen any care packages from your Sharon. I'm beginning to think there isn't a Sharon. I'm beginning to think you just made her up. A figment of your imagination."

"Sharon, Smaron, cut the crab, Rob. This ain't about Sharon, it's about you. You don't want to get an infection when you have to run. Remember none of us needs to be an invalid if we can help it. We need to be strong as rocks, tough as nails, and mean as hell. One of us down, we're all down."

Walt stepped away from the conversation and found a spot on

the cot and opened up one of the letters sent from a third-grade class in Iowa. Scrawly little nine-year-old signatures were positioned all around the card.

Dear Soldier,

We don't know you, but we want to thank you. Thank you for keeping us safe. Thank you for protecting us. Come home soon.

Love,
Lauren, Paige, Andrew, Ryan, Jacob, Kevin, Sarah, Katie.

Walt thought about Travis—the day he would be sitting in class and writing such letters. An image of him sitting on the floor of a classroom with folded hands, his attention on a teacher, came into his mind.

"You know, Boots, it's funny the things you take for granted."

"What are you talking about? I don't take advantage of anyone or anything."

"Granted goofy, not advantage. And I'm not really talking about *you*. I mean *you* as in all of us. It's funny how we all take things for granted." Walt leaned over and peered into Boots's grinning face. "Am I gonna have to give you another English lesson?"

"What do you mean *gonna*, Whitman? *Gonna* ain't a proper word, even someone as lowly as I knows that. Am I *going* to have to give *you* an English lesson?"

Walt ignored the comment. "All I have to say is that most of the time on a daily basis you and I and a lot of people I have come across over the years take for granted a lot of things we don't even think about. Things that we don't appreciate the way we should. I took for granted the fact that whenever I wanted I could go out to the store and purchase things. I could buy a fishing rod, new boots, parts for my Jeep. I had a washing machine and clean clothes. I had a great mattress. And I could pretty much go to the grocery and find any food that I might want and have the money to pay for it. And had a place to cook it. And I found that sometimes in the summer in Michigan, the sky was so damn blue! Where the hell did the blue go? Everything here is tan and gray and red. And the water would stretch for miles. Now I miss all that. And I didn't even really know I had them to begin with. Now I realize that all these things were gifts. Gifts that I hope I will never take for granted again."

"Okay, Mr. Michigan Mush, I get it. I understand what it is you are trying to teach me, okay? The word *granted.* I will use it in a sentence." Boots stood, stretched out his arms and lifted his eyes toward the tent ceiling. "Now, guys, all eyes on me. It's time for a lesson. An English lesson. One that I learned from Mr. Whitman. I am going to use the word granted in a sentence." He cleared his throat.

"I will never take for granted my nice dog Oh or the way he howls or the way he sets a bone at my feet in the morning so I'll rub behind his ears. I will be happy to clean up his poop when we go for walks after work. I will never take for granted that even though I lost my folks, I had some great parents that loved me and wanted me to do well. And I will never take for granted a nice half-pound burger smothered in cheese with grilled onions and ketchup."

Tommy James shouted. "Now that is something not to take for granted. Where the heck are the burgers when you need them?"

"Hush, jerk-off, let me finish!" Boots cleared his throat again; half-closed his eyes, and continued. "I will never take for granted that I have a girlfriend that I hope is going to wait for me and not run off with some other schmuck. I will never take for granted that I have a nice car and a place to hang my hat. And my underwear. I will never take for granted that I live in a free country and that I don't have to live in a war zone. Except, of course, when I lived in Los Angeles for a few months in the eighties. And finally, fellow soldiers, I will never take for granted that I have found such a fine English teacher like Mr....uh...Whitman here, who cares enough about me to make me speak good."

"Good?," Walt asked. "What he means, is to have him speak properly."

"I knew that Whitman. I was just testin' ya. You are such a wise guy."

"And to all my fellow soldiers, let's get through this thing and go back home so we can have some things to never take advantage of."

"For granted."

"Whatever, Whitman."

Boots took a brief bow, and with a flourish awaited the roar of the crowd. The few soldiers who were listening, applauded.

"And just for good measure," Eagle Eye shouted out from his cot, "let's never take for granted that we have warm, willing women waiting at home for us."

"Oh, c'mon, Rob, you never had a warm woman in your life. The only woman you have ever had has stared out at you from a magazine."

"Rob does too have a girlfriend."

"Oh, I got it wrong then, you are the one that is gay."

"Eat shit. You are the faggot."

The banter continued as it often did. Once the expletives had made the rounds and everyone had been insulted in one way or another, the men found their way back to their jobs. The voices and language of these men were additional sounds Walt would jot down in his journal when he got a chance.

Later at dinner, Walt sat across from Boots on a canvas-folding chair at a metal table in the makeshift dining room in tent city. There was a small Christmas tree in the corner to remind them that it was December. He watched as Boots wolfed down an MRE of rice and lima beans. He wondered how many nights before he could have a home cooked meal.

"You look like you really love the stuff," Walt said.

"Food, Mr. Walter Whitman, is one of the few things I enjoy right now, so if you don't mind, if you ain't going to finish those beans on your plate, can you please pass them over? I need my calories."

"Yeah, you need your calories to run your mouth." Walt handed over his plate and tossed Boots a cellophane-wrapped cookie.

"Well, you never know if this will be the last food you're gonna get," he mumbled as clearly as he could with his mouth full. "I was always told to clean my plate. And I wouldn't want to hurt the memory of my momma."

"Well, if I was home tonight, I'd have steak. And a baked potato with sour cream. And a glass of wine. And I'd end the evening with a backrub. And then…."

Boots groaned. "Please stop, Whitman, I can't stand all the braggin'. I'd play the violin for you, but then that would be too romantic."

"Oh, c'mon, Boots, you really think I'm braggin'? I have not one shittin' thing to brag about." As Walt spoke the words, he felt an aching in his gut. "I tell you who should be braggin' right now— that kid brother of mine." It was true. Pete was back home with a girlfriend he was probably going to marry and Pete was probably the one enjoying the steak and the baked potatoes and the backrub. Walt might be bragging about what he would do if he was home, but for now it was all wishful thinking.

"You are probably right, Whitman, you should be home with your kid. And we both should be ringing in the New Year with noisemakers and champagne and watching that lovely Times Square ball drop out of the sky."

But when the day was done, instead of noise-makers and champagne and Christmas carols, there was Trump silhouetted against a vast foreign sky that looked vaguely like the one back home, playing his nightly mournful songs that signaled to the soldiers that another day together in the desert was over.

After listening to Trump, Walt settled onto his cot and opened the letter from Grace. She had found the home of their dreams. How had that happened without him? What else was happening without him? Maybe there was a new friend she wasn't telling him about, maybe she had the flu and didn't tell him. Maybe she was having trouble with her nerves or maybe Travis wasn't developing as he was supposed to. He was out of the loop.

And there were a lot of things she didn't know about him either. Like the conversations he'd had with men she'd never met and the fear that gripped him when he considered the idea that any day could be the day when they would commence with active battle.

Even though he was happy to hear that Grace had bought the house, he was sad about it too. It was a part of their family history that he wouldn't be able to share when they looked back. At least he had been there for Travis's birth. There were soldiers here with pregnant wives who had their firstborns while they were cleaning rifles. So he was lucky for that. And as far as he knew, his family was healthy.

He opened up the note card with the American flag on the cover for the umpteenth time that day.

> Walter. Come home soon. I need some help painting. And I'm not real sure if you want your desk by the window or in the corner. Are they still stuffing you with lima beans? You'll probably never want to eat another one. I'm going to make sure to rid the pantry of the stuff. I think Dad is going to help repair the squeak in the barn door. Walt, please, never forget the barn. Remember that Saturday in January when we were pregnant with Travis? I would do anything to have that day back, to do it again. I can't wait till we get a chance to do that again. I don't care how cold it is! I will warm you up. I can't wait till we get a chance, just you and me and you and me and Travis, to make more happy memories. I miss those times and I sure MISS YOU!

> Love forever, Grace Ann

Walt thought of the day in the barn and his loins ached. Sex was another thing he had taken for granted. And something that he now tried to avoid thinking of. But that was not possible. He would just have to live with a hard dick and nowhere to put it. It was a common problem. The men in his battalion were young, virile, horny. And lonely.

Along with her written proclamation of love, Grace had sent him a copy of the *Sand Beach Times*. He went straight to his column, now being written by Dave Pollard with a little daily inscription that indicated that Dave was filling in for Walter Moore who was currently deployed in Saudi Arabia. He stuffed the letter and the paper under his pillow, but sleep eluded him amid the sound of an explosion in the distance and snoring.

TWENTY-FIVE

Grace decided to take the job at Art's. The lonely nights of staring at the walls and trying to entertain Travis and think about Walt were just too much. She needed the work to fend off fear and loneliness and she needed the company of her co-workers. She needed to know that she could manage on her own, and waitressing seemed the quickest way to earn a wee bit more than minimum wage. And so there she was, a new waitress at Art's, having arranged for Travis to stay with Fran and Paul on a night when Michael was not going to be around.

She was loaded down with a heavy tray of entrees when she noticed her dad enter the restaurant. It was the peak of the dinner hour, and it was all she could do to keep the orders straight. She set down the heavy tray on the stand and tried to remember which entrée went to whom. She had learned to position them according to the seating arrangement, but sometimes when people wanted separate checks and special orders, she got confused. She had developed a system of serving by placing the plate in the center for the person at the head of the table and then worked her way to the right.

"Smoked halibut and steamed broccoli?" She smiled and set the steaming plate before the diner and by stating the name of the entrée confirmed that he had in fact gotten what he had ordered. She knew if she got a sneer or a head shake that she had gotten it wrong. She had learned that it was easier to get any mix-up over with now, before the entire table started eating.

"Pasta with clam sauce? Ma'am, here is your rib eye with loaded baked potato."

The final dish on the tray was a turkey club with fries. Her stomach grumbled as she set down the meals, wishing she had ordered something to eat before her shift. Maybe she could catch a bite with Dad after work.

"Just a minute, Pop," Grace said as she swept past her father. "I'm real busy tonight, but I'll stop by your table when I get the chance." She took a second glance when she saw that Janice Nielson was by his side. She had forgotten about Janice after the closing on the house, because when she had questioned her father about her, all he had said was, "Yes, Janice is sharp. She is a wonderful lady."

It was now a shock to see her there, but kind of a nice shock—a pleasant change from the lonely father who would come in and sit awkwardly at a table by himself, occasionally making light conversation with the other patrons. Today he didn't need to busy himself with the newspaper or a book. Today he had someone to sit across from like most of the others in the restaurant. And Grace was under the impression that Janice was a good person.

She smiled at the woman on Dad's arm. "Hey, Janice, I'm still very happy about the house. I look forward to the closing, though I have to admit, it makes me nervous. We'll have you seated in a minute. Try the special. It is awesome!"

They were seated at a table served by Tammy, one of the other waitresses.

As Grace was finishing up with the rush, managing a section of eight tables, she ran into Tammy as the two stood at the kitchen serving window retrieving orders.

"Isn't that your Dad?" Tammy asked.

"Yep," Grace said. "I'll introduce you when it slows a bit. He's with the realtor who found our house! He denies it to me, but I think he has found a girlfriend."

"That's nice but weird, I bet. What happened to your mom?"

"That's a whole other story, not for now, but I really didn't know he was dating," she added as she piled four plates on her tray.

"Oh, Grace, get used to it. Men are just not good alone. My dad brought home a girlfriend *two months* after he left my mom."

"Yeah, but I bet he was seeing her before they split, right?" Just as the words slipped out Grace realized that was not such a nice thing to say.

"Yeah, *probably*," Tammy said, rolling her eyes. "Well, they're having dessert now. Why don't you let me keep an eye on your tables, and you go say hi."

In the short time they had worked together, Grace had noticed that Tammy was helpful and the kind of co-worker you could rely on.

"Thanks, Tam." Grace cleared her throat and sat down at an empty seat next to her dad. Janice sat across from him.

"Hi, Dad!" Grace gave him a quick peck on the cheek.

Turning to Janice, she said hi to her as well and then asked if they'd enjoyed their dinner.

"It was wonderful," Janice said. She looked so petite and more down-to-earth as a date as opposed to a real estate agent. A date of Dad's. "My steak was done just right and your yeast rolls with the honey butter are excellent." Janice did not look like she made it a habit of devouring yeast rolls. She looked more like she might eat tofu and spend time at the gym.

"Grace, have you started packing for the move to the house yet?" Janice asked.

"Not yet. I am waiting for my dear, deployed husband to return so he can move in with me. I'm not doing this one by myself. It was enough that I picked out the place, and I'm going to have to close on it without him, but moving in? No, I'm afraid that when that time comes, Walt will be with me. I will at least put some paint on the walls and replace some of the carpet, but the actual move in is not about to happen till he carries me over the threshold. I can't bear the idea of spending one night there without him. Well, anyways, Janice, enough about me. What about you? Where do you live?"

"I moved to Sand Beach three years ago. Before that I lived in Arkansas. My husband died and I wanted to get away from the heat and start fresh. I'm used to the small town, and when I came up here for a getaway and saw the ad for an agent at Crescent Real Estate, I just had to move. I got my real estate license when my kids left the nest, and when George died after a thirty year marriage I needed a fresh start. I sold my place and found a job here and I haven't looked back. And it must have been the right choice, because in addition to finding a pretty and quiet place to live, I also have met a fantastically handsome retired gentleman."

Janice patted Dad's arm, smiled up at him and pushed a small piece of gray hair away from his eyes. He didn't blink. He looked as though he rather enjoyed it! Grace swallowed hard. It was difficult to see her father with someone who was patting his arm and looking up at him fondly—someone other than her mother.

Janice turned her attention to Grace. "So have you heard a lot from Walt?"

"Oh, a letter here and there. You would think for a writer he would be more prolific in his letter-writing. I talked to him once, though, last week! He sounded okay. I let Travis get on the phone with him, and it was then that I realized that Travis is getting quite the vocabulary."

"Well, I know you are counting the days till he gets home."

"Yes, ma'am." Grace replied. "I wish I knew how many days it was going to be, but either way, I can't wait." She was surprised that she felt like talking. Janice seemed to be a good listener.

"Well, I've seen pictures of both him and Travis. Walt is very handsome, and Travis is adorable. Charles is lucky to have such a wonderful family."

As Grace eyed this pretty woman, she wondered how much Dad had talked about her mother and about the girls and their growing up years. She wondered if Dad had told her about Beck.

"Let me know if you need help with the house," Janice said.

"Oh, I think Dad has a lot of that covered, don't you, Pop?"

"Of course. You know I do, Gray, but somehow I think that Janice is better with the homey details, like paint colors and carpet. Your father is a cabinet, landscape, and plumbing man. You girls are the ones who add that special touch."

Had Dad just called them girls? Now Janice and Grace were the girls. Grace jumped up from the table.

"Well, you two, I gotta go! You would not believe the side work they have me doing. You would think I could leave when the customers do, but nope, I have to hang around and fill the sugars and roll the silverware."

"Well, Grace," Dad said as he rose from the table and took Janice by the arm. He smiled at his daughter. "You just let us know when you would like some help with that new mansion of yours."

"I will."

Dad had said "us." Dad had called them "the girls." She turned her back to the couple and scanned her tables to make sure the coffees and drinks were full and there was no one looking to get her attention. As soon as she could, she escaped to the bathroom.

Gazing in the mirror, she thought she looked older, somewhat different, more like her mother than she had ever thought before. And tired. Not even considering that she might mess her mascara, she splashed some cool water on her face and patted a paper towel against her skin to dry. There was at least another hour of work before she could leave and head to Fran's to pick up Travis. Another busy day was done.

TWENTY-SIX

At the start of the new year, Grace attended a twelve-step program with Fran and learned how miserable it was for people who lived with an addict. She learned that the illness made the sober one just as crazy as the alcoholic, and often when the drinker stopped drinking the co-dependent family member became unhinged. As Grace sat with Fran and they two put their behaviors under a microscope, she wondered if she had any addictions that needed healing. She knew for a fact she was addicted to thinking about the day that Walt would come home. There were few moments when he didn't pop into her thinking. So if Grace was addicted to anything, it was hope.

Grace now held title to the house, but she had decided not to move in until Walt returned. When she wasn't at Art's or working an occasional Saturday afternoon at the barn, she would search out a quiet place in the duplex. Sometimes she would sit in the overstuffed chair in the den by the window, sometimes she would lie on her bed, sometimes she would sit in the kitchen with a cup of black coffee topped with cinnamon staring blankly at the bluebirds feeding outside. Or sometimes she would go to sit in the rocking chair by Travis's crib and daydream while he napped. She found that the fantasies became a salve to the restless nights, an alternative to a sleeping pill or a glass of wine. She began to believe that if she wanted things badly enough and daydreamed about them, in detail, then maybe she could just wish them into being. She began writing down her fantasies.

It's a clear, crisp day and it is not yet spring. The ground has thawed a bit. There is a scent of cold damp earth rising into the air and a sound of trickling water plummeting through the downspouts. Melting icicles thaw from gutters as the sun pokes through the trees with the promise of warmer days. It's a cold Saturday, and Dad has Travis because Walt arrived home yesterday. He arrived home and it is now just the two of us. We are reconnecting after time apart. We have both changed yet we are still the same. We have several days planned with no distractions. I open a bottle of Chardonnay and pour some of it into chilled glasses as we sit down to his favorite meal—steak, baked potato, broccoli casserole, and chocolate chip cookies. I am smiling inside and out as he tells me some story about his tour of duty. I laugh as I watch him devour the food, relishing the sound of his voice and the brush of his leg against mine under the small kitchen table. I am relieved to have my soul mate back.

After dinner, I massage his feet, the feet that have been worn and blistered from marching and living inside sweaty boots. We communicate with our lips and our hands and our bodies. Both speech and silence are comfortable.

I tend to him and comfort him and he does the same for me.

We make raw, passionate love interspersed with conversation, talking more frequently now and sharing with each other things that have occurred while we have been apart, he in his world and me in mine. After our first evening together, we start a new day, with pancakes, laughter, and sunshine warming the kitchen. After breakfast, we hop back into bed like we love to do and open the pages of the *Sand Beach Times*, he reaching for the section containing the news and the editorials and me grabbing the horoscopes and the crossword puzzles. After we have showered and dressed for the day, I prepare him for the journey to our new home.

It's a cool day, and the sun is bright and cloudless, and the birds are just starting to sing the way they do when they promise spring. He gets into the passenger seat of the Jeep and I blindfold him. When we pull up to our new mansion, I open the Jeep door and lead him up to the house. I remove his blindfold and kiss him hard and we turn to see the view from the porch, the first view that made me know that this was our home, the view that I had when I first came to see the place with Dad and Janice. I want him to experience our new abode in the same way that I discovered it, first through the view of the barn, the cornfield, the blue skies seen from the front porch where we will spend time with each other, with Travis and our other future children. Where we will host luncheons and visit with his parents, Dad, Fran.

We will then open the front door to the smell of pine and the first thing that Walt will see, right in front of him is his office, complete with a thesaurus and dictionary sitting atop the new oak desk that Dad helps me pick out. There will be logs chopped by the fireplace ready for the return of the Sand Beach author. I will have hung his diploma on the wall, and for the morning I will let him spend time in whatever way he wants. Meanwhile, I will put on my old shorts and his t-shirt and start painting the kitchen. I will be warm as I bask in the glow from our lovemaking and ecstatic that we can begin anew. I will line the drawers with shelf paper and hum while he makes phone calls and goes through the house exploring every nook and cranny. Later that day, we will go to pick up Travis, and Walt will have time with his son and Travis will get reacquainted with his father. I now have some dreams of my own, dreams of our family, but also plan for a riding school, maybe a riding camp for disabled kids, maybe a few boarders. I will have my Walt back, but also a life of my own that stands out. I will have more confidence that I can make it on my own, and we both will benefit from this. And it will be this way because I now realize that if someday I have to live without him, I will have to be self-sufficient.

Over the next few days after his return, we find our way home again, into a new steady pace of life different from the one we had before, a bit more urgent, more reverent.

As she wrote, the present lost its grip on her as her mind traveled from past to future and back again. Her memories carried her to the Ohio River, a canoe ride with Walt when they were dating, laughter when the canoe tipped and she lost her balance and the two of them ended up drenched and scraggly and smelling like fish. Her memories carried her back to the moment she had first laid eyes on Walt. He had caught her eye and smiled, and she had seen her future.

Thinking back to his marriage proposal, she could clearly picture him on bended knee, shaking, his expectant eyes looking into hers, searching for her response, hopeful. They had been on a trip to Cleveland and had dined at The Cliffs, a swank restaurant on the twenty-sixth floor of the bank building, overlooking Lake Erie and the Flats. She still remembered the smell of the lobster, the cool air-conditioned restaurant, and the feel of sweat trickling down the back of her neck and the music in the background and the couples all around them tuning into the life-changing event in their midst. She remembered her red glittery dress and her black patent pumps and Walt in a black suit. That was back in the day when going out meant getting dressed up, especially when you didn't get out too often. It was grand. Grace had met Walt's parents six months earlier and now they were visiting a second time. This time she had met Pete. Things had gone so smoothly, a picnic on the beach, a visit to his Catholic grade school, a concert in the park. He had hinted to her that he would like being married, and they had discussed it on occasion, so when she saw that shiny rock in the blue velvet ring box, her heart skipped a beat. She had rehearsed her response. She wasn't going to leave him hanging. She gave an exultant "Yes!" and pulled him up from his knees and clasped him to her. All eyes in the restaurant were on them and there was clapping from a few of the other diners.

Writing these memories gave her a sense of power over her circumstances, as though in the act of writing she were actually embracing him, loving him. The act of writing seemed to keep her life from slipping through her fingers, like sand. Once the words were on paper, they were captive, they were real and they had a finite beginning and a finite ending.

Every week, she put her daydreams and fond memories in an envelope addressed to Walt. She mailed them along with photos of the new home, of Travis, of her in her waitress uniform complete with crisp white shirt and black pants and her newly highlighted hair tied back softly with a black ribbon. She threw in a few crossword puzzles from the *New York Times* along with some writers' magazines, gum, candy, and razors. She also sent him the most recent issue of the *Sand Beach Times*.

In a letter, she wrote of a fun night at Gloria's Café after closing time. People had brought in goodies for her to place in a care package for the men. She sent some photos from that night with each person standing and posing for the camera, holding signs containing their individual messages.

Go Tigers!
Thanks to our Soldiers!
Come Home Safe!
We Miss You!

She wrote about the teacher that had contacted her and asked for the address so the children could mail letters to the soldiers. She wrote a summary of the week. And she signed the letter with her customary 'Love, Grace Ann.'

TWENTY-SEVEN

Rain in the desert was infrequent, and when it did come it drenched the earth and offered a respite from the sandstorms and an excuse to stay in the tent. The rain tamped down the constant haze of dust that hovered and washed the air, leaving it temporarily clean and pure. It also gave Walt an opportunity to work on his new book about the orphans of war. While the others played cards, napped, did pushups, or worked out on makeshift exercise equipment, Walt pulled out his folding chair and sat biting his pen intermittently as he jotted down ideas. Along with plot development, he continued to build a list of sights, sounds, smells, and flavors. He had learned to engage all five senses when setting a scene and so he did this almost obsessively.

Sounds: war planes droning, wind whooshing, rain clapping on the roofs of the tents, distant artillery fire, Arabic voices yelling, men snoring.

Tastes: a cigar burning his lips; stale crackers and old bread; sand that blew into one's food; the taste of blood from running so hard and fast he felt his lungs would burst; the taste of fear.

Smells: old dirty socks and sweat in the small damp tent filled with men; gunpowder; vomit.

Sights: the grayish purple hue of the sky in the desert; a defeated man sitting on the edge of his cot; expressions of grief on men's faces; smoke burning in the distance; sand stretching to the horizon; Bedouins and their camels crossing the desert; Arabs in caftans; tanks moving clumsily over the sand; a bright, fiery sun; a thin veil of heat rising up to create a shimmery mirage.

He wrote about other things too. Like what had happened during the previous two weeks in his unit. The thing that had left them all shell-shocked. The thing that he hadn't yet been able to process in his mind—it was too recent and too painful. So when he wrote about the incident, it came out in short sentences that were abbreviated like sobs rather than a deluge of words.

Amos was a twenty-five-year-old from Georgia to whom Walt had not spoken much outside of an occasional "How you doin'?" Poor Amos had snapped in the middle of the night. And none of them could figure out why. But something must have been too much for the quiet young soldier.

On a dry clear night in the middle of December, Walt awoke to the sound of a shot firing. He had grabbed his protective mask and gun and stepped outside, but instead of encountering the enemy he saw Amos on the ground, staring blankly at the sky, his mouth hanging open and blood running down his cheeks and onto the sand. It was too late for the medics, of that Walt was certain.

Soon the others followed Walt out into that night. They all watched as the medics examined the body and then quickly removed what was left of Amos to be shipped back home.

Walt wondered who belonged to Amos, how his siblings, parents, children, or friends would respond back home to the tragic news—the somber announcement that Amos had died, not in battle with an enemy but rather by the enemy that must have been lurking in his own soul. And not in the middle of a fiery blast but rather in the calm of a starry night just before Christmas.

There was very little discussion among the men about what happened, so Walt had to deal with his feelings about it by himself. He chose not to mention it in his next letter to Grace. Why make her worry? There was nothing that could be done for Amos now.

But soon after finding Amos's body, Walt started having nightmares about death. All kinds of death. Old people dying. Babies in car seats getting catapulted into lakes. Women dying in labor. And Amos lying on the earth with his blank eyes staring up at the night sky. Walt thought maybe his dreams were trying to put events together like a puzzle that he could not solve in his waking life. He could not wrap his mind around the fact that a man who had come over there, just as he had, had avoided death or injury in battle and then just one day decided to take his own life. Why would anyone choose that when he probably would not be there very long and would soon go back home?

He wondered about Amos, the shy man who stayed to himself, and after he was gone he wanted to know more about the Guardsman from Georgia. He wanted to go back to just before the event and learn what had made Amos tick—to get to the root of the problem. He wanted to go back to the moments before Amos made the choice to put a bullet in his head, wishing he could stop him with some magic words, pull the weapon from his hands, find a way to make him change his mind. He kept thinking that maybe he could have said or done something to prevent this suicide. Maybe Amos didn't feel like he had anything to go to home to. Maybe he had just gotten a Dear John letter, like others around him had been getting. Like the one he kept expecting Boots to get from Sharon. Women sometimes didn't want to wait, even for a few months. Maybe Amos wanted to take his fate into his own hands and instead of waiting to get shot or injured; he had claimed and sealed his own fate. Who knew? He just did it. And left no explanation. No suicide note. And the event had left Walt and the other men wary and fearful and quiet. It somehow opened up the possibility that someone else could do it too. It broke the taboo.

So, though Walt did not share the news with his dear wife or his friends back home, he did add this dark experience to his writing, at least in bits and pieces. He tried to capture the emotion, the darkness of the event. He tried to liken the event to the tragedies that the children of war experienced, the orphans that might have lost one or both parents in another tragic way.

The rain came in spurts and along with his introspection about Grace and his life and the death of Amos, he also thought about the culture of the Middle East. He wondered about the children caught in the constant battle that it seemed the Arabs had been embroiled in for so long. He wondered what it would be like to get close enough to one of them, to get inside their brown skin to feel what they felt and to understand life from their perspective. If he was going to understand the orphans of war, he needed to get inside the person, the culture, the experience.

He wished he could spend more time there in his capacity as a journalist and peacefully sit down with some older children to ask them, in Arabic, what it was like in the day of a child in Saudi Arabia. He wondered if as he listened he would learn things he could only imagine as an outsider. What was it like to grow up here, rather than to be a soldier just stationed here from another foreign culture?

When he thought about the children here, he thought about Travis, fat and happy, safe, coddled, and secure. He felt a combination of sadness and anger that children anywhere might have to grow up with a war or the threat of a war in their midst. He thought about bringing one of the children home to Sand Beach, a big brother or sister for Travis. To pull one away from this culture and allow him or her to experience a small town in America—a cheeseburger, French fries, bowling, fishing. To grow up and live in a place of peace and freedom. He thought about his role as a soldier in all this, wondering if over the centuries if there had been enough intervention things would change or if the roots of this culture were just too deep for that to ever happen. A life without threats and bombings and death.

"What're you moping about?" Boots interrupted his reverie as he looked him square in the eye. "You look like you just lost your best friend."

"Just thinking, Boots. Why would you say I was moping? Do I look depressed?"

"Damn right you do, Whitman. You always look depressed. You think too much, and thinking can get you in a hell of a lot of trouble. Why don't you get that carcass of yours off that cot and come play some poker with us? It will be good for you. Get over yourself."

"All right, then," Walt replied as he swung his legs off the edge of the cot and slipped into his boots. "I'll beat you this time."

"Yeah, sure, that's what you always say and you always lose. I say we bet with some of that candy that Grace sent you."

"Deal!"

Walt had come to believe that Boots McCall offered way more than what was visible on first meeting.

TWENTY-EIGHT

At 4:45 a.m., Grace was rudely awakened by the sound of her alarm from a pleasant dream of sailing on the ocean. She reached for Walt's watch fob—the one his grandfather had given him when he graduated from high school—and held it to her breast as she stretched and thought about the day ahead of her.

Taking note of the time, she at first couldn't imagine why the alarm was screeching at such an early hour. And then she remembered. She was a waitress! She had to go to serve breakfast most days now. She clutched the timepiece, gently brushed her lips over the face of it, and closed her eyes.

It had been nine weeks since Walt had left. *I miss you baby!* And it was the anniversary of the day they had met! She hoped he was thinking of her too. It was already 12:45 in the afternoon in Saudi Arabia, the middle of the day—enough time for him to have already had something happen, an accident, breakfast, lunch.

She heard Travis waking and chattering to his stuffed animals in the other room. It was so early!

She rolled over onto her side and pulled her tired body to a sitting position, swung her legs to the side of the bed, and yawned. She slid her feet into her fuzzy slippers and plodded to the bathroom and stared at her reflection. She washed her face and started humming, realizing that the job was a good thing.

"Really," Grace she said to the reflection, "you must do something with those dark circles." The reflection scowled back at her.

"Travis." Grace opened the door to her son's room and found him standing in his crib, one hand holding his stuffed elephant and the other hand in his mouth. She brightened at the sight of his little round face and his happy smile when he saw her.

"How are you, sweetie?" She had to be there for this child who needed her so desperately.

"Mommy's going to work today, Travis. You want to go with me?" She lifted him out of his crib. "I think we need to go look at big boy beds—you are growing out of this tiny prison."

She hauled him off to the tub, removed his damp diaper, and placed him in the warm soapy water. As she lathered and rinsed and sang to him, she made a mental checklist of the things she would have to do when she had a day off: clean out the closets, pick up boxes, stop by the new house. After Travis was clean, she got dressed in the black pants and white shirt she had pressed the day before. She packed Travis's bag, gave him a Pop Tart for breakfast, and then took him to his sitter.

It was still dark when she arrived at Art's. Tammy was the only other waitress there, and the two of them remained half asleep as they brewed coffee and set the tables.

"Did you get to send the package to Walt?"

"We did get it packed, but I'll need to scoot out on break and get it mailed. I couldn't believe so many people could get together and be so generous."

"It must get lonely for you."

"I have no idea how single parents make it! I mean, come on! Work and then groceries, then play time and bath. And you might as well forget it if Travis gets an ear infection. I have a new appreciation for all mothers, even those who stay home! I am so glad this is only temporary. I only *thought* I appreciated my husband."

"That is why I'm going to wait to have children," Tammy replied as she walked past Grace to fold some napkins. "I want to make sure not only that I will have enough money but also that I have a man good enough to help me with all that stuff. I wish I had gone to school. Waitressing hardly makes me a living."

"Oh, school makes no difference! I went to school and got my degree and look where I am, right alongside you. A degree in liberal arts and four years wasted. I could have been traveling."

"I don't think those years were wasted."

"Yeah, you are right. I earned my Mrs. Walter Allen Moore degree. Plus, I guess if I ever had to put out a resume, it might look good that I have gone to college."

Grace went to all the tables checking the sugars and filling the creamers in the cooler before the breakfast rush. When her pre-shift tasks were done, she sat for just a moment at one of the leather booths and watched life go by the window. The day was foggy and damp. She watched another mother, about her age, scolding her child as she pulled him out of the stroller. She looked up the road to see the door of Gloria's Cafe and imagined Walt home soon going back to his morning routine. Or maybe he would switch to Art's for breakfast.

Her reverie was interrupted when the new cook plopped down in the seat across from her. "Well, look at Ms. Daydream. Give anything to know your thoughts." He was leaning across the table, looking through her.

She took a second to refocus. "Oh, nothing in particular. I just miss my husband. I do have a husband, Doug, haven't I told you that? If he were here, he might not appreciate hearing you flirt with me all the time. There are plenty of available girls in town. You need to get out more and meet one. And now, we need to get to work. I think it's going to be a busy day. Days like this one are always busy." She leapt from the table to get back to work.

"Well, he's a very lucky man. I don't think I could have left you behind. If I had been deployed, then I might just have told them that you would have been something I would pack along."

"I've got to open up, Doug," she said as she grabbed an empty coffee carafe and rinsed it in the sink. "'Something I would pack along,'" Grace repeated under her breath. She felt a knot in her stomach. What an idiot. Did he really think she might be attracted to him? Did he really think that she was a cheater? And then, him thinking that Walt had any choice but to leave her behind. She really wanted to slap him. Walt was perfect. Doug was rude.

"When will he get the hint?" Grace asked Tammy under her breath, as they greeted the first customers of the morning.

"When the cows come home," Tammy replied. "Or at least when Walt does. He's just a lonely, single guy. And he worships you, I think."

"Oh, great," Grace muttered, as she took one last glance at the morning special before approaching her table. It was times like this she wished that work at the barn was year-round. Horses were much easier to deal with than humans. And she would rather shovel hay than pour coffee. But the barn in winter was cold and the pay was sparse. And on some small level it was nice to be noticed. It was nice to have someone think you were pretty. It was nice to be appreciated.

The shift was hectic. A few items that Doug had overcooked were sent back, and one lady complained about a wilted piece of lettuce in her oatmeal. It was embarrassing when a customer sent food back with something in it that shouldn't be. It made Art's look like it wasn't all that clean. But, in fact, it seemed as though they were constantly cleaning.

TWENTY-NINE

Several weeks into the New Year, Walt awoke after a nightmare and reached for the thermos of cool coffee that he kept by his cot so he could sip at it before the others woke up. It seemed that he had been dreaming all night, and it took several minutes to shake the strange visions and to realize it was just him there in the desert at night in a tent full of men. His nightmares of death continued, but interspersed with these were pleasant dreams of Grace and Travis, of home.

He sat on the edge of the cot, trying to remember the details of the dream. In one of them, he was standing in the sand, knee-deep, with nothing around him, not a sound, not a soldier. As he stood there stuck, he saw Grace atop a horse gallop by into the sunset, not even giving him a glance. He was confused by her lack of acknowledgment. Simultaneously, hundreds of camels and tanks appeared and Arabs ran around screaming. Grace was wearing a winter coat that vaguely looked like the one she had worn when they had made love in the barn. This time Travis was with her in the saddle instead of Walt and Travis was seated in front of Grace. It was like that winter day, but this time in the dream, it wasn't winter and Walt couldn't connect with Grace or their son—he remained stuck deep in the sand and it had become heavy and thick. His feet wouldn't move—the gritty grains of sand had turned to concrete. He reached out for his wife, and just before she disappeared into the sunset she looked back at him and laughed, her skin, lips, and soft lilting voice inaccessible and elusive.

The dream that followed was just as strange. Pete had been deployed with him, and the brothers stood out in the middle of the desert, just the two of them, with maybe a few men in the background clanking metal or something. Pete was drinking a beer and refused to wear the uniform. Instead of obeying, he would laugh when given a command, and as he laughed a thin stream of blood trickled out of the corner of his lips. When he opened his mouth, Walt noticed that he had lost his teeth. His brother Pete was maniacal and defiant as he laughed. He was announcing to the men, after he removed his shirt, that Susan had moved to Sand Beach and that she was going to become a waitress and have their second child. He pulled out a picture of Susan, a small picture that quickly became the size of a large wall hanging. In it Susan was very pregnant, her stomach protruding. And as she stood with a small child by her side, Susan looked like Grace, though not exactly. Susan's hair was a fiery red.

The dreams were vivid. They left him anxious and disoriented.

Walt looked over to see Matusik sitting on the edge of his cot, reading a murder mystery under the dim light of a lantern. He was very glad to see that Pete was not there and that things were pretty much the same as they had been when he had drifted off. The air was cool and dry. He rose to get a bottle of water. Combing his fingers through his damp hair, he yawned and nodded to Matusik.

"Morning, Rob," he said softly, careful not to wake the other men. "I'm going to step outside for a minute if you need me.

Snorehead here looks like he isn't going to wake for a while."

"Hey, I need to stretch my legs too, I'll go with you." He marked his page, set the book down on the center of the cot, and pulled on a warm long-sleeved shirt.

When they stepped outside, Walt looked up at the night sky in which, despite the smoke caused by the fires and the bombings, a few stars were visible. Walt thought he saw some shooting stars moving across the sky but actually they were red firefly-tracer rounds, exploding in small flashes of light and burning out like meteor showers. There was a distant glimmer of a fiery oilfield burning on the horizon.

"So, tell me, Rob do you ever think about how huge the world is? I mean, look at that star up there trying to shine through this hell. Compared to those, we are just tiny specks. Those stars are huge and we are tiny. If you were sitting on one of those stars looking at this planet, you would have no idea that there were people running around. You would have no idea that we even existed. We are less than a speck in the vast scheme of things."

"I try not to think about stuff like that, Whitman. It just makes my head hurt. But when you put it that way, I guess you are right: the universe is big, and we are small."

Walt continued. "But even though I know we are tiny compared to the vastness of the universe, I still feel like our lives mean something. When I think about my life and the people I care about, it doesn't seem meaningless. It seems important." He pulled a Marlboro out of his pocket, held it between his lips, and lit it. He sucked in the smoke this time. Each time he had lit up since he had landed in the Middle East, the smoke went a little deeper into his lungs, filling his head and calming him, seeping into his veins and quieting the blood rushing through them.

"Do you know, Rob, that before we came over here, I never touched a cigarette, never even tried one. And, well, now I rather like it."

"Oh, come on! You trying to tell me that when you were fourteen years old you didn't try one?" Rob smiled as he settled into the metal chair.

"Not ever." He took another deep drag. "Maybe this will be a time for me to get my life in perspective."

Rob removed his nylon jacket as the air seemed to warm in the pre-dawn hours. "Yeah, I'm sick about Amos, and I wish that never had happened. And as for me, I just want to learn something. I want to learn what I want out of life, because honestly, I have no idea! I don't feel particularly good at anything, except for maybe following orders. So at least for now, I want to be a hero. I want to make my momma and my girl and my best friend proud. And it would be nice to let my baby sister know that her big brother can go out and save the world and protect her freedom. High school sucked, you know. And I will never get a scholarship to go to college because my grades weren't good enough and my folks can't afford it. Heck, I work at Blockbuster back home and was hoping to save money to figure out something for my future. What do I know? I'm still trying to figure it all out. So it really freaked me when I joined the Guard for some extra money and they actually deployed us! What the hell! Ain't that crazy? I must have been destined to be in a war, even though I never thought I would be. But isn't that what men are supposed to do? My father and his father and his father…and now me. How I ever got over here, I will never figure out, and it just scared my mom half to death. But what ya gonna do? When you sign up for something, you gotta do it. So here we are, Mr. Moore. Here we are."

Rob continued as he stretched his arms and legs and fell into a yoga pose, a kind of semi-sun salutation. "But I've been trying to look at it this way. Hey, as long as I get home safe and don't suffer any permanent damage, then it's an experience. And since I pretty much stayed in one place my whole life, I figure this may be my time to travel. And this place is way different from my home. Free travel. Be all you can be. Now I'm living a Blockbuster life, like something out of a movie. Now if I go back to work there, I can rent movies about people like this. Maybe they'll make a movie about the Guard being deployed during Desert Shield and one day, when I'm forty something and married with three teenagers, we'll rent it as a family. And I can tell the kids while we pile on the couch and stuff ourselves with popcorn. 'Hey, kids, your old dad was there.' And the kids will look at me funny and say, 'Yeah, right!'"

He bent down to touch his toes. "Or maybe I'll be an actor and I can act in a movie about being deployed in Desert Shield. Now that would be something! Maybe I'm doing this so that the next thing will fall in place. Wouldn't that be funny? An actor?" He paused to consider what he had just said.

"Yeah, Rob, that sounds great! An actor and a father! And you can tell your kids 'Hey, your dad did that!' And that will be the legacy you pass on through the generations. Every man needs a war story."

Walt pointed up at the sky. "See that dipper over there? I think that it looks down and knows everything about us—our fate, our dreams. I think it has all of our destinies sealed tight in its ever-present light. Written in stone they are and we just don't know it yet."

"Wow, Whitman, I see why you are a writer, dude, you really have some deep thoughts."

"A lot of the time, my thoughts are shit. But not all the time." He shrugged his shoulders and let out a long breath. "It's just that I feel clearest just before the dawn. That is when things seem the purest. Before the noise of day. After the sun comes up, my thinking goes downhill. Gets cluttered with other shit."

Rob replied. "Before I came here, I never got up early. Certainly never before the crack of dawn. I still lived with my mom, and most days I preferred to sleep in till ten or so before I had to work at noon at Blockbuster. And you know, much as I hate these MREs after three years of stuffing my face with Big Macs on my break, I don't miss them a bit. I would rather have a plate of rice and canned corn than another greasy burger. When I joined the Guard, they made me lose fifty pounds! And I like my six-pack abs now." He looked down at his abdomen and fondly patted the result of daily workouts. His fit, muscular frame was visible under his thin sweatshirt.

Walt finished the last of the cigarette and bent down to put it out in the sand. He then lifted it and walked over to the coffee can filled with smokes and dropped it in. The two became silent as a thin glimpse of red showed on the horizon, the break of a new day.

"Ready to run, Eagle Eye? Let's get Boots out of bed. I think we should run sixty laps around the perimeter today, shake the cobwebs out. Do us some good."

Days later, the warning siren jerked Walt to attention. He grabbed his rifle, placed his protective mask on his face, and stood alert as he prepared himself for an emergency. His comrades acted quickly too, flying out of the tent. They were all looking out over the sand, guns at the ready, when Walt spied two drab green Arab trucks loaded with olive-skinned men in caftans driving straight toward the encampment.

The entire unit stood facing the trucks with M-16s poised on shoulders. An interpreter stood at the head of the group and shouted something in Arabic. Walt recognized the Arabic word *Qef*, meaning halt, one of the few words he had learned. After a few exchanges between the groups, Walt was relieved to see the trucks retreat. Apparently, they had just gone astray in traveling across the desert.

THIRTY

Gary Martin woke from a deep slumber to the clamor of the phone. He opened his eyes and reached for the receiver.

"Captain Martin, sorry, I know it's Saturday."

Gary yawned and responded, his voice gravelly. "Yes, Chaplain Conner, it's Saturday. You never do take that into account." He squinted to see the lit digits on the alarm. Five-fourteen.

Why can't these calls come in on a Tuesday?, he thought as he struggled for consciousness. He knew the drill. He would meet Conner, a retired chaplain, at the armory to get additional details about the nature of the call. It couldn't be good. It never was.

He rubbed his eyes, rolled over, and pushed himself up to sit at the side of the bed. He had hoped to work on his airplane engine today. He had a Rolls Royce Merlin waiting in the garage for him along with a stack of technical books from the library that he had waited two weeks for. Today was supposed to be his day in his man cave with no interruptions. Why was it that whenever he had a personal agenda, life offered one that topped his?

He turned to look at Suzanne on her side, sleeping deeply, snoring in that quiet way she had, a light wisp of hair across her cheek. No need to wake her. There didn't need to be two Saturdays ruined. Gary opened the walk-in closet and removed his freshly starched Class-A uniform from the hanger. After carefully dressing and removing a few dog hairs from the trousers, he bent down over Suzanne and planted a light kiss on her cheek. He would set up the coffee maker to brew a fresh pot and leave a note on the table. He hoped he could make it home by early afternoon. They could have a late breakfast when he got back. He'd pop open some of those orange-glazed croissants, cook some sausage. And then he'd put on his sweats and spend time with the engine.

For now, he prepared a piece of toast and slathered it with crunchy peanut butter and raspberry jam, careful not to drip any on his uniform. He would stop and get a large coffee on the way to pick up Conner.

THIRTY-ONE

Grace awoke from a dream at the crack of dawn. In the dream, she and Walt had picked out a pale aqua color for the kitchen and had begun to roll it on the walls, inhaling the smell of fresh paint. She smoothed the paint onto the roller; spread it thick onto the dull white walls, and frequently stood back to admire her work. Their clothing speckled with paint, the two of them laughed and joked as they transformed the room to the color of water and sky with every stroke. As Walt continued to paint the walls, Grace set her roller aside, switched paint and brush, and started painting the trim on the windows a crisp white.

Walt was humming the same song that he often hummed when he was changing the oil on the car in the driveway, the one he sang to her on the day that Travis was born. The name of the song was elusive and, for the life of her, Grace could not pin down the title. But she could hear the humming. The mood in the dream took a turn when the humming turned into "Taps" and she realized that he wasn't wearing blue jeans or a t-shirt anymore. He was in his fatigues. And as he was humming, he put down the roller and stepped away from her.

He began to float away. The door opened up in front of him and he floated out over the porch and landed on the front lawn and started marching. With her paintbrush in hand, she stepped onto the porch and called out to him. But he wouldn't turn around. He had his back to her and continued marching. She was trapped in the doorway, unable to move. She yearned to join him but couldn't. She wanted to put an end to his strange behavior and reach out to him and hold him as he was out on the lawn, lonely and awkward, humming and marching in his fatigues in the middle of the afternoon. She started to cry.

Then she awoke and her throat felt very tight and she was choking in the dark quiet of the room. As her eyes adjusted to the real world, she realized that it had been a dream. And for that she was glad.

It still felt early as she turned to see the bright red digits on the alarm. Five-fifteen. She rubbed her eyes, pulled the journal out of the nightstand, and jotted down the details of the dream. She had started keeping a dream diary since Walt had left. She found it interesting to jot down the details when she awoke and to see if there was anything remotely related to the dreams in her waking life, and of course there was. It was just jumbled.

She stretched, yawned, and swung her flannel-covered legs over the side of the bed and slid her bare feet into her slippers. She was glad that she had the day off and that it was a Saturday, her favorite day of the week. Today she planned to have Janice and Dad over for breakfast, and they were going to help her look at the paint samples she had picked out. After breakfast they would go to the hardware store to get everything they needed for a day of painting and puttering at the new house.

She had the impression Janice was good for Dad. She could see it in his eyes, hear it in his voice. He had new energy and talked more than he ever had. She hoped that Janice wouldn't mind some of the clutter left behind in the living room from a night of popcorn and play with building blocks on the floor with Travis.

All the while she was showering and getting dressed, she hummed the song Walt had been humming in the dream. When she was ready for the day, she went down to the kitchen to make coffee and prepare the fixings for a breakfast of eggs, bacon and strawberry waffles.

When the doorbell rang, she checked the clock on the wall. Seven-thirty. They were right on time. Travis was still asleep, even though it was past his usual wake-up time.

She opened the door to a gray blustery morning and a gust of cold wind whipped into the foyer.

"Hi, Janice." Grace smiled and wiped her hands on her apron as she beckoned the couple inside. "Hi, Dad," she said as she turned to her father and planted a kiss on his cheek. "Come in, you two! It's freezing out."

Grace hung their jackets in the front closet, and her guests followed her into the kitchen.

"That coffee smells fantastic! I'm starved."

"I was hoping you guys were hungry. I've planned enough food to feed an army."

"An army of three." Dad chuckled.

"Oh, Grace," Janice commented. "You have the cutest apartment here. But I know you can't wait to move to your new home. It will be the kind of home you can spend a lifetime in. The kind of place to raise your family, host picnics, and board the horses you talked about. It's incredible! And I heard from your father that he has never even been on a horse. Maybe you can take us on a trail ride!" Janice looked up at Charles. "You would enjoy that wouldn't you, dear?"

From the sound of that, and the term of endearment, Janice planned to be around a while. At least until Grace moved.

Dad cut in. "Horses yes, but I am hoping that Grace will let me set up a woodworking room for Walt."

"Yes, Dad, another woodworking room for *you*," Grace said. "You two have a seat while I finish making breakfast."

Her father and Janice sat at the table as ordered and commenced to sort through the color chips.

"Travis is still sleeping and I have to heat up the waffle maker, but it is great to have company early in the day. I never realized how much I enjoy conversation in the morning. So please, fill me in on something exciting while I finish making the breakfast."

As Grace spoke, she smiled across the table at Dad and Janice. She noticed for the first time that they actually looked good together, not just made each other happy, but *looked* good together. Like they belonged that way.

As she poured half-and-half into the creamer and set it on the table, she smiled and exhaled a sigh of contentment. Breakfast was going to be perfect. And so was this day.

THIRTY-TWO

Gary Martin had a crummy job. Unlike the prize patrol who could visit the unsuspecting at their home and grant a million dollars, or the obstetrician who could go into a room full of expectant faces and announce to them that they were grandparents or aunts or uncles to a healthy baby girl or boy, Gary was a Casualty Notification Officer. He was the one with the lousy, crappy job of informing the surviving family members that their soldier had died in the line of duty. He wasn't sure just how he had been the one to get this job, other than a simple heart murmur that had prevented his deployment this time. But he was certain it was the most miserable job a person could have.

How did you tell someone that his or her loved one had died? This was his third notification. The other two had left him in a cold sweat. He couldn't forget the look of horror on the faces.

When you were asked to do something for the Guard, you did not say no. He was spared the active duty, and his master's degree in counseling made this position a natural fit. And counseling never was perfect anyway. When you were a counselor, you always had to deal with some kind of unpleasantness, divorce, addiction, depression. His unpleasantness turned out to be grief.

He was glad that his own experience with it was fleeting. He had lost a grandfather at an early age, a distant cousin, a childhood friend. He had been trained to be calm when he told someone about their dismal fate, the event that shouldn't have happened. He had to listen to the grisly details of how it had actually had happened, whether the soldier had been blown up or committed suicide or was run over by a Humvee. He was the final part of the clean-up crew, tidying up the lives that had been blown apart by disaster. He was the one who had to see the facial expressions, the looks of dread in the eyes of the survivors that accompanied his dire announcements. Then he was the voice of reason and calm, as he listened to the wracking sobs, telling the bereft person, often a wife or mother, that there would be a Casualty Assistance Officer available any time of the day or night to help with questions or if she just needed to talk. He would hand over a crisp business card with his emergency number and office phone.

Sometimes Gary felt as though he might as well have been the one to shoot the soldier in the first place. That's what it felt like.

Chaplain Conner had not given details, but had informed him that this day he had to visit a wife with a small child in Sand Beach. He hated it when there were kids, especially ones not old to remember going places like amusement parks or Disney World with their daddies. The little girls would not have a daddy to walk them down the aisle someday, and the little boys would not have a father to guide them into manhood.

Gary drove down dark, damp streets that glistened in the lamplight from the overnight drizzle. He lifted his coffee mug and gulped, wondering how much of his day this visit would consume. He mentally rehearsed the words and the way they needed to be said. He didn't want to make it worse by the way he handled it. He knew from experience that times like these, the words, the approach, and the demeanor were important.

Gary drove into the parking lot of the base that was just now becoming light with the dawn. He spotted the lone figure in familiar uniform. He pulled up to the curb and remotely unlocked the door. Conner flicked his cigarette and entered the car and rubbed his hands together. "Damn, it's cold this morning." A puff of frigid air escaped his lips as he spoke. "I couldn't tell if it was smoke coming out of my mouth or just the frozen air."

"Well, if you didn't insist on sucking on those cancer sticks, you could have been wearing your gloves."

"Whatever." Conner turned away and looked out the window. "Thanks for getting up. The address is in Sand Beach. Apparently, the soldier was a writer for the newspaper over there. He was driving a Humvee at night and ran into a damn wadi. He was killed immediately. He was the only casualty, but two of the other guys were injured and are recovering in a Kuwaiti hospital. You make the initial announcement. Give the specifics. I'll be the supportive one. You know how it works. You deal the shit and I'll be there with you to clean it up."

The two men fell silent as they drove past farms and country homes covered with a soft layer of morning frost. The horses and cows in their thick winter coats appeared oblivious to the sparse traffic on the road driving by. Gary sighed as they entered Sand Beach and drove through the small town, passing closed shops, Laundromats, bakeries, and churches. He flicked on his right blinker as he turned onto Main, took a left on Oak Street, and slowed as he neared the duplex with the number 1017 on the mailbox and a red Jeep and a silver minivan in the drive. The house was easy to spot with the string of Christmas lights still hung outside and the yellow ribbon on the tree and the star in the window. Gary wondered if the lady of the house had kept lights up in expectation of the newspaper man or if she was just too exhausted to take them down. For a flash of a second, the thought crossed his mind that the extra vehicle might mean a boyfriend.

Gary took a deep breath and prepared himself for the most dreaded part of his job. "This is it." He turned off the ignition and looked over at Conner. "Let's get this over with."

They stepped onto the porch and rang the bell. Seconds later, a pretty young blond with her hair pulled back, wearing an apron, came to the door with an older man right behind her. She looked surprised.

"Can I help you?" Her voice shook. The older man joined her in the doorway and grabbed her elbow. The two stood frozen in the doorway and stared at the men.

"Mrs. Moore?" Gary initiated.

"Yes, what is it?" Her face dropped. The man didn't look like a boyfriend. Maybe a father. He detected the scent of bacon and it made him suddenly nauseous.

"Mrs. Moore?" Gary repeated, his mouth gone dry as he spoke the words he had been trained to speak. "On behalf of the Secretary of Defense...." He linked the formal and meaningless words together in a hurry to get it over with. He didn't have a chance to finish.

The blood fell from the young woman's flushed face. There was usually nothing to say immediately beyond those first words. At that point, you just had to wait to see what the reaction was and then respond. Mrs. Moore looked as though she was trying to scream, but nothing escaped. Instead, she fainted. Small blue paint samples fell from her dainty hand onto the floor, and the burly older gentleman caught her before her head hit the ground.

THIRTY-THREE

The following day was cold and gray just like the one before, and the rain had stopped, but the penetrating dampness remained. A large black crow cawed incessantly outside the duplex. Captain Martin had left Grace with a business card telling her that a Casualty Assistance Officer would be contacting her soon and instructed her to please call anytime.

Grace was numb and only vaguely aware of Travis, who was clingy and clutching, sucking his small fist as he followed his mother everywhere, hung on her hip, tugging at a wisp of her hair, staring at her in that quiet way of his. The telephone had become her lifeline.

Her first call was to her in-laws. When she got on the phone with Molly, she burst into tears and told her the news through her sobs. The two women wept and talked until late in the evening. Grace finally had to hang up the phone when she felt she would collapse from fatigue. Molly told her that she and Lou were on their way, to just sit tight, that they would be there as soon as they could pack up a few bags and lock up the house.

When her in-laws arrived, Grace searched her mother-in-law's face for answers. She hoped that Molly's motherly instinct would take over and make some sense of all this, provide comfort, make

— 231 —

things right. She waited for some wise and hopeful comment. But none came. Molly was just as devastated as Grace and her face was drawn and pale. She looked as though she had aged a good twenty years since the time that they had seen Walt off at the airport just a few months earlier.

"I can't believe my boy is gone! It can't end this way. He is too young. I am supposed to be gone way before my children! I wonder what he was thinking? I hope he didn't suffer. I wonder if he will be buried in full uniform?" Wracking sobs accompanied the unanswerable questions. And then more questions.

"Where in the world is he going to be buried?" Another downpour of tears.

"The cemetery by the lake," Grace answered. "He loved that place."

The women became quiet and Molly fidgeted with her clothing and her watch as Grace smoothed Travis' fine hair. As the women sat speechless, Grace remembered walking through Lake Gardens Cemetery with Walt in the cool of a late summer evening several years before Travis was born. She remembered holding hands and calling out the names on the gravestones, witness to the people who had once lived in Sand Beach. Walt had told her once that if he were to go before she did, he wanted a spot at the edge of the cemetery overlooking the lake, closest to the lighthouse.

"Oh, Walt, don't say such things." She had curled her arm around him and nuzzled into his chest. "Let's not talk about stuff like that!"

"You are right, Gracie," he had answered as he swooped her up in his arms. "Let's talk about ice cream and…what I am going to do to you when I get you home alone."

They had been irreverent then, laughing, and skipping to the edge of the cemetery, feeling their aliveness amidst the stillness of the graves. Now that day seemed like it was a hundred years ago.

The news of Walt's death traveled like wildfire throughout the town. Grace had told only Fran, but Fran must have dropped her combs at the beauty shop and announced it to the others. And once Shelly was aware, it might as well have been on the six o'clock news.

In fact, the following Saturday, it actually was on the local six o'clock news. Grace promptly lost her lunch when she saw a picture of Walt flash across the screen, the professional photo that was used for his column with the *Sand Beach Times*.

Grace's front door remained open over the next few days. Neighbors and friends brought tissues, casserole, drinks, flowers, and sympathy cards and offered moral support that was often expressed awkwardly in their search for the right words. For Grace, the faces and voices of these visitors merged into one huge sympathetic sigh. The opening of the door became both a distraction and a comfort. She couldn't have survived if she'd been left alone in the abyss. She wished that all the visitors would spend the night to distract her from the feelings that bubbled inside. She clung to Travis and wouldn't let him leave her sight. She felt similarly toward Dad and Fran. She embraced everyone who spoke to her and held them for an extra few moments, because she now realized that anyone at anytime could leave you. Out of the blue.

Art came by with a large box of fresh-baked bread from the restaurant and six gallons of iced tea. "Don't worry about waiting tables, Grace, I have you off the schedule. You just let me know when you want to work. If you need a month off, we'll manage. Whatever works for you, my dear, works for me."

He had brought a peace lily from her co-workers and a sympathy card and a large tray of chocolate chip cookies. But she wasn't hungry and the smell of food nauseated her. The words that came out of her mouth felt dry, tinny like she were inside of a can as she formed the hollow sounds.

"Grace I'm so sorry." She turned to follow the voice and found Linda, who had dark lines of mascara streaming down her cheeks. Grace shared the damp box of tissues she had been holding all day. "I can't believe it, honey, it seems so unreal."

Grace trembled.

"Do you know what happened?"

"A little."

"You don't have to talk about it if you don't want, but if you do I'm listening."

"They will be transporting him here in one to two weeks. Apparently, there were two other guys. And they are in the hospital. I would like to know how they are doing."

It was helpful to think that there was still life after the wreckage. The idea of the two men lying somewhere alone in the hospital in a foreign land was stored in the far reaches of her awareness with the thought that someday she might meet them. She didn't know if they had families, but she knew that if they did, those families were better off than she. Those families still had hope that their soldiers would survive and return home.

"Well, dear, you know we are here for you anytime," Linda said, and Grace knew she meant it.

Somewhere in the midst of the chaos, Grace found herself in the funeral home wedged between Molly and Lou in a red-embroidered chair across from Frank Hammonds, the funeral home director, his red, blotchy face speaking words she could not comprehend. She saw his lips move, but she wasn't quite sure what he was saying and had to ask him to repeat things. She didn't have a notebook and new information did not sink in. He spoke foreign words and inside those words he mentioned something about the plans being coordinated by the Guard. He said something about military procedure. Something about the body being brought back with the utmost of care and respect and then there would be a full military funeral. She saw his diploma on the wall, but it was blurry—everything was blurry—and the damn headache lingered. The headache that had arrived at the same time the two strangers had come to the door was excruciating, the worst she had ever had.

Funeral arrangements were not what she and Walt had discussed in the days and hours before he left. Though the Guard did have him filling out paperwork that was foreboding such as wills, survivor benefit paperwork and powers of attorney, those were not the papers they dwelled on. When they took a dental impression as Walt was getting ready to deploy, it was just one of many routine preparations. They had together pushed these preparations to the back of their mind, and instead talked about the dreams they had, the children they hoped for, the travels they would take, the new home they would buy, and the books Walt would write. Funeral preparations were for the aged—for her parents' generation—as they retired and moved toward death.

After listening to Mr. Hammonds, she and Molly went and carefully chose a deep blue satin-lined casket. It was a hue that Walt would have loved. They also picked a song for the ceremony, the damn one that he had been humming in the dream. And Grace reached into her purse and pulled out a tattered copy of a poem to be read, the same poem that Walt had hanging above his desk etched on parchment and framed, the prose about footsteps and sand.

It took ten days for the body to arrive. On the day of the funeral, Grace wore a black dress with a lace collar. She had put a light dusting of powder on her face to cover the days and nights of tear stains. The day started out wet and cold but as the day wore on there were glimpses of pale sunlight cutting through the trees. Little Travis clung to her dress. Molly, Lou, Pete, Susan, Dad, and Janice always remained near her, and Janice had a never-ending supply of tissues for her.

At the funeral in the Methodist church, the pews were completely full. Grace sat in the front row, clutching Travis, her empty stomach churning throughout the service. When Molly's warm motherly arm enveloped her, she melted into the embrace. Molly wore no makeup and her aging face looked dry, wrinkled, beaten. Her eyes were red and swollen, and as she held her limp arm around Grace, her own tears kept bursting out in small explosions of grief.

When the pallbearers carried the casket down the aisle, Grace felt her muscles clench as she held Travis and sat in the hard pew. The men who made the slow procession included Pete, Lou, Stu, Jim, and Hank Higgins along with a soldier from the guard. There were attendees from the Guard Grace did not recognize.

After the casket was placed at the front of the church, the eulogy was given by Jim, and then several people stood to speak. The first one was Hank Higgins, who placed a war medal that he had gotten in Vietnam inside the still-open casket. Hank was cleanshaven and wore an oversized Goodwill jacket, his longish hair pushed behind his ear. His hand shook as did his voice, but he was sober and sincere.

"Now, I first must say that I know what it is to serve our country. I left this town in 1969 because I was drafted to serve in Vietnam. There isn't a day that goes by that I don't wonder what my life would have been like had I not gone over there. I know that Lieutenant Moore was not planning on going over to serve in this conflict. But he followed the call of duty, and now we have lost a great man.

"If Walt were here right now, he would probably know something about everyone in this room. He would probably know when you got married, when you had your first child, and where you were born. When I came home to Sand Beach after Vietnam, things weren't so good for me. They still aren't most days." He paused as he said this and looked into the sea of faces.

"My comrades and I served in a war that changed many of us from young men with hopes for the future to young men who had lost something important. I'm still not sure what that important thing was, but it's real and it's real to me every day. When I came home, there weren't any flags waving or bands playing or open arms awaiting my return." Hank cleared his voice and lowered his eyes.

"I lived with my folks for a while, then got married. But my marriage lasted only three months. Something inside me was missing. It felt like a piece of my soul. And I never got over it. I feel like I never made anyone proud after that. I didn't even really know after I got back why I went in the first place. But I do know one thing. And that is that Walt Moore made sure I knew that I mattered. He didn't look at me like I was a misfit. He cared. He knew my name, treated me with respect. And he thanked me most times when we talked for serving in that war. He made me feel somehow that even though I had lost something essential in Vietnam, my life wasn't a mistake; that I was still living and there was still hope for something to fill my emptiness.

"And I bet all of you would agree that when Grace Walker married Walter Moore and brought him to Sand Beach, she brought a man who cared. Walt gave me something back that I thought I had lost over there in that hell hole. He gave me recognition for my service to our country. And I thank you all for letting me talk today. God bless."

Linda stood and walked up to the podium, paused a moment, and looked out at those in the pews. "Hank is right. Most times if a big city fellow or lady comes to town, they just feel like we are a little too comfy for them. Not Walt! He just fit right in from the day Grace brought him home before they were married. The first time he came in to Gloria's, he asked my name and where I was from, and he never forgot. And what a tipper! We will miss Walter Moore. But I promise you, Walt, if you are out there somewhere and can hear this, that we will look after your young son and your Grace. And we will never forget you."

Stu Warner made his way up next, his body clumsy and large. "The *Sand Beach Times* will never be the same. What can I say? I can say that Walter was always here ten minutes before everyone else, and before I even stepped in the door, he would have had his morning coffee and would be laying out his work for the day on his desk. Walt took every project we ever gave him. He was never late on an assignment and never failed to bring truth and compassion to the stories he wrote for our town paper. After he learned he was being deployed, he didn't complain. He just told me he was going and continued to come in and gave two hundred percent like he always did. He didn't grumble and make excuses about how he should get a break with the extra load on his shoulder. He must have been worried about how this was going to affect his family. But it never showed. My condolences go out to Grace and his family at this time of grief. The *Times* will miss you, Walt. God be with you and your family."

When Stu mentioned that Walt never showed his worry, various memories surfaced in Grace's mind as she sat in the stiff pew. Walt's nakedness, his sleeplessness. The moments he snapped and crumbled. She heard Molly gasp intermittently and felt Dad's strong sweaty hand reach out to give hers a squeeze every now and again.

His other hand belonged to Janice.

Pete was last person to get up to speak before the Methodist minister spoke the final words. Pete had been silent in the pew behind Grace, and when he got up he left Susan behind, quiet Susan who nervously wadded up a tissue as Pete claimed the podium. Pete's skin was moist from sweat and tears. His voice cracked as he began. "You know I have to admit, that most of the time, I felt that my brother was just a little too good. I mean, Walt was the one who brought home the great report cards. He was the one who got the girl way before I found my lovely Susan."

Pete paused and wiped his face with a tissue. "You would think he might have picked on me, but he never did. He put up with my BS. He was my older brother, but for the most part I really didn't see him for who he was. I saw him as someone to be jealous of, but now, *now*"—his voice cracked—"I would give anything to have a chance to go fishing with him, to tell him that he really was the kind of man I would like to have been. And now"—he hunched his shoulders as though protecting his heart—"now I am going to show him wherever he might be that he has a brother who admires him. And if I am ever lucky enough to have a child or two, I will make sure that I tell them about their uncle Walt."

Pete looked more helpless than Grace had ever remembered him, with his cracking voice and his stammering words. He seemed much smaller, and the smirk he usually wore was absent. He held his gaze to the ground as he stepped down and made his way back to Susan in the pew.

After the funeral, the long procession drove to Lake Gardens Cemetery for the interment. The military presentation was formal, the men with their white gloves, somber expressions, and stiff posture. The men played the part reverently as they removed the flag from the casket and folded it with precision, as the lone soldier played "Taps" on his trumpet. At that moment, Grace realized this ceremony was a part of something bigger. The loss of Walt was a loss for her country and her community as well as for her family and her son.

The day was bleak, and the people surrounding the casket extremely sad. And when Walt was lowered into the ground, it was as though the curtain had been lowered on the happiest, most meaningful chapter of Grace's life.

THIRTY-FOUR

When Charles Walker first learned that Caroline had cancer, he attempted to deny it as though the word had never been spoken. He was working then as the editor of the *Sand Beach Times*, and Grace was living in a dorm at the University of Michigan, and Beck was just a sophomore at Our Lady of Angels. Every day, he would come home and go into the woodworking shop in the basement in an attempt to get a grip on the feelings he had about Caroline and the C word. He felt guilty that he couldn't hold her hand all the time through the whole thing, but it drove him crazy to have to face her mortality. Of course, cancer wasn't always fatal, but sometimes it was. He needed some things in his life that were predictable and those things, at the time, were his career and his hobby. He desperately needed control.

When cancer claimed Caroline two years later, something inside of Charles died with her. His heart stopped beating the day hers did. The caring woman who had been by his side for much of his adult life had just disappeared and he realized at that point that it didn't matter what your plans were and it didn't matter how good things were. Everything was a gift, and at any point in time, a gift could be snatched away. The experience devastated him.

And then, in his darkest hour, his little Beck just up and left as well. Her graduation from high school occurred two months to the day after the funeral. Eight days after she accepted her diploma, she told Charles that she hated him and all he had put her through, and now that her mother was gone and she had finally graduated from that "damn high school," she saw no reason to hang around without a mother in a "stifling, gossipy town with a father who works all the time and a sister who thinks she's better than everyone else."

Grace had been visiting for the weekend, and she and her father had watched, helpless, as Beck packed all of her clothes, stuffed animals, and personal items into a suitcase Charles and Caroline had gotten her for her eighteenth birthday just a few months earlier. After she left, Charles couldn't help but question all that he was and all that he had been as a father. Children didn't run off and leave good parents. Or, in this case, one remaining parent. What had gotten hold of her?

After she moved away and Grace returned to college, he was left with an empty nest. But his home was the one thing that didn't up and leave. The home would never replace a life, but it was tangible and was there for him at the end of the day when he returned from wherever it was that his day had taken him. He purchased new furniture. He liked his new kitchen table but realized it was nothing compared to the old oak table on which Caroline had served the girls blueberry pancakes and freshly squeezed orange juice on Saturday mornings.

Beck's bedroom was gradually turned into an office, but the new office furniture couldn't erase the memory of Caroline sitting by Beck's bed reading to her when she was small, or taking her temperature and wiping a fevered forehead when she was sick, or watching the door slam behind her when she turned thirteen and became all secretive and started wearing black nail polish and had her ears pierced without parental consent. Sometimes he wished he had left everything just the way it was the day Caroline died and the day that Beck left, her posters of the Rolling Stones on the wall and her pink bunny slippers still under the bed. The only female in his life who hadn't let him down before he had met Jan was his eldest daughter and if that hadn't been the case, if she too had left, he might never have even spoken to a woman again, might never have left his home for groceries, might never have shaved again and might have taken on the appearance of Father Time, with a long beard and a broken heart. Despite the fact that he had patiently redecorated and refurbished his home, it was still empty for the most part and the rooms still harbored the ghosts of Beck and Caroline.

Over time, the fact that Beck had left made a little bit of sense to him. For all of Beck's outrage he realized now that she was probably the one whose emotions had been fully expressed. They were raw and authentic. While he and Grace had quietly accepted their loss and did their duty, Beck was angry and showed it. Beck could not take it lying down and in fact was not going to take it at all. The whole course of events during what he came to term as the "dark years" etched themselves into his psyche, leaving an open, gaping wound. He supposed that others could see his pain, but he tried to hide it. Especially from Grace, as he wanted her to think that her father was strong.

It was at this time in his life that things became very quiet. Quiet enough to hear a still, small voice tell him that he had to, no matter what, set the alarm every day and get up and do something productive. And that for survival's sake and for the sake of his remaining daughter and eventually his new son-in-law, he had to make things look good on the outside. He knew how to work, and he had learned that if you stuck with a task, you usually had something to show for it. And he owed it to Caroline and to the way that they had taught the girls to always make lemonade out of those lemons. His moment of loss was the point in his life where the rubber met the road. It was the time to prove that when life handed you the sourest of lemons you still had no choice but to make the sweet lemonade.

And the way Charles made his personal brand of lemonade was from objects that would not leave you, that could not die. Before retirement, words were one of those objects. When he was an editor, he had found something very soothing about words and the way they could be shaped and formed. And once they were on the page, they were permanent, set in stone, like the Bible, which had withstood so many generations. After retirement, the object was wood. Wood was permanent. Or at least it felt more permanent than flesh and the people that could leave you.

After his final days with the *Times,* he added new equipment to his woodworking station in the basement and continued to find comfort in sawing and sanding. There was something about the wood and the way he could shape it that calmed his nerves. Wood did not expect him to talk or perform in any way. Heck, it didn't care if you gouged a hole in it or pulled a splinter. Wood was forgiving and compliant.

So Charles looked to his creations in the hope that rebuilding his home was something like rebuilding a life. He had hoped that in all of the activity, the sawing and shaping and sanding and polishing, that things would become new. He had hoped that when he went through the closets in his lonely home he would find his heart and that it would be pulsing and alive. Maybe he would find it buried deep in the closet, inside the photo boxes, or maybe out in the garage where for years he had piled up tools and all of his "toys," as Caroline had called them. He had hoped he would find it somewhere, anywhere, red and healthy, pulsing with life, just as it had been when he had loved Caroline, when he still had both of his parents, when he had been blessed with two young daughters, and when he had the little family that had provided him with a purpose.

But it never happened. The heart that he was searching for was not magically going to be found inside an old box somewhere to be revived. Instead, broken as it was, it beat slowly inside his chest, where it had been all the time. It was dried up and used. The only way for this heart to be revived was going to be through love again. The love that made a heart skip a beat, made a heart sing. The love that healed all wounds. The love that made an old man feel young again. Over the years, women had tried to get his attention, but none of them had succeeded. Oh, yes, the single, divorced, and widowed women in town were more than willing to cook him a meal and send him an occasional card. But he would have nothing to do with them. Women were to be avoided. They had the capacity to destroy his world. And before too long, the available women in Sand Beach gave up on him.

So it was a surprise to Charles that the moment he laid eyes on Janice Nielson he realized that he did, in fact, still have a heart that had been beating all along, it was just dormant like the trees in winter. When he first made eye contact with her, he felt something he had never imagined he would feel again. It was almost as if Caroline had stepped back into his life—he felt the same excitement, the same obsession when he thought about her.

He felt a little guilty that someone other than Caroline could have this effect on him. He hoped that Caroline wouldn't mind— and in his heart he knew that she wouldn't. On her deathbed, she had whispered to him that she hoped when she was gone he would find someone and remarry, because she knew that he needed that in his life. Charles had told her that no, that no one could replace her, but in some part of him he hoped that somewhere there might be a replacement as he watched his once-vibrant wife fade into the sheets and wither under the covers.

He had known soon after he had met Janice that she was the kind of woman he just might be willing to take a chance on, to ask for her hand in marriage, but the right time had not come. It had been too soon to make such a bold claim, just weeks after they met. It just wasn't proper for a man to meet a woman and then impulsively ask for marriage so early in the relationship. Well, sometimes they did, but it wasn't practical. But then that was precisely what he had done with Caroline.

He knew it was important to be sure that a life with Janice was what he wanted, that she was right for him and for his remaining family before he invested every last drop of faith in love. He wanted to make sure she did not have some hidden tumor or some crazy quirk that would be the death of him. He wanted to make sure that she wasn't the leaving kind, but he somehow knew that she wasn't. She had stayed by her husband for thirty years—at least that was what she had told him when he asked if she had been married before.

And then, when he and Janice were just realizing that they had a spark that might last, he lost his son-in-law. Proposing in the wake of a loss so great seemed irreverent—even though that loss sparked his desire even more to make things permanent. So he had waited. Waited for the right time and waited for the bond between them to strengthen and to make absolutely sure. For some reason, the straightforwardness and the sincerity of Jan had made him feel safe. Just as he had been able to trust her with finding the perfect home for his daughter, he knew somehow she wasn't going to let him down.

So now the only thing left to do was to ask Janice for her hand. After fifteen months of dating her, his heart still skipped a beat when she stood next to him.

So, this day, a year after Walt's funeral, was the day Charles picked to pop the question. He finished shaving, ran a comb through his silver hair, and straightened the collar on his dress shirt that was covered by the emerald-green sweater Janice had given him for Christmas. He splashed on the cologne that she had also given him "just because." He wasn't sure if that was a hint or not, but he realized that he had not noticed till he had met Janice how lazy he had become about his wardrobe. When the doorbell rang, he smiled to himself, took one last confident look in the mirror, and winked at his reflection. "You can do it, old man," he muttered, as he sauntered to the door.

"Hi, Darling." The name for Janice seemed natural.

As she stepped into the foyer, he embraced her. He closed his eyes and kissed her gently and then with more passion as she returned his kiss. The petite brunette who stood in his doorway had become a treasure to him, and he was comforted as she pulled him close to her. They stood for a moment as he felt her against him, his heart thudding beneath his shirt, as her shapely female form awakened his desire.

"Are you ready? I'm glad you wore your warm coat."

"I always wear my warm coat in February, sweetie. I'm starved, aren't you?" She looked up at him, her brown eyes sparkling in the dim hall light.

"I am indeed, but before we go to eat, I have a plan, an adventure. I was over by the lake earlier today and noticed the snow had left an exquisite dusting on the sand. It is just so pretty! So maybe you will take a ride out there with me. Besides, there is something I want to tell you."

He watched as Janice's expression changed. "Don't worry, dear, it's not a bad thing that I want to say, it's a good thing!" He smiled as he pulled out his gray wool jacket, his cap, and the pair of warm gloves that had also been a gift from his sweetheart.

The ride to the lake was silent and Charles kept touching his right pocket making sure the ring hadn't fallen out.

"Charles, you seem so quiet, honey, what is on your mind? And I wish you hadn't said that you have something to tell me. That worries me." She clenched her jaw and looked out the window into the dark of the winter evening as the snow fell onto the pavement.

"Well, I do have something to tell you, but I also have something to show you. No worries." He decided to change the subject. "How's little Jeremy?" he asked, referring to the new addition to Janice's family. Her daughter had had her second child not too long ago.

"He's finally sleeping through the night," Jan replied, eager to talk about "the Grans," as she called them. "At least Melissa can rest now. She's going back to work next month." Her daughter Melissa worked as a nurse in the emergency room at Sand Beach Memorial, and had re-located to Sand Beach to be close to Janice.

Charles steered the car into the small parking area by the pier, and it slid on the freshly fallen snow. He made sure he had the best parking space, the one closest to the small white form atop the snow-covered sand, the form with the view of the lighthouse.

"I know it's cold, dear."

"We are going to get out of the car?" She eyed him suspiciously. "Can't whatever it is you have to tell me about happen with the heat on? I'm freezing!"

"I'll make sure to warm you up, Jan Bear, I promise. But you must humor an old fool, just this one time."

"You've said that before, Mr. Walker. I will humor you. But Valentine's Day in the middle of February in Michigan is best spent by a warm fire rather than a brutally cold lake."

"A warm fire is best, when it follows a brisk winter's walk, don't you think? I promise it will be worth your while, and I promise that before you know it, we will be settled in a corner of Art's, sipping champagne and thawing out."

"Okay," she said as she pulled her wool scarf close around her neck.

He opened up the trunk and removed a large canvas bag and then walked around to the passenger side as he had become accustomed to doing with his sweet lady friend. He held out his arm for her to exit the car and then closed the door behind her. They crunched their way through the snow, toward the ice sculpture by the lake. The shifting sand underneath the snow made the short walk unsteady. A lonely foghorn bellowed.

As they looked out toward the lake, Charles said, "Janice, seriously look out there, isn't it pretty in the dark of the night? All that light coming from the snow and the lighthouse! Think of all the ships that have come to harbor and the feeling the captain must have when he knows that he has a safe shore to land in. The same kind of feeling I had when I met you. And," he added, "there is no one else around. We have our own private little wonderland, right here. For free. So, my dear, let's just take a few more steps to that little pile of snow over there."

"What is that?" Jan asked, as they neared the white shape. "It looks like some kids must have been out here trying to build a snowman or a fort."

As they neared the form, the white sculpted chair became visible. "I know it doesn't look like it, but it's a chair, honey, complements of Yours Truly."

"Charles, it looks like a throne! It's beautiful. I didn't know that you were just as good carving snow as you are carving wood. You are so talented!"

Charles reached into the large sack and pulled out a red satin pillow and set it on the snow chair.

"I know it's cold, honey, and I promise this won't take but a moment. Before you know it, we will be at Art's, enjoying the fire. So, would you be so kind as to honor me by sitting on the throne I have built for you?"

Janice looked at him and smiled. "How can I say no, when it's obvious that you have spent a good deal of time making this for me." She shuddered and pulled her coat down so that it covered her behind. After she sat, he pulled out a small red woven rug, obviously new, and set it below her feet.

He bent down on one knee in the snow and looked up at her. "Janice Nielson, you have been the center of my life since the moment I walked into Crescent Real Estate and you came out to greet me. I came in there looking for a home for my daughter and her husband, and I ended up finding not only a lovely home for Grace but also a lovely home for my heart. If you only knew what you have done for me and the happiness you have brought me this past year. I'm not perfect, and I come with a past life. I have a family and you have a family. But I know that when I see you, my heart sings. And I know that you are the person I would like to spend the rest of my days with. My house has been so empty! I have been the king of my castle lacking a queen. You fill up my life. I want to wake with you every morning, and I want the sun to set every evening with you by my side."

He fumbled in the pocket to pull a diamond solitaire out of a blue velvet box. "So, Janice Nielson, with this ring, I ask you, would you marry me?" He felt awkward and old-fashioned but glad to have spoken what was in his heart.

Then Charles saw the expression on Jan's face, and a warm feeling radiated throughout his body. He realized that he had done the right thing. Janice Nielson looked ridiculously happy.

Her warm breath escaped in an icy mist as she answered his question. "I will, Charles, I will!" She rose slowly from the frozen chair and offered her hands to pull him from his kneeling position. She embraced him. "Thank you, Charles, I would be more than happy to share your castle with you."

With the foghorn still bellowing in the distance, the two remained in an embrace and shared a passionate kiss. Before pulling her leather glove over her cold red hand, she spread out her fingers to admire the diamond engagement ring that was now on her ring finger. Charles looked into her deep blue eyes and touched her soft fur coat. Her eyes sparkled with love and her smile could have lit up the whole planet.

Charles Walker had thought that his heart had stopped beating the day his Caroline died, and in a way it had. But now, years later, on an icy winter evening by the lake, his heart was restored. He had handed it to Janice Nielson and she had accepted it for safekeeping. She had said yes! The lonely days for Charles were officially over. The Sand Beach lighthouse rhythmically blinked on the rocky shore, winking at his fate.

THIRTY-FIVE

Ultimately, it was Fran who finally prompted Grace to decide to move into the new house. Grace had been resistant, with little motivation to lift a finger, much less move a house full of furniture and memories to a new location. It was when Fran announced that she had filed for a divorce and was putting her home on the market that Grace felt she could no longer stay in the stifling duplex.

Fran had approached Grace on several occasions and had told her that she thought it might be a lovely idea if they moved in together. She had given the pitch that there was so much space in the new house, so much to be done to the place. She had convinced Grace that moping around the duplex day after day could in no way be good for Travis. She had made a list of reasons it was time to go, reasons that Grace couldn't argue with any longer. She had asked Grace a series of thought-provoking questions. What happened to the dream of the riding school? Did she think that Walt would have wanted Grace to stay stuck in the old home? So the move was no longer avoidable.

Grace had purchased the home in anticipation that she and her husband would have a beautiful life together. She had pictured time after time that he was going to lift her over the threshold of their new home. After Walt died, Grace had a dark year of sadness. Despite the purchase and her plans, she was immobilized by her grief. But now it seemed Fran was right—the moping had to end and she had to move forward despite her pain. She had to do this for herself, for those who cared for her, and for her son. She had to do this because it was something Walt would have wanted her to do. Would have expected her to do. So she listened and followed her friend's advice.

On moving day, Grace, Fran, Linda, and Bob carried box after box out of the duplex and into a rented moving van.

"Fran, did you get the box marked Toys?"

"Of course, I did!" Fran hoisted a box on her hip and strode up the ramp to the van. Grace's neighbors in the duplex had been coming and going all day, asking questions.

"Leaving, huh? You have lived here a long time, haven't you?"

"It seems like a long time, but sometimes when I think of moving in, it seems like it was just yesterday. So I'm not sure if seven years is a long time or not."

"Well, you will be missed. We have enjoyed watching Travis play, and you have been a good neighbor, Grace. Hope that boy of yours likes his new home!"

Grace lifted the plastic storage box she had bought at Raymond's. It was in this box that she had stashed Walt's letters, the pictures she had sent him, his belt, his patrol cap, and the notes he must have been jotting down for a book or an article. When his things had arrived, she had clutched each item and studied it, hoping that somehow the item could bring Walt back. But they were just things, and she carefully arranged them in the box, one by one. And when it was full, she put on the cover and placed it on the top shelf in her closet.

Now she put it in the front seat of the van with her, so that when they unloaded, this particular box was not going to get lost in the move. She would take it directly to her new bedroom and place it in the top right-hand corner of the closet. She didn't care if she lost everything else in the shuffle. But she was not for the life of her going to lose track of Walt's box.

When the last item had been removed from the duplex, Grace stood on the street in front of the house and looked back to acknowledge her emotions. She now had to say goodbye to the home whose threshold she had been carried over by Walt when they first moved in. Goodbye to the porch on which she was sitting when her water broke and Walt had gone into a panic. Goodbye to the bathroom in which she had found out she was expecting Travis. Goodbye to the home Walt had returned to every evening after work.

She realized at that moment that a house was much more than a place with a roof and four walls. A house became a home when memories were made, both good and bad, and on this moving day it felt as though part of her was supposed to let go of some of the memories as she closed the duplex door behind her for the last time. She looked at the home that held so much love and she waved goodbye.

"Goodbye 1017 Oak Street! I hope you have some great young couple move in, and maybe they will have a baby too!"

She felt a sense of sadness and relief at the same time. It was the same feeling she'd had the day she left her dorm at the college with a mixture of sadness and excitement about the future. Strange how two conflicting emotions could inhabit the same person.

Later that week, Fran arrived with her furniture and other belongings. She also brought several cans of wall paint. Painting was one of the pastimes that Fran enjoyed most. She had once told Grace that pain could be transformed just by adding the letter t and that paint had a way of making the "whole world look better." Grace quickly realized that painting the whole interior of the house would be their first joint task.

"Oh, Grace, thank you for letting us move in! I promise we will help you clean and work on the projects you have around here. And Paul and Travis can enjoy each other's company. Right, Paul?"

Paul, now eights years old, was pale and fidgety as he stood with his head down, picking at a bandage on his finger, unwrapping and rewrapping it until it loosened and sagged. He appeared older and more tired than most boys his age. Grace shuddered to think of what he might have witnessed in his short life. At his tender age, a divorce could not be easy.

"Hi, Paul, you are going to have a room with Travis, okay?" She took Paul by the hand and showed him the room with the "big-boy bed" for Travis that she had gotten from Dad's house, the old bed that had been hers when she was a kid.

Paul stepped cautiously into the room. Paul's bed was topped with a worn beige bedspread. He went to the bed and sat on the edge of it, his shoulders slumping as though he was protecting his heart. Travis came into the room holding a banana and headed straight over to Paul to offer it to him. Paul brightened as he accepted.

"Sure, why not, a banana! Oooo,oooooo oooooo oooo," Thanks, Travis."

Travis smiled and looked at Paul. "Monkeys eat bananas!"

"Yes, they do, Travis. You know what a monkey sounds like?" Paul made an ape sound and Travis giggled. Every time he giggled, it elicited more ape sounds from Paul, who now had the banana stuffed in his cheeks.

"Oooo,,ooooo,ooooo, ooo aaaahhhh, aaaaahhh." He held the remainder of the banana in the air and ate it like a monkey. Travis laughed some more.

Paul tilted his head back, egged on by the eruptions of laughter from the captive two-and-a-half-year-old. He repeated the ape noises, holding his hands under his armpits. Each time Travis laughed, he was an image of pure delight as he threw his head back and clapped his hands.

"More! Do it more!" Travis shouted.

Paul began bouncing on the edge of the bed, each time sailing higher into the air.

"Fran, I think that having you and Paul here will be good. We can have fun! And I look forward to having such a talented decorator in the house. Does Michael know where you are?"

"The only thing that Michael knows is that he can have supervised visits with Paul."

"But do you think that he knows that you will be staying here?"

"I haven't told him, but it's not like we live in New York City or anything. On any one given day, he can just follow my car from work and find out where I live. It's not that hard. But even though he's pissed at me, I think he is hooked in enough with Mavis and that drama that he can let this drama go for now. I'm sure that if he doesn't know already, he is going to find out where I am staying. The good thing, the thing I never thought I would say about him, is that I don't think he cares about me anymore. I didn't think I would ever be glad to say that, but at least I don't have to worry about him showing up in the middle of the night, unexpectedly drunk, or stalking me. He has permanently moved all of his affection elsewhere, to Mavis. Mavis." Fran repeated the name, this time shouting, her body rocking with laughter. "Remember driving by her house that first time? I couldn't believe his car was there. And now? Well, it would seem strange if it wasn't there! And now I actually hope that it is there! I *want* him to live with Mavis! I want her to inherit my agony. She worked hard for it. But I will miss the house. It seems strange to see the For Sale sign out front."

Grace thought of their pretty cottage by the lake, all white and blue like the magazines. Even magazine homes had their tragedies.

"It's a shame that you couldn't stay in that house, Fran. You were the one who picked it out. And you were the one who did so much decorating. It was yours!"

The women had stepped from the room away to be out of earshot of Paul and Travis, though Grace was pretty certain they weren't listening to their mothers, so intent they were on romping around and playing. Fran followed Grace into the kitchen, where Grace began to fill up the teapot with water.

"It's okay, Grace. It's all okay! I am finally okay with this new life of mine. In fact, now I really want it. I want a fresh start. Those walls in our house have too many secrets, dark ones, and I don't want the memories screeching out at me every time I go to the bathroom and remember looking in the mirror at a black eye, or remember hauling Paul in there with me, waiting till Michael was done with one of his tirades. Oh, my gosh, I am so relieved! I finally realized, when I went to Al-Anon and listened to others talk about their dramas, that if I had stayed with Michael, I would be attending Al-Anon till I was old and gray, needing it to heal a sickness like a diabetic needs insulin. I would need it for survival."

She bit her lip as she spoke. "And I did need Al-Anon, oh, I did. I waited for those meetings when I could share my shame. The best part about the whole thing is that I found out that I wasn't alone. That other people had family members who had erratic behavior because of the drinking. That alcohol may appear to be a choice, but deep down, for an alcoholic, it is an illness, a soul sickness that causes its victims to lose their jobs and their dignity. It is insane the kinds of things that people experience with addictions! It was pretty depressing listening to all that, but at the bottom of it all, what I learned is that my actions were normal. Not normal for someone who wasn't married to an alcoholic. But normal for someone who lived with one. Drinking is one of the worst illnesses I know! When I used to chase Michael and drive by Mavis house? I was acting just as crazy as he was. And I learned that in a sense, I was a co-alcoholic. He was addicted to the bottle and I was addicted to the one that drank out of the bottle. I was addicted to the idea of making him what I wanted him to be. We all were one great big addicted mess. And poor Paul. He will probably have years of therapy ahead of him."

"Which I'm sure his mother will gladly pay for."

"Not on my salary! But maybe I'll win the lottery." She laughed and pushed a wisp of hair behind her ear. "There was one woman there who had been an Al-Anon member for twenty years, and when I listened to her stories about her husband going on and off the wagon, his losing his job again and again, his inability to communicate with her or have any kind of dignity, well, it just opened up my eyes. I realized that just because I attended Al-Anon meetings, that wasn't going to make Michael stop drinking. And it just hit me in the middle of a meeting on a Tuesday night. I can still almost see the clock on the wall and feel the heat of the emotions in the room. It was as if in a split second, I saw my future. I saw myself in twenty years and I imagined being fifty-something, still having the same conversations, but maybe having a few old broken bones in the wreckage, having Paul be an alcoholic himself and having Paul learning from his father to be a wife-beater. And the whole prospect of that kind of a future, just, well, scared the hell out of me!

"I couldn't tell that woman that she saved my life because I didn't want to be like her, but I did tell her thank you. I told her that she helped me more than she would ever know and that she was a strong lady to endure such things. But in my heart, I thought maybe she would have been a stronger lady to have left. And in that moment, I knew that I didn't want to be like her. I've never been to another meeting, Grace. I can't. I knew when I left the Al-Anon meeting at the church that night I would never be back because something inside me had changed. My tolerance just went down to zero for Michael and his crap. But I've been praying for that woman every day, and when she shared her story I then realized that people may look like they are doing okay, but if you dig down inside, they carry such burdens! There are many times, that I wonder where the Michael I fell in love with went."

"The Michael you fell in love with, Fran, was an alcoholic. You just didn't realize it when you met him."

"You are probably right. Why is it that love at first sight is so hard to let go of? But like loosening a piece of gum from a patron's hair, I am going to loose this thing that's got hold of me, Grace, one day at a time. And so don't worry, I'm not going to chase him down and beg him to come back, because my mind is ruling things now. My mind knows what is good for me. And I think, no scratch that, I *know* that I have made the right decision. Because I know that he hasn't changed, not one bit. And if he has at all, it is for the worse. His temper is still there and he never did stop drinking. And he would have kept on and on with Mavis, and the whole world would know that Fran Baker is a fool. It is a horrible illness. I couldn't bare it. And now, now that it's over, I actually feel some relief. This whole thing has been going on for too many years. When I look back, he was drinking on our first date and drank through much of the time when we dated. And he was so funny and charming when he had a few, I really thought nothing of it! Oh, Grace, I am such a fool!"

"You are not a fool, Fran, you are a hopeless romantic who believes that if you love someone that is enough. So maybe I guess you are a wee little bit of a fool for love."

"And, Grace, I know I have told you this, probably a million times, but I admired what you and Walt had. So much. You seemed like the perfect couple. And, I mean, you just loved him! And you should have. He was a great guy!"

The mention of his name touched the usual spot in the center of her being. "Yes, he was, Fran, and the more time I have without him the more I realize it."

She turned off the teapot and moved the whistling kettle to a cool burner on the stove. She let it sit for a moment while the cups with the tea bags waited for the hot steamy water.

"The more I realize what we had and see how rare it is, the more I realize, Fran, that I have probably had the one true love of my life. And when that thought comes to me, I get the feeling that I probably should never look for love again, because I know that there is no one out there who will match up to Walt. And it feels like, even though he is gone, I still have a relationship with him on some level. With his spirit. I mean I still go down to talk to him most days at the cemetery, and I still have all his clothes—which, I must inform you, I have actually hung up in the spare bedroom."

"Well, don't feel too crazy, Grace. I know how much it must hurt, but I have learned that everything happens in its own sweet time, when it is ready. When you are ready to let go, it will just happen, just like it did with Michael. So you know you might have Walt's clothes in the spare room for many years and then one day out of the blue, like the second I realized I was leaving Michael, it will just be time."

Grace hoped that was true. She really most days still felt like Walt might walk through the front door. She felt it and hoped it. Fran was right that it had been time to move to the new house.

"Yes, don't push it. Just when it is time, let it be time! And, Grace, knowing that you got it right has just inspired me! I know that maybe there is someone out there for me who will be just as right for me as Walt was for you. And I can see now that maybe Michael never was 'the one.'"

"Oh," Grace smiled at Fran as she poured the hot water into the cups. "I know there is someone out there for you, Fran!"

"But I will need to be smarter next time, not to choose an addict."

"I suggest you give it time, Fran, focus on yourself and on Paul."

"Yes, but it's hard you know, not wanting a man in your life. Not wanting a man in your home. In your arms."

"Oh, yes, I know that! But the single men in this town are slim pickin's, and it might be best for both of us to come to terms with what we have been through. Get us ready, so to speak."

"Things sure worked out for your father, Grace."

"Oh, yes, they have, and I'm tickled pink for him. I can't believe the wedding is five months away! And the craziest thing is that he has been getting more and more cards from Beck, and from the sounds of the last one, she may be up here. Maybe, just maybe she will make it up here in time for the wedding!"

"Now that would be crazy—Beck coming back after all these years."

The two women sat at the kitchen table while the boys played hide-and-seek throughout the house. The sounds of the children's voices were pleasant, calming, like wind chimes in the breeze.

Yes, there was a time for everything, Grace thought, as she sat next to her lifelong friend and sipped the tea, inhaling its minty aroma, the heat of it burning her lips, and listening to the laughter of two young boys at play.

THIRTY-SIX

It was late July and the gazebo in Sand Beach Park was decorated for the mid-afternoon wedding of Charles Walker and Janice Nielson. The weather cooperated, offering a deep blue sky and a spattering of puffy clouds as seagulls sailed and dived over the lake in the unseasonably cool and pleasant afternoon air. Dad had rented a horse carriage from a livery near Detroit. Mr. Mathis from the barn had agreed to be the coachman, and he sat patiently in the driver's seat, his black top hat and white suit giving him the appearance of a character out of a Dickens novel. The two large brown geldings tethered to the carriage stood still with their blinders on, occasionally biting at a fly or whinnying.

In the hours before the wedding, Grace was accompanied by her sister, the two of them wearing identical violet-colored bridesmaid dresses. Beck Walker appeared rougher around the edges, her voice husky from smoking, her eyes tired, and her complexion ruddy. A bright butterfly tattoo was visible on her back that hadn't been there in the years before she had left Sand Beach.

Fran had set up a spot at a picnic table and was weaving braids of babies' breath, miniature roses, and violets into the female wedding attendants' hair. After Grace's tresses had been laced with the flower braid, she bent over to wipe a bit of graham cracker from Travis's face. She admired his small suit, the one she and Janice had picked out a few weeks earlier—her three-year-old might as well have been school age, he looked so grown up in his formal attire. The women also had the flower girl with them, the five-year-old granddaughter of the bride.

"Grace, you look beautiful," Fran whispered. Grace felt a lump in her throat.

"Thanks, Fran, you do an awesome job weaving those flowers. I think you should start a side business of wedding hair preparation. Doesn't Dad look handsome?" Grace nodded toward the group of restless and awkward men who had gathered around Charles. The way they stood in a circle, jangling change and cracking an occasional joke, made it appear as though they were waiting for the whole thing to get started or maybe for the whole thing to be over. Dad stood out from the men not only as the groom, but he had a patient demeanor, as though he had been waiting for years for the moment and did not mind waiting a few more hours. And he positively glowed.

Grace wondered what his and her mother's wedding had been like so many years ago. She had seen pictures, but these had been put away a long time ago. She wondered how the young couple must have felt and behaved before they knew they were going to be blessed with two daughters and a mortgage, before they could even fully imagine their future together. They had honored their vows— "till death do us part"—and Grace thought that this wedding of her lonely father was the happiest moment she had experienced since the birth of Travis three years earlier.

As the guests began arriving, Gabe Jordan, a friend of Dad's from high school who was wearing a lime-green suit, went out to the parking lot to direct the cars to available spaces. Once the cars were parked, Gabe and his brother George escorted the ladies to the gazebo, which had been decorated and readied for the nuptials. Rows of metal chairs faced a faux stage surrounded by fresh-cut flowers. The breeze blew ever so slightly, just enough to welcome the guests. A medley of voices and conversations wafted into the afternoon air.

"Grace, it's time to line up." The attendants followed Fran's calm instruction. Grace felt the pinch of her tight shoes as she clutched Travis's hand and followed Fran to the back of the gazebo. Grace looked nervously over at the groomsman she'd been paired with, a friend of Dad's from church named David. Suddenly, she realized that the last wedding she'd attended had been her own.

She thought back to that day her father had walked her down the aisle to meet Walt at the alter where they were joined in the bond of matrimony. Today was the first day since his personal items had been returned to her that she wasn't wearing Walt's watch, the one he had been wearing when he was deployed. As she lightly brushed her finger across the dog tag that lay hidden beneath her dress, she wondered if Walt knew that Dad was getting married from wherever he was now. She wondered if those who had passed had memories. She wondered if they were there with her now. Was Walt also remembering the special day when the two of them had said their vows in this same town, with some of the same people attending?

Beck cleared her throat and giggled. Grace had not heard that giggle since Beck had been twelve or so. She turned to face her sister whose small chest was heaving with contained laughter.

"What's the matter, Beck?" she whispered.

"I'm just nervous. I've never attended my own father's wedding before."

Grace didn't say it aloud but she thought about how Beck hadn't attended her own sister's wedding.

"Me neither. But you must hush!" Grace felt like she used to, the older sister keeping the younger one in tow.

At three o' clock, the voices in the gazebo fell quiet and the clear crisp music from the organ floated out over the small crowd. The processional began with Grace and David, followed by Beck and her partner, and then the remainder of the small wedding party made their way down the aisle. The group gathered on the small stage and formed a protective half circle around the bride and groom.

All eyes fell on Pastor Hagan. Without a microphone, his words were soft and barely audible. He looked down onto his open Bible and cleared his throat. "Ah, dearly beloved."

Grace felt for her sister's hand and gave it a quick, sweaty squeeze.

"We are here today to witness a bond, a bond of holy matrimony."

Grace swallowed hard, certain those were the precise words spoken at her wedding to Walt. A thin line of sweat trickled through the weave of flowers in her hair and down onto her shoulder. She stood and focused her attention on her father and Janice, who seemed strangely shy for their age. They appeared very serious as they stared at Pastor Hagan and waited for his prompts.

"Do you, Charles Henry Walker, take this woman, Janice Priscilla Nielson, to be your lawfully wedded wife? To have and to hold from this day forward? To love and to cherish till death do you part?"

"I do."

Right on cue, Travis handed the ring to the best man. Grace was grateful that he didn't blurt out anything embarrassing.

"You may now kiss the bride."

The small crowd let out a cheer and Grace breathed a sigh of relief. Dad was married! And she had no doubt that he would honor his vows, as he had with her mother.

She and Beck were standing in the same place at the same time to witness this miracle. And Travis had performed for the first time as a little ring bearer.

Travis ran to Grace after the bridal kiss and raised his arms to her, asking to be picked up.

"Gampa got the wing, momma. He special!" Travis squealed.

Grace felt her heart flood with love for the little boy, looking so grown up and special himself. The little boy whose ears and nose were just like Walt's. She lifted him and held him close.

"Oh, Travis Moore, you special too!" She planted a big kiss on his cheek. You did such a good job! Grandpa is very proud of you."

"Daddy proud of me too, Momma?"

Grace looked into the young boy's pale blue eyes. "Why, yes, Travis, Daddy is very proud of you!"

"Good, Momma, I glad he proud. I'm proud!" he added.

The guests tossed rice on the couple as they made their way to the carriage. Some let go of balloons. Jan looked lovely as she lifted her flowing gown and stepped up into the carriage with her new husband beside her. The reception hall was just a few blocks away. Grace and Travis joined the boisterous crowd of guests and attendants that meandered behind the carriage, some hobbling in tight dress shoes, making their way to the VFW hall.

The reception that followed, catered by Art's was fabulous— among the highlights were roast beef, artichoke hearts, French bread, and strawberry tarts. There was a cash bar and fruit punch. The wedding cake was perfect with a light peach frosting and a middle-aged plastic couple sitting atop it. The happy couple made the first cut and fed each other. The entertainment was provided by a DJ from Sammy's. The afternoon music and the wine flowed.

And then the part came where Janice Nielson Walker stood in the center of the dance floor with her back to the single women. She gleefully tossed the bridal bouquet backwards as the ladies shouted and jostled each other.

As the bouquet sailed effortlessly through the air, Fran Baker was there to catch it.

THIRTY-SEVEN

The air was warm for mid-autumn and Grace went to the stable in the back of her home to tack up Glo and take a ride along the beach. She found that Saturday mornings were perfect for this, and ever since she had urged Mr. Mathis to let her move Glo to her barn, she had made it a Saturday morning ritual. Besides, Dad and Janice loved having Travis over on Friday nights and Janice would make him a pile of pancakes and let him watch cartoons on Saturday morning. Or Grace and Fran might swap dates for babysitting. Grace found that this time to herself allowed her to think, ride, and visit the cemetery.

Grace pushed her hair up under her riding cap and listened to the snorts from the three horses that now inhabited the barn. She filled a scoop of grain from the large bin and proceeded to pour several rations into each horse's bucket—even before the grain hit the bottom, the crunching commenced.

"Hey, girl, how's my beauty this morning?" She pulled a carrot from her bag and offered it to Glo. As the aging horse crunched on the treat, Grace pushed the mare's pale gray fetlock to the side and eased on the bridle. After brushing and saddling her, Grace hoisted herself onto the mare's back and adjusted the straps of her backpack, which she had filled earlier with a small blanket and some handwritten letters.

As she settled into the worn leather saddle, Grace breathed in deeply and exhaled a sigh of contentment. She leaned over to pat Glo's sides and clicked under her breath, and as they got onto the two-lane highway, she urged her into a trot. The two were a familiar sight on Saturday mornings to the neighbors out on the roads. The traffic was sparse, and Glo trotted the several miles to the beach. Then Grace urged Glo into a canter, the wind whooshing as they sped by trees sporting fall foliage. Glo's hooves tamped down the sand, and she fell into a steady cadence. Grace saw several families walking along the lake with small children pointing at the sight of a horse cantering by.

Horse and rider galloped the two miles along the path by the lake and stopped at the small cemetery where the familiar military flag waved its daily salute to the man who meant so much to a woman, a child, his parents, and his town. Grace arrived at the familiar grave and as always felt heaviness in her chest. She dismounted Glo and dropped the reins as the mare stood patiently by her side. Grace released the backpack from her shoulders and pulled out the blanket and a piece of crinkled-up paper and found her spot on the ground near Walt's grave. She read aloud from her letter, though Glo and the waving thin reeds by the lake blowing in the breeze were her only audience.

October 17, 1996

Dear Walt,

I miss you sweetheart, every day. Every day when I wake, the first thing that comes to my mind is you, your face and your love and your memory, and I can't believe that you aren't here anymore.

It's so unreal. Even now, I keep wishing that it was just a dream and that you will come back to me, through the front door of our new home and things will be just exactly as I had hoped they would be. There is not a day that goes by, that I don't wonder where you are now. I wonder what it felt like for you when you died, and I wonder what would have happened with our lives, if you would have come home to me. Now, I am left wondering whether we would have had more children, wondering how our lives together would have played out. I have finally learned that life is full of surprises, good and bad, and that every day that I wake, I wake to the unknown.

I have just finished putting together a book, and I hope you don't mind, but I am publishing it with a pen name. My pen name is Walter Allen Moore, because I couldn't stand the fact that the one thing you had dreamed of and wanted as much as anything— to publish a book—was left undone. I had a counselor after you left, and he suggested it to me. And it has been the thing that has saved me. I used all the notes that came home with your things, and I have been amazed by all the details about life that you took the time to write about. I know that this was important to you, and I loved reading your lists of things. Your list of sounds, like Trump playing his instrument in the evening and the sharp sound of an explosion and mosquitoes in your ear. I would have never thought to do that. So I used those things in the book and some of the letters that we wrote back and forth.

I want people to know you, Walt. I know that so many have. But I wish they could have known the Walt that I knew—playful, sweet, and just about the best husband the world has ever known. I know there is no way that the book will be anything like the great American novel you would have written or the dozen or so you would have followed up with, but the book is my gift to you. I used all your notes in the writing of it. It's a tribute to you and to all the soldiers who served. It is my thanks to you for giving me ten wonderful years of your life. For being there for me after Mom died, for being such an excellent son-in-law to Dad. Just having your love for the time that I did has changed me in so many ways.

And if it sells, a portion of the money is going to start scholarships for those children that have lost their mommies and daddies in Desert Storm. I will also use some of it to make sure that our son gets the best education ever.

You would be so proud of Travis, he made it through first grade this past year, and I can hardly believe he is going on to second. His teacher says that he looks just like you. She says that he sits so quietly and listens and really pays attention, and she thinks he will do well. It was so crazy his first day of school to see him all dressed up and to walk him to the front door. I so wished you could have been with me and with him. I know you would have been the kind of father to take him to Cub Scouts and Little League, and you would have been his troop leader or coach. I am sending him to St. Matthias, just like you wanted for him. And I make sure that I tell him about his daddy and how proud his daddy was of him, and sometimes I see him looking at the picture of you two at his christening. Or the one with you and him on the front porch steps when you were wearing your uniform and the leaves were on the ground under the big oak tree and you looked so large and handsome and he looked so tiny in your arms. He asks me questions about you and I love to tell him how his daddy loved him so, even though every time I do, I want to cry.

I'm living in the house now, sweetheart, the one you never got to see. I wonder again how things turn out like they do, because, frankly, if I had stayed in the duplex, I would have gone insane with the memories. I have not found anyone to date yet. No one measures up to you. But we are okay, and Fran and Dad and everyone makes sure that I have what I need to raise our son.

And Fran lives with me, she finally left Michael.

And I didn't ever write to you about this because I wasn't sure it would last, but my Dad met this woman, and now I have a stepmother! At my age! It was a beautiful wedding, and I am so glad for Dad because now he once again has a home filled with laughter and love. And it is just what Mom would have wanted for him.

And it's unbelievable how much can happen in five years, sweetie. I know I probably told you this in one of my other letters, but I can't get over the fact that Beck came back—my dear, sweet sister Beck—just in time for Dad's wedding, and we were bridesmaids together. I'm still having some issues with forgiving her, as she wasn't the maid of honor I needed her to be at our wedding, but Fran has really been my sister of sorts all these years, so it somehow doesn't hurt so bad. Beck didn't stay long, Walt. She was here just a few months and then disappeared again. At least I got to see her. I think the drugs got her again. Now I know she didn't hate us, she was suffering. I don't think I will ever come to terms with the years that I lost my one and only sister.

On a happier note, my father was not the only one who had a wedding. I still can hardly believe that Pete finally got married. I'm sure you would have been his best man, and I know for a fact you were his role model, because he told me that frequently after you left us. I wonder if you knew how he looked up to you? You, my dear Walt, would have had a sister-in-law named Susan. And I expect that any time now there will be a little Pete Moore or two running around the Cleveland streets. And I'm sure Pete will tell his children stories of his childhood, of his big brother Walt, and the times the two of you had growing up. I wouldn't be surprised if Pete names one of his children after you. Since you have been gone, Pete has told us all kinds of stories about the two of you growing up that I don't think you ever told me about. It's funny what we remember.

And you know what? Two of the men who said they served with you came to Sand Beach the summer before last, just out of the blue—a guardsman named Rob Matusik and Boots McCall, the guy you used to write to me about. I had almost forgotten your stories about Boots. Just out of the blue, they knocked on my door. I have no idea how they knew where to find me, but they did. They were very nice and respectful, and they asked Fran and me if we would like to go down to the lake and have a picnic and then visit your grave. Apparently, the day you were killed, both Rob and Boots were injured too. Rob has a titanium leg, and Boots lost a finger on his left hand. Boots told us about the Dear John letter he had gotten from his girlfriend Sharon while he was over there. And then he told us how he has learned that sometimes things turn out for the best. Fran and Boots hit it off. He's kind of a goofy guy, but he seems so sincere, and I think he really loves Fran. And he is sober! And for the past year, they have been visiting back and forth and talking on the phone. I get the feeling something might just last with them. She told me last week that they are going to Niagara Falls, and I agreed to watch Paul, who is a teenager now. Paul, little Paul, can you believe it? A teenager!

I still have so much to tell you. I feel the time slipping away since you have been gone. So much yet to tell you, so many lost times without you.

So, Walter, you keep a spot for me up there wherever you are. I hope it's heaven, because I know that someday I want to see you again, and I hope you feel the same. It sure is not going to be the reunion I had hoped for, sweetie, the one where you get to see our house for the first time, but it will be what it will be. I have learned that life can change in a heartbeat, and if you don't just treasure each moment, well, it will slip out from under you. And life shifts so unpredictably and can make your legs buckle, kind of like running in the sand.

So I am going to make you proud, Walt. Our book will be published. I know you are looking down on me. I know you are waiting for me. But till that moment when we meet again, sweetie, I have our son to raise. And a few new horses in the barn that need me to go home to put out a few scoops of grain and some hay.

So don't you worry, honey, we'll make you proud. And Travis is going to be just like you. Until we meet again, Travis and I will be fine.

Love,
Grace Ann

Grace sighed as she clutched the letter to her breast. She wondered if this would be her final one, as she gently placed her lips against the paper. She carefully rolled the letter, tied a red ribbon around it and placed it in the steel canister along with the large stack of aging notes, yellowed photographs and drawings Travis had made for his daddy. She placed the canister in the spot in the ground made especially for these mementos next to the fresh flowers by the grave.

She looked over at Glo, who was swishing her tail and biting at flies, and then out at the lake. The sky was as blue as blue can get, and the birds were singing their little hearts out in the warm October air. She heard the clear song of a bluebird and noticed that he was alone, perched on the wooden post that outlined Lake Gardens Cemetery. Insistent in his shrill call, he seemed to be telling her something. That she was going to be okay and that her life was not in vain and that as long as there were songbirds and sunrises, the strong hoof beats of a horse, and a child to raise, life still had meaning.

She stood, her legs wobbly from kneeling, and put her backpack on. She mounted Glo.

As she sat atop the horse and felt the breeze, she glanced over at the bird on the post. She was sure that little bluebird was Walt.

EPILOGUE

Grace spent many years trying to come to terms with the death of her husband. As she had learned from her father, grief was a heavy cross to bear. She realized in her grief that she was not alone, that people every day were losing children and parents and friends. The book that she published went to help others, but most of all it allowed her some closure, knowing that the husband she had been so blessed to have found had left a legacy.

On the dedication page of the book, she wrote:

This book is dedicated to all of the families and the soldiers who served unexpectedly in Desert Storm. For many of you, it was just a brief interlude in time, an experience you will carry with you. For some, like myself, it changed everything. For those of you who lost loved ones in the Storm oversees, this book is especially for you.